DRAMA CITY

A NOVEL

GEORGE PELECANOS

PHOENIX

A PHOENIX PAPERBACK

First published in Great Britain in 2005
by Orion
This paperback edition published in 2006
by Phoenix,
an imprint of Orion Books Ltd,
Orion House, 5 Upper St Martin's Lane,
London WC2H 9EA

1 3 5 7 9 10 8 6 4 2

The Orion Publishing Group's policy is to use papers that
are natural, renewable and recyclable products and
made from wood grown in sustainable forests. The logging
and manufacturing processes are expected to conform to
the environmental regulations of the country of origin.

All the characters in this book are fictitious, and any
resemblance to real persons living or dead
is purely coincidental.

A CIP catalogue record for this book
is available from the British Library.

ISBN 0 75381 939 2
EAN 978 0 75381 939 5

Printed and bound in Great Britain by
Clays Ltd, St Ives plc

www.orionbooks.co.uk

To Jeanne Georgelakos
and Alice Karangelen

DRAMA CITY

ONE

LORENZO BROWN OPENED his eyes. He stared at a cracked plaster ceiling and cleared his head.

Lorenzo was not in a cot but in a clean, full-size bed. In an apartment with doors that opened and shut when he wanted them to. A place where he could walk free.

Lorenzo swung his feet over the side of the mattress. His dog, a medium-size mix named Jasmine, rose from her square of remnant carpet, stretched, and shook herself awake. She came to him, her nails clicking on the hardwood floor, and touched her nose to his knee. He rubbed behind her ears, stroked her neck, and patted her flanks.

Jasmine's coat was cream colored, with tan and brown shotgunned across the fur. Lorenzo had saved her from the shelter on New York Avenue the night before her scheduled euthanization. He passed by scores of doomed animals every day but had never taken one home. It was her eyes, he supposed, that had caused him to stop in front of her cage. He tried not to think too hard on the ones he'd passed by. He couldn't save them all. All he knew was, this was one good dog.

"Morning," said Lorenzo. Jasmine looked at him with those beautiful coffee bean eyes. Seemed like she was smiling too. The stand-up fan in the corner of the room blew warm air across them both.

The clock radio that had woken him played on. He kept its dial set on 95.5, WPGC. Huggy Low Down, a comedian in street-fool character, was talking with Donnie Simpson, the morning deejay, who'd been on the air in D.C. since Brown was a kid. It was their morning conversation, conducted by phone.

"Donnie?"

"Yes, Huggy?"

"Donnie."

"Yes, Huggy."

"You know what time it is, don't you?"

"I think so, Huggy."

"It's time to announce the Bama of the Week."

The last word, reverbed in the studio, echoed in the room. Same back-and-forth, every day. Huggy could be flat-out funny, though. And when he spun music, Simpson tended to play old school, which Lorenzo preferred. Lorenzo couldn't get behind that death romance thing anymore.

Lorenzo Brown peed and brushed his teeth. He swallowed two ibuprofens to fend off the headache he knew would come. He washed down a C and a multivitamin as well.

Still in his boxer shorts, he returned to his room,

where he did stretching exercises and crunches on a camping mat he'd laid on the floor. He then worked out with forty-pound dumbbells in front of a wall mirror, pyramid sets that left a rope of vein popping on each of his arms. He did some triceps curls as well. He finished with pull-ups on a bar he'd hung in the door frame, bending his legs at the knees to accommodate his height.

Lorenzo no longer did push-ups. They reminded him unpleasantly of the five hundred push-ups he had done for eight years, every day, in his cell.

. . .

RACHEL LOPEZ got up on one elbow, reached for the snooze bar on her clock radio, and silenced the banter coming from the morning deejay and his provocateur partner. She let her head drop back onto the pillow. Her stomach flipped, and a dull ache came from behind her closed eyes.

This will be my morning: three aspirins, no breakfast. Coffee and a cigarette, then out the door. Today is a road day. Get up and do your job.

She opened her eyes and kicked weakly at the sheets, which smelled faintly of cheap male cologne. She got herself up to a sitting position on the edge of the bed and turned the alarm off. The clock radio, a graduation gift from her father, was a Sony Dream Machine, a simple white cube that had looked ultramodern back in '92.

"To wake you up for work now, little girl. No one is going to do that for you anymore. You're going to need the alarm, the way you light the fire on both ends. But that won't last too long. Your body will reject it. Too many late nights; you can't mix them with work."

I'm still mixing them, Popi. The bad Rachel and the good.

Rachel showered, shampooing her hair and thoroughly washing her sex. In her bathrobe, at a small table set by an open window, she had her coffee and smoked the day's first cigarette. Afterward, she dressed in a loose, lightweight cotton shirt worn out over relaxed jeans and sneakers. The clothing was utilitarian gear of the Gap school of conformity, the styles chosen to hide her shape. She put on no makeup and added no shine product to her shoulder-length black hair. She was not trying to look unattractive. She was simply aiming to discourage any sexual feelings on the part of the men and women she encountered every day.

At the front door of her functional apartment, she stopped and gathered her tools: several manila files, a clipboard holding forms called "pinks," field sheets used for notations, a couple of pens, her cell phone, her badge, and the keys to her car. She glanced at the mirror hung above the table and looked into her dark eyes.

Not bad, she thought. Even without the war paint, and with what I did to myself last night, I still look pretty good.

• • •

LORENZO BROWN ate a bowl of Cheerios while standing in his Pullman kitchen, then showered and changed into his uniform. Walking to the front door, he passed a worn sofa and armchair, and stopped to adjust his grandmother's hope chest, centered behind the sofa's back. The hope chest sat on an old oval throw rug; beneath the throw rug was a rectangle that Lorenzo had cut out and replaced snugly in the hardwood floor.

At the apartment's entrance, Lorenzo picked up a chain leash with a looped leather strap that hung on a nail he had driven into the wall. Jasmine heard the clatter of the chain and joined him at the door.

Lorenzo's landlord, a man named Robie who lived on the second and third floors of the row house where Lorenzo stayed, had left him a long plastic bag, the one the *Post* got delivered in, on the porch. As he always did, Robie had put the bag under half a brick so that it would not blow away. Lorenzo slipped the bag into his pocket and went down concrete steps to the street. He and Jasmine walked east on Otis Place, up a grade into the sun, along brick row houses with wooden porches fronted by columns, some of the homes painted and kept up nice, others in disrepair. Sturdy oak trees grew on the government strip along the curb.

Lorenzo went up the block, stopping at the short, run-down stretch of 6th Street that was the cut-through from Otis to Newton as Jasmine peed beside a tree. Down there at the corner of Newton and 6th, where Nigel Johnson's mother still stayed, Lorenzo could see a cluster of parked cars, new and late model Lexus and BMW coupes and sedans, with a black Escalade, tricked with spinners, in the mix. A couple of young men leaned against their rides. The Lexus, a black GS430 with dual pipes and aftermarket rims, belonged to Nigel.

Lorenzo assumed that Nigel was in there behind that tinted glass, sitting under the wheel, talking on his Nextel. Few in Nigel's profession had their troops up and on the street at this early hour, but that was Nigel through and through. He'd had that kind of ambition, and an almost blinding work ethic, since he was a kid. The two of them had run these Park View streets together, going back almost twenty-five years.

As Jasmine finished her business, Lorenzo pulled

gently on her leash. They passed the home of Joe Carver, another of Lorenzo's old neighborhood running boys, now living with his aunt. Joe's pickup, a red-and-white F-150 of midnineties vintage, was not along the curb, which meant he was already gone for the day. Joe had been getting steady work as a bricklayer, a trade he had learned in the federal facility in Kentucky, since he'd come out. He'd been on a construction site on North Capitol, south of New York Avenue, for the past six months.

Lorenzo walked along Park View Elementary, where he had attended grade school. The summer-school kids had just begun to arrive, some holding the hands of their mothers, grandmothers, or aunts. He passed the mural painting of successful black folks, Frederick Douglass and George Washington Carver and the like, that covered an entire wall. They'd had pictures up of folks like them in just about every classroom Lorenzo had ever been in, but the pictures hadn't stopped him or anyone he knew from going down to the corner. Lorenzo realized that people meant well, but still.

At Warder, the wide north-south street that paralleled Georgia Avenue, Lorenzo cut left, then hung another left on the east side of the school and went down Princeton Place, where his grandmother still lived in the house in which he'd been raised.

A little girl he recognized, a six-year-old name of Lakeisha, came toward him on the sidewalk, swinging a clear book bag by its strap. Right behind her was her mom, a pretty young hairdresser named Rayne. Rayne was a single mother who undoubtedly led a stressful life but seemed devoted to Lakeisha and always kept herself looking good. She and her daughter lived beside his grandmother, in the next row house to the south.

Lorenzo stopped to let Lakeisha bend down and pet his dog. She had a pretty smile, like her mother's but near toothless, and cornrows with tiny seashells fitted on the ends of her braids.

"Jazz Man's her name?" said Lakeisha.

"Jasmine," said Lorenzo, looking at her fondly, barely knowing her but loving her, as she reminded him of his baby girl.

"Is she good?"

"Most of the time."

Lakeisha touched a finger to her chest. "Does she love people in her heart?"

"Yeah, she loves people. 'Specially little princesses like you."

"Bye, Jazz Man," said Lakeisha, abruptly standing and going up the hill toward her school.

"Thank you, Lorenzo," said Rayne, smiling shyly.

"For what?"

"For being so nice to my baby."

"Ain't no thing," said Lorenzo, smiling back, puffing his chest up a little and laughing at himself for doing so. Wondering how she knew his name, remembering that he had made it a point to find out hers from his grandmother. Maybe she had done the same.

"I better catch up to her," said Rayne.

"See you around," said Lorenzo.

Down the street a bit, Lorenzo entered a pedestrian passageway between the school playground and a neighborhood park surrounded by a fence but accessible through an always open gate, and walked onto a field covered in high grass. This was the usual morning route for Lorenzo and his dog. Jasmine stopped in the middle of the field, put herself back on her hindquarters, and defecated in the grass.

Lorenzo looked around, slightly embarrassed, as he always would be, at what he was about to do. He retrieved the plastic bag from his pocket, slipped his hand inside it, formed a glove, then reached down and picked up Jasmine's feces. He turned the bag inside out and tied it off. He and Jasmine left the park, exiting by the south-side steps, and went back down Otis the way they'd come.

Passing 6th again, he could see Nigel, now standing outside his car, talking to the ones on his payroll. Nigel had on a nice powder blue Sean John warm-up suit, with a simple gold chain hung outside the jacket. One of the young men, wearing an Oakland Raiders cap sectioned like a pizza pie in alternating black and white, turned and looked at Lorenzo, made a comment to the tall boy next to him, and laughed. Lorenzo could only imagine what had been said as they looked at him, a square in a uniform, working for rent money and nothing more, holding a bag of shit in one hand and the leash of a dog, and not even a fighting dog at that, in the other. Time was, Lorenzo Brown would have laughed at the sight of his self too.

Nigel Johnson said something to the young man who had made the comment, and the young man's smile vanished. Nigel nodded at Lorenzo with an uptick of his chin. Even from this distance, Lorenzo could still see the boy in Nigel's eyes. He nodded back and went on his way.

• • •

LORENZO LEFT FOOD and water for Jasmine, turned the stand-up fan so that it blew directly on her carpet bed, and exited the house. He got into his Pontiac and went down to Georgia, where he drove north, toward the office. There he would clock in, check his messages, and take one of the white trucks out for his calls.

Up around 9th and Upshur, in Petworth, he stopped to pay Rodel, the man who cut his hair in the shop set in that commercial strip that ran along the avenue. He'd been light at the time of his last shape-up, and Rodel had let him slide. Coming out of the barbershop, he saw a big man with a dog, a muscular tan boxer, out on the sidewalk. The man, broad of shoulder and back, his hair lightly salted with gray, was turning the key to his business, had that sign with the magnifying glass over its front window. That sign was always lit up at night. Man had been in business there Lorenzo's whole life. You'd be driving down Georgia at night, from a party or a club, or from laying up with a girl, and you'd see that sign? You *knew* you were close to home. Lorenzo had heard the man coached kids' football too, held practices on the field of Roosevelt High. Joe Carver's boy was in the program. Joe had told him this man was all right.

"Pretty animal," said Lorenzo to the man's back as he passed.

"First time anyone called Greco pretty," said the man, turning his head, checking out Lorenzo in his uniform. The man pushed on the door of his business. "Well, let me get on in here and do some work."

"I heard that," said Lorenzo. "I got to be off to work my own self."

"Have a good one," said the man, the boxer following him inside.

Off to work, thought Lorenzo as he got behind the wheel of his car. Feeling a kind of pride as he turned the key.

TWO

B Y ELEVEN-THIRTY, Rachel Lopez had already put in a
fairly productive day. She'd gone into PG County for
her first calls, one in Barnaby Heights and one off Addison
Road, a couple of young offenders freshly out on drug-
related incarcerations, the most typical cases in her files.
Next she'd driven toward a men's shelter down off Central
Avenue to check on one of her older offenders, a man
named Dennis Coles, but on the way she'd been held up
by crime scene vehicles that had converged on a strip shopping center up ahead. The traffic reporter on 1500 AM told
her that a robbery-murder had occurred in the area and that
a roadblock had been set up by police. She turned her
Honda around and drove north to Cheverly. She parked in
the lot of a garden apartment complex, where she found
the unit of a young man named Rudolph Monroe.

Monroe's mother, Deanna, answered the door. She was around thirty, heavy and unkempt. She wore a family reunion T-shirt over jeans. Big gold hoops hung from her ears.

Rachel could hear the sound of a cartoon show blaring from a TV set somewhere back in the apartment. That would be Jermaine, Deanna's youngest, age four. Rachel made a point of learning, and remembering, the names of an offender's kin. Jermaine would be sitting in front of the set, Rachel guessed, drinking sugar-heavy soda, his hand in a bag of Doritos or potato chips.

"Hey, Miss Lopez," said Deanna. Her eyes were welcoming, but she did not ask Rachel in.

"Hi, Deanna."

"Rudy ain't here."

"We had an appointment," said Rachel. Not sounding annoyed, but stating a fact.

"I *told* him you was comin'," said the mother.

"Do you know where he is?"

"He went to talk to this manager."

"What manager?"

"Up at the Popeyes."

"On Landover Road?" said Rachel, hoping that was the one. She had spoken to the manager there before; he had two brothers who had been incarcerated and was not averse to hiring offenders.

"Yeah. I seen they had a position open there, had one of those signs up in the window. Rudy knew y'all had a meeting, but I told him, you need to jump on that opening quick. You understand?"

Rachel said that she did understand and that she was glad Rudolph was motivated in that way.

She wasn't angry at all when this kind of thing

happened, because the time an offender spent actively pursuing employment was quality time, much more important than any meeting with her could be. That is, if Rudy really was out looking for a job.

"Tell him I came by," said Rachel.

"I will."

"Nice earrings," said Rachel before she said good-bye.

"Thank you," said Deanna with a smile.

Out in her car, Rachel checked her NA schedule, which she had printed off the Internet, then glanced at her watch. There was a meeting on East Capitol about to convene. If there wasn't much city-bound traffic, she could still catch the tail end of it, sit for a while, and relax. While she was resting, say a prayer.

• • •

THE DOG WAS a black rottweiler with tan socks and tan teardrop markings beneath its eyes. It stayed under a rusted rust-colored Cordoba, up on cinder blocks, parked in the paved backyard of a row house in the two hundred block of Randolph Street, west of North Capitol.

Lorenzo Brown had seen the dog before. He had left an Official Notification form on its owner's door back in July. The shelter violation had been reported by a neighbor. Next to chaining, it was the most common call.

Lorenzo sat in his work van, a Chevy Astra, idling in the alley behind the row house, looking through the lens of a digital camera. The dog had come out from under the Cordoba and listlessly barked one time. Now it was staring at Lorenzo curiously and without aggression, its tongue dangling out the side of its mouth. Lorenzo snapped off a shot and took note of the home address, which had been stenciled on a No Trespassing sign hung on a chain-link fence. Then he drove out of the alley and went around the block, parking the van on Randolph near the front of the house.

As was his habit this time of year, Lorenzo left the motor and air-conditioning running to keep the van cool. Once outside the Astra, he locked the door with a spare key. He surveyed the block, a typical D.C. strip of brick row houses topped with turrets. Here, near Florida and North Capitol, the rep of drug dealing and gang activity was strong. But there was no evidence of criminal enterprise today. Construction vans and pickups dotted the curb. Spanish music, thin vocals and surging horns coming trebly from the low-end boom box of a housepainter, blared from the open windows of a house. A white girl in a pantsuit, a real estate agent, Lorenzo supposed, stood on the sidewalk, talking on a cell while she nervously smoked a cigarette.

Several longtime residents sat on the porches and stoops of their homes, watching the white girl, their eyes showing amusement. Behind the amusement was discomfort. They realized that in the near future their corner of the world as they knew it would cease to exist.

"Uh-oh," said a man sitting on a rocker bench on his porch as Lorenzo crossed the sidewalk and went up the steps of a residence. "What J. J. do now, cause the police to make a house call?"

"You see a gun hanging on his side?" said a neighbor sitting in a similar type of chair on the porch of his own dwelling.

"I can't even see your wide behind without my glasses."

"That's the dog man, fool."

Lorenzo heard such commentary often when he entered a neighborhood. To the street-challenged eye he did look like some kind of police. If not police, an official, or something more than a meter man. He wore a sky blue shirt with a Humane Society badge pinned to his chest. He wore dark blue cargo pants and heavy black boots with lug soles, useful for climbing fences. He carried no form of protection, either clipped to his belt or concealed.

Black folks weren't shy about discussing his presence, in his presence, in the same way that they would tell a stranger, straight up, if they did or did not like his outfit or new car. On the flip side, when he entered the white, wealthy neighborhoods of Ward 3 on business, there were no Greek choruses and few questions.

"Look here, J. J. ain't home." It was the one who had identified Lorenzo as the dog man, shouting from his porch.

Lorenzo ignored the man, continuing on until he reached the house, one of a few fronted by a portico rather than a porch. There he saw detailed stonework arching the entrance and colorful tile inlaid on the floor.

Lorenzo knocked on the door, despite having been told that "J. J." was not home, suspecting that even if he were home, he would not answer the door. Lorenzo began to fill out an ON form, set on the clipboard he carried, as he waited. Soon he heard footsteps behind him and the voice of the middle-aged man who had called out to him from the neighboring porch.

"Told you he wasn't home."

"Thought I'd try him anyway," said Lorenzo, keeping his eyes on the form as he filled it out, feeling the man beside him, smelling the hard liquor on his breath and the perspiration coming through his pores.

"You ain't gonna find him at this residence."

"What, he doesn't live here no more?"

"I'm sayin', he ain't never gonna be in *at this hour.* J. J.'s got a day job."

Lorenzo had met this fella before, the last time he'd come through, and he'd smelled this same way. Man in his fifties, still young enough to work, not working, drinking liquor while the sun was straight up overhead. Bags under the eyes, teeth missing, "retired" with fifteen good years still in him. He was wearing one of those tired-ass Kangol caps too.

"Jefferson's my name. I'm a friend to J. J. — John Jr."

"John Jr. got a last name?"

"Aaron."

Lorenzo Brown wrote the full name of the resident on the form. It was easy enough to get from the criss-cross directory back at the office. But office time was not Lorenzo's thing.

"I'm a Humane Law Enforcement officer, with the Humane Society. My name's Brown."

"I know who you are," said Jefferson, in neither a friendly nor an unfriendly way. He did not offer Lorenzo his hand. "You came through here earlier this summer."

"Don't look like much has changed. What I can see, the situation with his dog is still the same."

"He been meanin' to get around to it, though."

"You say you're a friend to him?"

"I am," said Jefferson with weak pride.

"I'd like to show you what J. J. needs to do to keep his dog. I'd hate to have to take it."

"You mean you'd snatch that girl?"

"I wouldn't take pleasure from it. But I'd do my job."

"Damn."

"How 'bout you meet me in the alley?"

Jefferson looked around the street as if to consider it, as if he had anything else to do.

"Okay?" said Lorenzo.

"Gimme five minutes," said Jefferson. "I need to urinate."

You mean you need to have you another drink, thought Lorenzo. He nodded at Jefferson before going back to the van.

Lorenzo drove around to the alley and waited. Five minutes stretched to fifteen. He whistled softly at the rottie, and when the dog came to the fence, Lorenzo put his knuckles through the diamond space of the links. A dry muzzle touched his hand.

"All right, girl," said Lorenzo. "You all right with me."

The dog's eyelids had curled inward and appeared to be growing into its eyes. Besides this bit of sickness, it seemed to be well fed and in decent shape. Its owner had left a stainless steel bowl of water beside the car, though the water, most likely, had now been rendered hot by the moving sun. Health issues aside, there was no real shelter for the dog, except under that shaky car. Maybe the owner felt he had done enough. Lorenzo surmised that this was not a crime of deliberate abuse, but rather ignorance.

The alley smelled of excrement, garbage, and something that had once been alive and was now in decay. The August heat and the lack of breeze made the smell strong and sickening.

Two boys wearing long white T-shirts over blue jeans walked down the alley, going by Lorenzo Brown. They chuckled at the dog, which moved back a step as they passed. The T-shirt-and-jean combination was the uniform of choice for young men in the lower ranks of the drug game, but Brown had noticed both white and black kids in the suburbs, straight kids, honor students, whatever, wearing the same hookup. The suburban kids got their fashion sense out of *The Source*, off CD covers, and from the hip-hop videos run on *106 and Park*. For all Lorenzo knew, these two could have been playing studio gangster as well. They gave him cursory eye contact but made no remark as they passed. If it had been his partner, Mark, white and therefore fair game, back here, these boys would have said something, made him the butt of some quick joke. They'd have to, because it was in the contract. But Mark wouldn't have cared.

Jefferson came up the alley and stood near Lorenzo. He smelled more strongly of liquor than he had before.

"Awright, then," said Jefferson.

"Let's start with the shelter," said Lorenzo.

"Go ahead, I'm listenin'."

"Dog needs a structure, some kind of real shelter. And I ain't talkin' about leaving her to lie under that old Plymouth."

"That's a Chrysler."

"Whatever it is. Car ain't even on tires, could come off those cinder blocks and crush that animal. But the point is, the dog needs to be out of the elements. Needs to be protected, case some of these kids around here go throwin' rocks at it, somethin' like that. You understand?"

"Some kids just be evil like that."

"I left a notification, last time I visited, for your friend. I detailed all this."

"I know for a fact he got it, 'cause we discussed it. Said he was gonna act on it too. When he got the time."

"Time is now. This animal needs some attention."

"Look at her, though," said Jefferson, smiling with forced affection at the animal. "Dog's healthy. Ain't nothin' wrong with that dog."

"Not exactly. You see how her eyelids are growin' in like that?"

"She been sleepin'. Her eyes be puffy, is all."

"Called entropia. It's a disease, something rottweilers are prone to get."

"She gonna die from it?"

"Nah, you can treat it. Antibiotics — *you* know, pills. Or it can get cut out. Point is, this dog needs to be cared for."

"Uh-huh."

"We got a misdemeanor law in this city for failin' to provide veterinary care."

"That right."

"And you see the feces there?" said Lorenzo, pointing to the turds strewn about the paved backyard.

"Fences?"

"No, *feces*. Crap."

"Dogs do that, young man."

"So do folks. But we don't leave 'em layin' out in the yard. It needs to be cleaned up, 'cause that crap there, it carries disease and attracts flies. Not to mention the stink."

"I'll tell J. J. he got to clean it up. But that ain't gonna make no difference. You know, this alley just stinks natural."

"I heard *that*," said Lorenzo, writing on his clipboard, finishing the form. "What you're smellin' today is a rat. A kitten, maybe. Somethin' got itself dead in this alley."

"Whole lotta shit *stay* dead back in here," said Jefferson.

"Give this to the dog's owner," said Lorenzo, handing

the form to Jefferson. "Tell him I'm gonna be back, check on the progress he's made with this animal. Tell him it's gonna be soon."

As Jefferson rounded the corner at the T of the alley, Lorenzo turned the dial of the radio to 1500 AM for the traffic report, issued every eight minutes. He needed to get over to Northeast, down by the big wholesale food market off Florida Avenue. There was a Subway shop near there, made good tuna salad. He had an appointment in the parking lot with Miss Lopez. They could have lunch and do their business, all at once. Miss Lopez liked the tuna they made there too.

THREE

I WAS IN NEW YORK CITY this mornin'," said a man named Rogers, seated in the chair reserved for the guest speaker at the head of the room. "Well, it was New Jersey, way up north in Jersey, if you want the exact location. I was doin' some business up there, buying some automobiles at this auction, for my lots? I left out of there, like, two and a half hours ago. Now, I know you thinkin' it takes three and a half, four hours by car to get down to D.C., right?"

"'Less the car got wings," said a man in a green Paul Pierce jersey, seated in the front row.

"Oh, it had some wings on it today," said Rogers. "Like an angel has wings. 'Cause this morning, it felt like an angel was driving the car. I mean, I was on some kind of divine mission — to get to this here meeting, you feelin' me?"

"Yes," said a small young woman in a halter top, seated in the second row.

"I didn't care how fast I was goin'. One hundred, one hundred and fifteen miles an hour. I ain't even glance one time at the speedometer, 'cause I just didn't care. I wasn't worried about no police or nobody else. I'm sayin', I would have rather gone to motherfuckin' *jail* before I missed this meeting. I'd *go* to prison before I'd go back to where I was. 'Cause where I was, when I was at the bottom? Boy, I was tired."

Now, thought Rachel Lopez, you're going to tell us just how tired you were.

"What was I tired of? I was tired of seein' my grandmother staring at the floor when I spoke to her. 'Cause if she looked in my eyes, the woman who raised me and held me in her arms as a child wouldn't see nothin' but a lyin'-ass thief and fiend." Rogers, gray salted into his modified Afro, snaggle-toothed but handsome in a Lamont Sanford way, paused for effect. "Tired. Tired of watchin' my children turn their backs on me when I walked into a room, for fear that I might put my hand out for a ten-dollar bill. Knowin' their pops was gonna go right out the door with that Hamilton and cop the first rock he could."

"Tired," said a few people in the group, getting into the rhythm.

"Tired of smellin' the shit in my dirty drawers," said Rogers, lowering his voice dramatically. "'Cause most of the time? I had so little love for my gotdamn self that I was too disinterested to wash my own ass."

"*Tired!*"

"Lord," said Rogers, "I was tired."

Rachel sat back in the folding chair. She'd heard

Rogers speak before. He'd lost a business and a family to crack, hit bottom, gone straight, and come back as the owner of several used-car lots east of the Anacostia River, starting a second family well into his middle age. Clean for ten years, he still attended three meetings a week.

Rachel was in the back of the room, which held a scarred lectern, a blackboard, and about fifty seats. Many of the seats, situated in a four arcing rows, were taken.

The room was in the basement of a church on East Capitol Street in Northeast. Rachel attended Narcotics Anonymous meetings throughout the city but preferred those held in this part of town. The most honest stories, both poetic and profane, were to be heard in the classrooms, church basements, community centers, warehouses, and bingo halls of North- and Southeast.

Rachel was not in recovery, but she frequently dropped in on these meetings. The struggles, setbacks, and small victories related here gave her perspective, and a spiritual jolt she had never found in a synagogue or church. Also, this was business. She often ran into her offenders, past and present, in these halls, and kept herself involved, informally, in their lives.

"So I just wanted to come here to thank you all," said Rogers. "These meetings we be having right here? And you? I'm not lyin', y'all saved my life." Rogers sat back. "Thank you for letting me share."

"Thank you for sharing," said the group in rough unison.

After a few program notes from the group's volunteer leader, a basket was offered for donations. When it came to her, Rachel contributed her usual dollar bill and passed the basket along. The leader opened the floor for discussion, and the young woman in the halter top spoke first.

"My name is Shirley, and I'm a substance abuser."

"Hey, Shirley," said the group.

"I saw my little girl this morning," said Shirley. "She been stayin' with my grandmother since the court said she can't stay with me no more. . . ."

Rachel Lopez felt her stomach grumble. She was past the nausea stage and ready for lunch. She had an appointment with Lorenzo Brown, over at that Subway near the market off Florida Avenue. She liked the tuna they made at that one, and Lorenzo liked it too. Lorenzo Brown, one of the lucky ones who had found a job above the menial level, seemed to be doing all right.

". . . I was watchin' her from the corner. Well, really from behind a tree. She was goin' off to summer school. She about to go into first grade, over at Nalle Elementary, in Marshall Heights? She had this purple T-shirt on, got shorts go with it. And a pink backpack, had little cartoon kids on it. She looked happy. I mean she was *skippin'* off to school."

"My baby girl went to Nalle too," offered a woman on the other side of the room.

Shirley nodded at the woman in commiseration. Rachel could see that Shirley's eyes had watered up.

"I was just watchin' her," said Shirley. "I didn't want to bother her or scare her or nothin' like that. Lord knows I scared her plenty back when. I'm not ready to come full into her world just yet." Shirley wiped at one of her eyes. "You know, it hurts me to think of how I neglected her all those years. When she'd be cryin' for milk or food, or just to be held or loved, and me in some room with the blinds drawn in the middle of the day. Sittin' around with a bunch of fiends, suckin' on that glass dick."

"Uh-huh," said a man, like he knew.

"All those years I cannot get back," said Shirley. "But my eyes are lookin' forward now. We gonna have us a relationship, me and my girl, the kind I never did have with my own mother. I ain't bitter or nothin' like that. You can't change the past nohow, so you best put it behind you. I'm lookin' ahead. . . ."

Rachel dozed for a second. Maybe for minutes, she couldn't be sure. Her head snapped back up and she opened her eyes.

". . . so thank you for letting me share," said Shirley.

"Thank you for sharing."

A lean, hard-looking man in a dirty red T-shirt pushed the dirty Redskins cap he was wearing back on his head and raised his hand. The group leader nodded his chin in the man's direction.

"My name's Sarge . . ."

"Hey, Sarge."

". . . and I'm a straight-up addict. Now, I been comin' to these meetings for a long time, listenin' to you all talkin' 'bout support. How we all in this together, how we ain't never gonna make it individually 'less we stand together, lean on each other while we walk through that dark tunnel to the other side. All that talk, that's real good. But when it's *just* talk, it's just bullshit."

Sarge shifted his position, the chair creaking against the mumbles in the room.

"I ain't never been one for hugs and shit like that. I don't have many friends. The boys I ran with when I was young, they either incarcerated or deader than a motherfucker now. My family? My mother and my brothers? To them, I might as well be dead too. That's all right by me. I'm a lone wolf, you want the truth. That's how I like it, most times.

"But other times, even I need someone to talk to. And y'all always talkin' about, 'When you get weak, when you about to *do* that thing, you can call us any time.' Y'all passed out a list with phone numbers on it for just that purpose. *Didn't* y'all?"

"That's right," said a quiet voice.

"Remember that barbecue the group had last weekend?" said Sarge. "Over there by Fort Dupont? I was there. Not that y'all could recall it. No one talked to me much. But I was there. I got tired of standing around with a soda in one hand, my other hand jigglin' the change in my pockets while y'all was talkin' to each other and laughin' and havin' fun. So I left out the place and went home.

"I got this little efficiency off Bladensburg Road, down by the Shrimp Boat? Got a concrete patio out back; anyone in my unit can use it. Someone went and set up a grill back there, like a hibachi or somethin', a cheap old thing you pick up at the CVS. So I decided I was gonna have a little cookout my own self. Went down to the corner market and got some charcoal and a package of hot dogs and some buns. I lit the coals up and started to cook a rack of dogs on the grill. Had the box playin' this old tape I got, a Frankie Beverly mix? And it just reminded me of some shit, summer and cookin' out and all that bullshit, you know how that go. I got to cravin' a Heineken and a blunt. Nothin' better than that in the evenin', in the summertime. You got Maze on the box and you pokin' at some food on the grill? Goes hand in hand with a cold beer, right?"

"Damn sure does," said a man.

"One thing you got to understand about me," said Sarge. "I love to get high. I'd step over a hundred naked females if I thought there was a chance to get my head up on the other side of them. That's how in love with that shit I am. But much as I love to get high, I didn't *want* to, you see what I'm sayin'? And I didn't know what to do to stop myself.

"So what I did was, I thought of y'all. How y'all always be sayin', 'Make that phone call when you get the urge.' And I got that list out, the one with the numbers on it. And I made some calls."

Sarge cleared his throat. "I called a few of the male names on the list. I didn't want to talk to no females. I ain't no faggy or nothin' like that, understand. But I was lookin' for help, not no relationship. I just use females when I get with 'em, anyway."

"Hmph," said a man.

"And you wanna know somethin'?" said Sarge. "I got nary a call back. Not one. I got that answerin' service thing for every number I called, and I left my number on it too. But I just wanted y'all to know: Not one of you called me back."

No one said anything for a moment. And then Shirley said, "You just called the wrong numbers, is all."

"I called the numbers on the sheet," said Sarge.

"You didn't call mines," said Shirley. "I would have returned your call. And it wouldn't of mattered to me whether you did or did not like women."

"I ain't *say* I didn't like women."

"Well, you got no use for them, then. Look, I ain't lookin' for no relationship with a man, neither. But I would have called you back, despite the way you feel, because you needed help. And even though you seem to be, I don't know, antisocial or somethin', that wouldn't have stopped me from calling you. 'Cause I don't judge nobody, hear? I ain't got no *right* to. None of us do."

"Tell it," said a woman from the back of the room.

"'Cause if you judge," said Shirley, "you don't matter. And if you matter, you don't judge."

Sarge adjusted his cap so that it fit tightly on his head. "Awright, then. I can accept that. I ain't mean to bring no negativity up in here. Just, *you* know." Sarge looked down at his shoes and spoke softly. "Thank you for lettin' me share."

"Thank you for sharing."

"If there's no one else," said the group leader, "why don't you all come forward and form a circle."

A handful of people, who felt uncomfortable for their own reasons at this overtly spiritual and distinctly Christian portion of the meeting, left the room. Most stood and came forward, forming a wide circle, putting their hands on one another's shoulders and bowing their heads. Rachel Lopez stood beside Sarge, the angry man in the Redskins cap, touching his muscled shoulder, feeling his calloused hand on the back of her neck. She closed her eyes.

"God, grant me the serenity to accept the things I cannot change, the courage to change the things I can, and the wisdom to know the difference."

After the Serenity Prayer, the group recited the Lord's Prayer and said "Amen."

"Narcotics Anonymous," said the leader.

"It works if you work it!"

Outside the church, Rachel shook a cigarette from a pack of Marlboro Lights. She lit it from a matchbook she had gotten in a hotel bar the night before. She stood there on the sidewalk smoking, watching as the group dispersed, many in twos and threes to cars whose drivers had picked them up to ensure they had attended the meeting. Others walked to a Metrobus shelter and had seats on a bench. A few walked down East Capitol toward their dwellings or jobs.

Shirley, the girl in the halter top, approached Rachel and stood before her.

"'Scuse me," said Shirley. She was tiny, with almond-shaped eyes, Hershey-colored skin, and a pretty smile. She looked to be thirty, but had given her age as twenty at a previous meeting. Her drug use had stolen ten years from her looks. If her daughter was in first grade, Shirley had given birth to her at fourteen.

"Yes?"

"Can I get one of them Marlboros?"

"Sure."

Rachel shook one from the deck. Shirley took it, and Rachel offered her a light.

"That's okay," said Shirley, slipping the cigarette over her right ear. "I'm gonna save it."

"You'll need these," said Rachel, handing Shirley the matchbook.

Shirley smiled. "You have a blessed day."

"You also," said Rachel Lopez.

Shirley went to the curb and stood with her hand on her hip. Rachel crushed her cigarette under her sneaker and walked to her car.

FOUR

THE SHORT WOMAN, looked like an addict to Lorenzo Brown, had bulging eyes, ill-fitting clothing, and a bandanna covering her ratty scalp. The woman, along with Lorenzo, Rachel Lopez, and many others, was in line at the Subway shop near Florida and New York avenues. She was standing in front of the Plexiglas that separated the employees from the customers, raising her voice at the employee, a Hispanic woman, who was building her sub.

"How you gonna put mayonnaise on my sandwich when I asked you for mustard?" said the woman.

The employee did not look at the woman or answer. There was no need to argue or even reply. Also, there was a problem with communication, as the employee spoke little English. She simply replaced the top portion of the sub roll and used a knife to spread mustard on the bread.

"I want some more cold cuts on that motherfucker too," said the woman. "More turkey and shit. You listenin'?"

The small customer space was near filled with blacks, whites, and Hispanics, many in uniforms and some in low-end office outfits of the Docker-and-poly variety. No one told the woman to mind her manners or to simply keep her mouth shut. A few of the customers, insecure about their own place in life, enjoyed the woman's rant. Most, Rachel Lopez and Lorenzo Brown included, were uncomfortable with the scene but did nothing to stop it. If they did, it would only end with more aggression, and anyway, a person filled with so much self-hate could not be changed. Still, many in the store, Rachel and Lorenzo included, felt mildly ashamed for not coming to the employee's defense.

"See that?" said the woman, who turned to Rachel Lopez, saw the Latina in her skin and eyes, thought better of it, and turned away. She focused her gaze on Lorenzo Brown, who stood beside Rachel. "*You* see, right? People come in here, takin' our jobs, can't even speak our language, how the *fuck* you think they can do some simple-ass shit like fix a submarine sandwich?" She looked back at the woman making the sub. "That's right. Put some more meat on there like I told you to." She rested a hand on her hip, her voice dying down to a mumble. "Tryin' to cheat a woman up in here."

Rachel Lopez and Lorenzo Brown got their subs, paid for them separately, and walked out into the sun.

• • •

THEY SAT IN RACHEL'S Honda because Lorenzo said the van smelled like piss. The day before, Jerry, one of his fellow officers who was driving that particular Astra, had transported a cat in a cage, and the cat had shaken and peed all the way to the shelter. Jerry had apparently forgotten to clean the bottom of the cage at the end of his shift.

Lorenzo couldn't help noticing that Miss Lopez's car was as messed up and unclean as the van. Empty Starbucks cups and gum wrappers littered the faded mats, sprinkled with ashes, that covered the floorboards. A whole rack of paperwork and files had been carelessly tossed on the backseat. A couple of green little-tree deodorizers hung from the rearview mirror, but the interior of the Honda still carried the smell of nicotine.

Least it didn't smell like urine. Cat pee was the worst. Lorenzo hated that smell. Unlike the earnest patchouli-oil-wearing types he worked with, he could never get used to that sour, nasty stench, and he couldn't seem to get it out of his clothes. Now that he thought of it, patchouli oil, whatever that junk was, it turned his stomach too.

"Tuna's good at this one," said Rachel, wiping a bit of it off the side of her mouth.

"They do it right," said Lorenzo.

Rachel dug into the rest of her sub as Lorenzo devoured his. She had asked for hot peppers, and the woman behind the counter had been generous with them. Rachel craved the spice. It was always like that when she was feeling poorly behind drink. Her body had been depleted of something and was begging to get it back.

They finished eating without speaking further. Rachel had turned on one of those radio stations played country, her music, and a song Lorenzo did not recognize and would never want to hear again was coming at a low volume from the dash. The two of them were out of the same era but had different taste.

"So," said Rachel, after consolidating all of her trash in one bag and dropping it behind her to the floor of the backseat. "How's it going?"

"All good," said Lorenzo, his usual reply.

Rachel Lopez nodded and looked at Lorenzo directly, trying to draw his eyes to her. She was good at this, pulling him in.

"It *is* good," he said.

"Nice to hear it," said Rachel. "Piece of cake, right?"

"Got its ups and downs," said Lorenzo. "Most times I get up in the morning, I'm anxious to get off to work. But some days? I just don't feel like dealing with people. You know, all those things people do that get on your last nerve. I'm talking about the politics and all in the day-to-day. Gives me headaches."

"Welcome to the grind."

"But still, it's goin' fine."

"You feel that way, you're doing better than most."

He looked at her, and her eyes smiled. Miss Lopez had pretty brown eyes, even without makeup. She tried to hide her looks, tried to hide the things about her that were physically attractive, her figure, everything. But she couldn't hide that nice spirit. With good people it just came through.

Showed you, the way you judged someone up front, it could be all wrong. But how she'd acted the first time they'd met, he figured that was deliberate.

When he'd first come out of prison, he'd been contacted with a written notice and follow-up phone call, and told to report to a Miss Lopez, his probation officer, out in some office building in Prince George's County, over in Maryland, within seventy-two hours. After going through a metal detector, he sat in a waiting room like a doctor's, had girl magazines all round: *Rosie, Good Housekeeping,* stuff like that. He was wondering why they didn't have any reading material for men, car magazines or *SI,* 'cause it had to be mostly men waiting out in this lobby. Then Miss Lopez came in, wearing a middle-age lady outfit like she had on now. She shook his hand, her eyes cool, telling him that this was business and she was all business, and that was how it was going to be.

They went into a room, looked like any interrogation room he'd been in at any police station, scarred table, blank walls, all of them like the rest. She didn't offer him coffee or a soda or nothing like that.

Miss Lopez then went over form number 7A, which described the conditions of his probation, point by point. Most of the rules any fool could have guessed. He couldn't commit any more crimes, couldn't own a firearm or any other "dangerous device" or weapon, and had to "refrain" from the use of controlled substances. As he was a convicted drug felon, he also had to submit to regular drug testing. He couldn't leave the judicial district (for him that meant D.C., Maryland, and Northern Virginia) without permission, was required to notify his parole officer as to any change of address, refrain from frequenting places where illegal substances were being distributed, refrain from excessive use of alcohol, notify his PO of any arrests (including traffic violations), and meet his "family responsibilities," which meant child support. He was to tell the truth at all times. And, Miss Lopez said, the most important requirement was he had to maintain lawful employment.

"It means you've got to hold down a job," she'd said, like he didn't understand the official words.

"That's not gonna be a problem."

"I know it's not. You have to work."

"What I mean is, I'm close to gettin' something already."

Miss Lopez sat back and folded her arms, the universal don't-bullshit-me sign. "What would that be?"

"I'm about to get a position with the Animal Rescue League," said Lorenzo.

"Over there on Oglethorpe?"

"Yeah. *Yes*. They gonna hire me, I expect. I'm pretty sure I gave a good interview. And I didn't hide nothin', either. The man in charge there, he knows all about my incarceration."

Miss Lopez pointed to number 13 on the form. "He would have to. Understand, any job you get, I'd visit you from time to time at the site."

"I figured all that," said Lorenzo. "Anyway, I should know if I got it or not real soon. Couple of days, tops."

Miss Lopez had looked at him different right about then. The cool in her eyes kind of melted away. She didn't act all nice to him sudden or anything like that. That would come later. She'd do her home visit, and then he'd start to meet with her in her own personal office, not in that box. And she'd gradually begin to treat him like an acquaintance and, later, almost like a friend. She was like those teachers you'd have back in grade and middle school, the ones you didn't think you were gonna get along with. The ones who acted the toughest in the beginning, who laid down the ground rules from the start. Those were the ones you ended up respecting most, and remembering long after the school year had passed.

"Why?" said Rachel Lopez.

"Why that job?"

"Yes."

"I believe I can do it, for one. Matter of fact, I *know* I can."

Lorenzo went on to explain about the program he'd gotten hooked up with in prison. They had this thing where the inmates could get involved in the training of dogs. These were animals that had been selected to be guides and companions to blind folks, handicapped, the elderly, shut-ins, and the like. Lorenzo had signed up for the program and, once involved, found he had the aptitude for it.

"You like animals?" said Rachel, her arms now uncrossed, the tone in her voice less hard.

"Always did," said Lorenzo.

"You grew up with dogs?"

"No, I never did own no animals myself. Well, that's not right, exactly. I did have this kitten I hid for a while, from my mother, when she was around. Before I went to stay with my grandmother."

Lorenzo shifted his position in his seat. The chairs they had in that room were hard. Plus, he was uncomfortable talking about himself to this stranger. But he had started it now, and the words, for some reason, were tumbling out.

"I found this kitten in the alley where we stayed at the time, in Congress Heights. Down there near Ballou, in Southeast?"

"I know the neighborhood. I've had a few offenders down there over the years."

"That ain't no surprise."

Rachel Lopez, with an uptick of her chin, told him to keep talking.

"I was just a young kid," said Lorenzo. "Seven, somethin' like that. This was just before my mother went away.

Before I moved over to my grandmother's in Northwest. I came up on these kids in the alley, they were gonna drown these kittens in a washtub back there, said one of their mothers had told them to do it. I snatched one out of there right quick and ran to my house. I couldn't save them all, so I just took the one.

"I knew my mother would get all siced if I brought an animal into our house. She was . . . she couldn't handle much of nothin' by then, you want the truth. An animal in the house, I knew that would set her off. So I kept it hid for a while. Looking back on it, wasn't no way my mom didn't know. You can't hide that smell. I was takin' tuna fish and bits of chicken out the fridge for that kitten too."

"What happened?"

Lorenzo shrugged. "Kitten got out. I suspect my mother *put* it out. Dog in the alley got hold of it, killed it dead. My first lesson in the laws of nature. I wasn't angry at that dog or nothin'. Dog was just doin' its job."

Seemed like Rachel Lopez stared at him a long while then. Finally she said, "Well, I hope you get that position."

"I aim to get it," he said.

He did. But he didn't last more than a few months on Oglethorpe Street. They were just warehousing animals there, doing nothing active about helping the ones in peril on the street, and he was no more than a paper pusher. After all that time in a cell, he didn't want to be walled in, sitting behind some desk. From a coworker at the Rescue League, Brown heard about an opening at the Humane Society, where officers were honest-to-God investigators, empowered through a charter of Congress to seek out violations and violators of animal health and rights.

Irena Tovar, the woman who ran the Humane Society office on Georgia Avenue, gave him an extensive interview. First thing off, she asked him about the specific nature of his criminal charges. Brown figured she wanted to know if he had a rape or domestic abuse or something like it on his record. He told her of his drug offenses, leaving out the violent acts of his past and anything else for which he had never been arrested or charged. She said she had no problem with the fact that he had done time or that he was under supervision. She said that she believed in redemption and she hoped that he believed in it too.

Miss Tovar had hired him, and he had been at it since. He had found it odd, at first, to be wearing a uniform and a badge, especially while he was still on paper, just strange to be on "the other side." Strange too that he took to it so quick. From his first day out there, it was like he had slipped his hand into a broke-in glove.

"Lorenzo," said Rachel Lopez, pulling him back into the present. He stared out across the parking lot at the Capital City Market, where all those Asians and other ethnics had their wholesale food businesses.

"Yes?"

"You been by the clinic lately?"

"I been meaning to go."

"You need to get by the clinic and drop a urine."

"I will. You know I'm gonna drop a negative too."

"No doubt," said Rachel. "You still need to do it."

"I will. But look, I did have a beer or two this week."

"I don't have any problem with that. Your agreement talks about excessive alcohol use. Doesn't mean you can't live a life."

You live one too, thought Lorenzo. I can smell that wine or liquor, or whatever you had last night, coming through your skin right now. In the summertime, when you sweat, it's real plain. Also, when we meet real early in the mornings, I see how your face is kinda puffy and your eyes be all red. So you're human; you got your problems like everyone else. Like they say at the meetings: Don't judge.

"How's everything else?" said Rachel, cutting her eyes away from his, reading his look. "How's your daughter?"

Lorenzo nodded, seeing a little Chinese girl standing outside one of the markets, holding some kind of toy in her hand. "I guess she's good."

"Her name is —"

"Shay," said Brown. "I see her, but her mother doesn't let me talk to her."

"Ever?"

"Shay don't even know who I am. I went in a few months before she was born."

"You talked to the mother about it?"

"I tried. Sherelle ain't lookin' to bring me into my little girl's world. I been putting some money aside for Shay. Just a little bit, understand? But I been doin' it every month. It'll help with her college someday, she wants to go."

"That's good, Lorenzo."

"I'm gonna stay on it. I want her to know me. I don't expect her to love me or nothin' like that, but still."

"Maybe in time."

"Speakin' of which," said Lorenzo, glancing at his watch. "I got some calls."

"Me too. You just keep doing what you're doing, hear?"

"I plan to." Lorenzo shook her hand and opened the passenger door of the Honda. "Have a good one, Miss Lopez."

"You also."

She watched him go to the Dumpster in the Subway lot, deposit his trash, then walk to his van.

Lorenzo was trying. He was not as pure as he made

himself out to be in her presence, but he was one of the better ones. He had chosen a road now and he wanted to stay on it.

She had felt the day she'd met him that he would make the effort. The fact that he worked well with animals, that was a good sign. Most of the time she put little stock in reports and statistics, but studies did show that animal-friendly inmates had lower rates of recidivism. She believed that people who were good to animals had more human potential than those who were not. That was just common sense.

Rachel wasn't naive. Lorenzo had committed some crimes, most likely, that were not in his jacket. To go as far as he had in the game, he almost certainly was involved in acts of violence. Perhaps he'd even killed. At the very least he had done some bad things beyond the mechanics of dealing drugs. But she did not think that the Lorenzo Brown she knew in the present was a bad man.

She could tell this by looking in his eyes.

FIVE

IGEL JOHNSON'S SHOP stood on the 6200 block of Georgia, between Sheridan and Rittenhouse streets in Northwest, with the neighborhoods of Brightwood to the west and Manor Park to the east. From the sidewalk, concrete steps went up to its second-floor entrance. There Nigel sold pagers, disposable cells, cigarette lighters, chargers, condoms, and everything else his young, mobile customers might need on the street. He even had a fax machine and a copier, a pay-per-use kind of thing. Sign said NJ Enterprises right there out front. "NJ" was in script, like he'd used his hand to write it himself.

Nigel used the shop as a front for his real business, and as a place to run through some of his cash, put a few of the dollars on the books, so to speak. You had to show something to the IRS, and he sure wasn't looking to go down on tax evasion charges, like many had been known to do. There was no safe here, and, it went without saying, guns and drugs never passed through the front door. He ran the place as any retail-and-service merchant would, the difference being that he kept it open whenever he liked. Dealers all over the city did the same thing, with barbershops, beauty and nail parlors, variety stores, and such. White dealers, moving cocaine, mostly, did it too, at those antique shops in Adams Morgan and at boutiques on the western edge of the new Shaw.

Johnson liked the location. The neighborhood was cleaner and safer than down in Park View, where he did his dirt. The presence of the Fourth District police station, two blocks away, between Peabody and Quackenbos, kept the lowlifes in semicheck and the fiends off the sidewalks. His friend Lorenzo worked out of the Humane Society office up there around Fern and Geranium, north of Walter Reed, where all those tree-and-flower streets were at. He didn't see his boy much anymore, because of the circumstances, but it felt good knowing Lorenzo was close and breathing free air.

Most of the stores were legitimate on this particular strip. One of them, the Arrow dry cleaners, went back eighty years, still owned by the same family of Greeks. Nigel Johnson's spot, it used to be a Chinese laundry back in the sixties. There was a good story about that laundry too. Nigel had not yet been born when this story happened, but old-time residents had talked about it often, and he knew the tale by heart. Nigel liked to tell it, especially to the ones under him. Some of his people were grouped around him now.

"'Round the time that black folks started moving into this neighborhood, I'm talking about *before* the riots, there was some armed robberies got pulled on this block. Right here on the avenue. The most famous was when the Theodore Nye jewelry store got knocked off. Like most of the nice stores, that place is gone now. There was another one, though, didn't get too much publicity: the Chinese laundry robbery, right on this spot."

"Where we at now?" said DeEric Green.

"That's right, right where we sittin'. A Chinaman, his wife, and the Chinaman's mama san, old lady looked like a yellow prune with eyeholes, worked here, all together. The man's kids, a little boy and a girl, were always running around in here too. Whole family livin' together, then they'd go off and work together, *together*, all the time. *You* know how those Asians do.

"One day, couple of young brothers, full of fire and speed, came in and put a gun to the Chinaman, demanding all of his cash. Man naturally wasn't going to give up what he'd worked so hard to get, so one of the brothers, high as he was, got nervous and busted a cap in the Chinaman's face. Chinaman must have turned his head at the last second, because the bullet grazed his temple. Legend was, right after? You could see the smoke coming off the man's skin. And listen: Forever after, that square head of his had a burn mark on it too. You know, like the way a brand is, on a cow?"

"Chang got his self the mark of Zorro," said DeEric Green.

"Okay," said Johnson, keeping on, not wanting to lose his rhythm, though Green was doing his best to stop the flow. "One of the brothers, let's say it was the gunman, 'cause it make the story better, jumped down off the stoop, coming out the shop, and landed on a wrought-iron fence they had out there at the time, came down right on his dick. Fence had those spikes on it. No, *spires*, that's what they called those things. That spire, it took a piece of that boy's manhood, just tore off a slice of his testicles. People still talk about the way he was runnin' down Georgia, all in pain, blood on his drawers, to a waiting car."

"Story good," said DeEric Green.

"Hold up," said Nigel. "I ain't finished. I ain't told y'all the best part.

"The Chinaman, his wife, and the old lady continued to work that laundry for a bunch more years, even though that was just the start of the violent shit that would come to the block, and even though their store, in the summer, was hotter than the devil's own attic, 'specially in the back, where Mama San toiled. And because of all that hard work and sacrifice, those two kids of theirs, they did more than all right. The son became a three-star general in the army and shit, and the girl went on to become a doctor, one of those chemists over at NIH or a new-clear scientist, somethin' like that."

"What kind of car she drive?" said Green.

"I don't know the woman personal. What difference does that make, anyway?"

"Bet it's an Avalon or somethin' like it. Bet she went with a spoiler on it too. Chinese do love their Japanese cars."

"Point is, you keep working hard, despite adversity, you gonna come out all right. Not just you, but the people around you as well."

"I know what you trying to say," said DeEric Green, pursing his lips, nodding his head rapidly.

"You do?" said Nigel.

Lawrence Graham, Nigel's enforcer, chuckled low.

"Sure," said Green. "You talkin' about, like, that Boy

Scout thing. Be prepared to fuck a motherfucker up. If Chang had been strapped his own self, that shit never would have ended up how it did."

"It ended all right," said Nigel. "Ended real good for the kids."

"But the Chinaman musta carried that scar forever. Might as well had a sign on him said 'I got my ass punked.' How you gonna face your people after, when you got that shit tattooed right on your grille?"

Nigel Johnson, seated at his desk behind the customer counter, tented his hands and felt himself tighten beneath his Sean John sweats. Green, one of his seconds, was just dim like that. He never could see past the obvious.

"Story wasn't about the robbery," said Nigel. "Story was about how the man hung in, kept on doing his j-o-b. Passed on the legacy of hard work to the ones around him."

"I feel you," said Green. "I'm sayin, though, for *me?* I'll just go ahead and murder a motherfucker, he finds the need to put a gun in my face."

Nigel breathed out slow. He looked past Green, slouched with his elbow on the counter, his Raiders cap cocked on his head, wearing his look-at-me hookup of a thick platinum chain worn out over a bright FUBU shirt, to Michael Butler, standing by the window fronting the shop. Butler just nodded at Nigel, talked with those smart brown eyes of his, telling him he understood, that there wasn't any need to make further comment.

The boy was mature for his age. At seventeen, he had more sense than DeEric Green and most of these other knuckleheads on the payroll. Respectful, hardworking, and he thought before he spoke. Focused. Butler reminded Nigel of his own self when he was coming up, though Butler was nowhere near as tough. He had a little Lorenzo in him too, with the way he stayed quiet unless something needed to be said. Butler was good.

"Nigel?" said Green.

"What."

"I had a little thing I had to take care of this morning."

"Talk about it."

"Saw this boy they call Jujubee, one of Deacon's kids, toutin' his shit on our real estate. Had to pull over and show him what I had in my waistband, you understand what I'm sayin'? Him and his boys, they walked off slow. I don't see no problem, like reoccurin' and shit, but I thought you might want to know."

"Where was he standin'?" said Nigel. "Exactly."

Green described the exact corner on Morton. When he was done, he smiled proudly.

"Well, then," said Nigel, "you fucked up."

"Huh?"

"That ain't our corner."

"Huh?"

"I'm sayin', that's Deacon Taylor's corner."

"It's close to ours."

"But it *ain't* ours, DeEric. It's Deacon's. I got an arrangement with the man."

Green lowered his eyes.

"Look," said Nigel. "I appreciate you takin' some initiative, but you need to get me on the Nextel, or Lawrence here, if you not sure what's ours and what ain't. You gonna start a war out here, and that is something I don't need."

"Right."

"Yeah, okay. Right." Nigel was tired of talking to Green, tired of trying to impress things upon him that he would never understand. Boy had the chrome, the outfits, the chains, the Escalade with the spinners . . . all the *things*. But there wasn't no reasoning behind it, no plan. Boy wasn't going to last.

"Anyway," said Green, "'bout time I went and picked up the count."

"Take Michael with you, hear?"

"*Ni*gel," said Green, protest in his tone.

It's Ni*gel*, thought Johnson, not correcting Green, seeing no advantage in correcting him. Man had been working for him for two years now and he still couldn't get the name right. Said he had a problem with it 'cause his cousin, boy name of Nigel Lewis, pronounced it "the English way."

"Take Michael," said Nigel, repeating the order. "Boy needs to learn."

"Let's go, youngun," said Green without looking at the boy, resentment plain on his face.

"Your mom need anything?" said Michael Butler to Nigel.

"She good," said Nigel, nodding at Butler, thanking him for asking after his mother without thanking him by word. He watched Green and Butler leave the shop.

"DeEric call you *Ni*gel," said Lawrence Graham, seated near him behind the counter. Like many of the deadlier young men in the city, those with the fiercest reputations, he was short and slight.

"I know it," said Nigel. "He got a cousin or somethin' who say it the wrong way."

"DeEric stupid."

"You think?"

"He right about one thing, though," said Graham.

"What's that?"

"If that slope had had him a shotgun, a cut-down or something like that, hid in that laundry basket of his? He'd a lit that boy up."

You stupid too, thought Nigel. But he didn't say it. Graham followed orders to the letter. It was hard to find people like that. Nigel liked having him on his side.

. . .

THROUGH THE WINDSHIELD of a Mercedes S430 parked in a space on the east side of Georgia, Deacon Taylor watched DeEric Green and Michael Butler walk down the sidewalk toward a black Escalade. Beside Deacon sat one of his lieutenants, Melvin Lee, spidery and small, an NY baseball cap worn sideways on his head. Slumped in the backseat was a young man named Rico Miller.

"That him?" said Deacon, thirty-three, handsome, wide-shouldered, and immaculately groomed.

"Way Jujubee described him," said Lee. "Said he had on that orange FUBU when he told Jew to move on. Said he came out that 'Lade, with the spinners and shit."

"DeEric Green, right?"

"Yeah. I ran with his brother, James, long time ago. The Greens stayed over there on Lamont when I was livin' on Kenyon. Me and James, both of us went to the same middle school."

"Tubman?"

"Yeah. I remember DeEric when he used to tag along at the basketball courts. He wasn't no more than seventy pounds, but he talked like he was full grown."

"His brother still out here?"

"Nah, James *been* dead."

"What happened?"

"James couldn't control his self around females. Made

the mistake of gettin' his grind on with some girl even though he got warned that this girl had a George."

"Man didn't take kindly to it, huh?"

"I'd say he took it to heart."

Deacon nodded. One thing about Melvin, he made it a point to know a little something about everyone who was gaming on their side of Park View. Boy just had a talent for learning about the players, their histories, their alliances, and how they'd fucked up. Eventually everyone made that one big mistake. No one knew this better than Melvin Lee, who'd recently come uptown off a three-year sentence.

"Who that slim boy with DeEric?"

"New kid, name of Butler."

"What you know about him?"

"Nothin' yet. Nigel groomin' him. But to me he don't look like much."

"Must be one of Nigel's projects. You know how he gets all hopeful about them young ones." Deacon tapped a manicured finger on the steering wheel. "Nigel got his corners, I got mine. That corner, the one his boy told Jujubee to step off of? That was mine. Nigel *know* this."

"No doubt."

"Me and Nigel, we ain't never had no big problems. I been knowin' him since we was Rough Riders."

"Roosevelt," said Lee, enjoying this part of the conversation, the history.

"I ain't sayin' either one of us wore the cap and gown."

"Nigel's main runnin' boy, he was there round that time too, right?"

"Lorenzo Brown. Boy was fierce."

"Yeah, well. He ain't shit now."

Deacon Taylor removed his shades, used his shirttail to clean the lenses, and replaced the glasses on his face. "I just can't understand why Nigel would want to start some bullshit at this point in time."

"Maybe his boy did it on his own. Green do tend to act bold like that."

"That could be," said Deacon Taylor. "Still, even if Nigel ignorant to the situation . . . I mean, a man needs to control his niggas, you feel me?"

"Damn sure do."

"Sharin' those corners is gettin' old," said Deacon. "That's a situation I'm gonna have to fix."

"What can I do?" said Lee.

"For now, we gonna need to send Nigel a message," said Deacon. "I can put Griff on this, you don't feel up to it."

Griff was Marcus Griffin, twenty-one, Deacon's enforcer, feared even by his own. The mention of his name made Lee answer quickly.

"*I* want it," said Lee, knowing he had to step up to keep proving his self to Deacon.

"Can I help?"

It was the voice of Rico Miller, seventeen, coming from the backseat. In the rearview, Taylor saw a strange, gap-toothed smile spread on Miller's thin, wolfish face.

Like many of Deacon's younger people, but in a magnified way, Miller claimed to be indifferent to the prospect of an early death. He was also cunning and at times uncontrollable. Most saw Miller's willingness to jump into any kind of fight as bravery, but Deacon saw it differently. There were those who did violent acts out of necessity, and a certain few, like Miller, who did them out of plea-sure. Deacon knew that Miller had not yet acquired the maturity needed to take on a supervisory position, but he did not feel that he could hold him back. Miller had just appeared one day, seemingly out of nowhere. His promo-tion from lookout to tout to lieutenant had been swift. He was one of those Deacon wanted close.

"What you say, Melvin?" said Deacon. "You mind if Rico hang with you on this?"

"I don't mind," said Lee. "Rico a beast."

Rico Miller clapped Melvin Lee on the shoulder.

"Sooner the better," said Deacon. "I want Nigel to know that I'm on it."

"We'll do it tonight," said Lee.

"You workin' your paycheck job this afternoon?" said Deacon.

"I was s'posed to. But they changed up my schedule. I got to be in there tomorrow."

"You still on paper, right?"

"Yeah."

"So you definitely need to report to that job."

"I always do," said Lee.

Deacon exhaled slowly. "What you doin' today?"

"Me and Rico, we was gonna check out a thing, east of the river."

"What kind of thing?"

"Fat Tony say they got some dogfights in the woods."

"Take care of this thing with Green tonight, then," said Deacon. "Not too soft and not too hard."

Lee said, "We will." He tried to say it real strong. But inside him, already he was dreading what he had to do.

Rico Miller felt no such dread. Rather, he felt a familiar kind of warmth in his thighs at the thought of confronting Green. As he imagined stepping to him, he fingered the sheath in his deep pocket. In the sheath was a Ka-Bar knife with a six-inch stainless steel blade.

The sheath had the word *Creep* burned vertically into its leather. Rico Miller's mother had given him the name.

SIX

LORENZO BROWN STOPPED BY the D.C. Animal Shelter on New York Avenue to take a pee. It was a large facility that over the course of a year warehoused more than 13,000 animals, mostly stray and unleashed dogs, or those who had bitten or attacked people. These animals would eventually be reclaimed, adopted, or euthanized.

Mark Christianson, the closest thing Lorenzo had to a partner on the job, had worked at the D.C. Animal Shelter early in his career but had moved on to the Humane Law Enforcement team when the opportunity had arisen. Lorenzo and Mark did not deal with strays, lost dogs, or cats stuck in trees. The animals in the kennel at the office on Georgia Avenue were either humane holds — animals impounded due to cruelty complaints — or surrenders, which were animals simply given up, voluntarily, by their owners. Lorenzo and his fellow officers were not empowered to make physical arrests, but they could paper offenders and serve search and arrest warrants. They also worked closely with the U.S. Attorney's office to prosecute their cases.

Lorenzo didn't feel superior, exactly, to those who worked animal control at the shelter on New York Avenue. They looked very much like his coworkers on Georgia, dogooders with a touch of punk rock, D.C.-style, in their eating habits, ethics, and manner of dress. But he did feel that what he was doing as a Humane Law Enforcement officer was more productive, and exciting, than the work done by others in the animal protection field.

After using the bathroom, Lorenzo headed out through the kennel, passing barking dogs, dogs wagging their tails, and dogs with their faces pressed up against the links of their cages, desperate for love and the human touch. He stopped once, to let a pointer-terrier mix named Judy press her nose to his knuckles, then went on his way. He didn't like to linger in the kennel too long.

Near the door, he was greeted by Lisa, a compact woman with short blond spiky hair, a young shelter employee he had seen from time to time at barbecues and picnics. Lisa had started as a Humane officer but now worked in animal control. She was well-intentioned but, it was said by some of her former coworkers, unprepared for the conflicts that often flared up on the street. City people tended to be resentful of uniformed folks in general, a resentment that graduated to outright hostility when those folks were attempting to impound their dogs. There were different productive ways of handling the conflicts, but showing fear was not one of them. Mark said that Lisa once left the scene of a necessary impound without the animal when a couple of women had begun to get into her physical space and address her as a "white-ass bitch."

"Well," Lorenzo had said to Mark, "her ass *is* white, isn't it?"

"I don't think they meant it as, you know, a physical description," Mark said.

"You tell me," said Lorenzo. "I mean, you done had it, right?"

Mark had blushed then. It was common knowledge around the shelter and the Humane office that Mark and Lisa had rocked a bed. But Mark, who had come out of the straight edge thing, felt it was wrong to discuss women in "that way," even though, as Lorenzo had pointed out to him, he liked to do them every *which* way.

"C'mon, Lorenzo."

"Okay, so they were testin' her. The woman shoulda shook that shit off. *You* do. Shoot, sometimes I don't even think you hear the insults they be throwin' at you, man."

"I hear them," said Mark. "But it comes with the territory. Lisa just wasn't suited to that kind of fieldwork, is all."

"You mean she's got a color problem."

"I don't think so. She was intimidated, is all it was."

"By bein' around black folks."

"By the conflicts, more likely."

"City's black. You afraid of black people, you ain't got no business working out in the streets. Those women? That's what they were tryin' to tell her."

"Maybe."

"So about that ass . . ."

"It is white," said Mark, one side of his mouth up in a reluctant smirk.

"Looks like it's nice and round too," said Lorenzo.

Lorenzo spoke briefly with Lisa, then got back in his van and put the air conditioning on high. Since he was in the area, he went through Ivy City, past horribly run-down row houses, some with plywood in their window frames. He drove on to Mount Olivet Road, the thoroughfare that bordered the Gallaudet University campus and led eventually to the Olivet Cemetery and beyond to the National Arboretum. There on the four-lane he parked along the curb and walked to a set of low-rise warehouse structures grouped across the street from a drive-through burger house and a Chinese sub shop, the ubiquitous Kenny's. Lorenzo often wondered why so many Asians used that name. Wasn't like it was the coolest one you could pick.

He went along the sidewalk of the warehouse that fronted the street. To the left side of the structure was a parking lot that had been converted into a holding area housing several high chain-link cages. There were no dogs in the cages today. He had warned the woman who lived in the warehouse about leaving the dogs out in the sun, especially at the height of the August heat.

Lorenzo went to the front door of the warehouse and knocked. He could hear the deep, insistent barks of large dogs coming from behind the door.

He waited, then knocked again. The woman was in there, he knew. She rarely ventured outside.

Lorenzo stood on the stoop for five minutes, sweating, waiting, and rapping his fist on wood. Eventually the woman, a stocky, milky-eyed Korean with wildly unkempt hair, opened the door. She recognized him immediately, as he had visited her the previous week. Through the open door, he smelled ammonia.

"I did!" she said, stamping her foot petulantly, like a child. She wore sneakers without backs.

"I'm just checking up on you to *see* you did," said Lorenzo, careful to inject no animosity into his voice, but raising it some so she could hear him. The barking had intensified.

"No dogs outside," she said. "All inside. I clean!"

"Where are they now?"

"Right there!" she said, pointing to a hallway. In the center of the hall, set in a cut-out of the drywall, Lorenzo could see a large interior window, glass streaked with saliva and clouded by breath. The barks were coming from behind the glass. The barking, teeth-bared heads of dogs appeared, disappeared, and appeared again.

"Can I come in?" said Lorenzo.

"I did!"

"Need to do my job and confirm that, ma'am."

The woman shook her head and stepped aside.

"They all in that room?"

"All, yes."

Lorenzo entered the hall. His eyes burned immediately from the ammonia. His lungs burned too. He went to the window and looked through it. Had to be twenty, twenty-five dogs in that room, running around, sniffing at one another, barking at him, wagging their tails at the woman who stood beside him. All were large long-haired shepherd mixes. All had similar brown-black coats. Some appeared to be inbred through generations.

There was some sort of portable kitchen hookup along one wall in there, a trashed, barely cushioned chair and a sofa, looked like it had lost a firefight. Set against another wall was a bed, its sheets rumpled and dirty with grime and hair. This, he guessed, was where the woman slept.

Lorenzo walked down the hall to the open warehouse. Stand-up industrial-sized fans were situated around the warehouse floor, drying the concrete, which had been hosed down. The last time Lorenzo had been here, the floor had been littered with feces. She had taken care of it, as he'd asked her to do.

"I clean shit," said the woman.

"I see that," said Lorenzo, taking a handkerchief from his pocket and wiping his eyes. He was sickened from the ammonia and could not stand to breathe it much longer. "You can't have those dogs in here with this ammonia. It's poison."

"Ammonia for clean," said the woman, who seemed entirely unaffected by the fumes.

"But it's poison. Do you understand?"

"Yes, poison. That why dogs in room. When no smell, I let dogs out." The woman looked at Lorenzo with a smile in her eyes. "Okay, police?"

"You need to keep this place free of clutter and feces," said Lorenzo, ignoring her remark. "Let those dogs outside, but not too long in the middle of the day."

"Too hot."

"That's right. And put water out in those cages when they're out there too."

"Okay."

"I'm gonna leave now," said Lorenzo. "But I'll be back."

"I clean," said the woman tiredly, looking around the warehouse, making a limp sweeping gesture with her hand.

"Right," said Lorenzo.

Out in the van, he dry-swallowed two ibuprofens. The ammonia fumes had hastened the return of his headache.

The Korean woman was one of several "hoarders" he had been introduced to on the job. Generally they were decent people who seemed to love their animals and want to do their best to give them good care. They often lived in filth and maintained little contact with other humans, preferring the company and security of animals. Like the Korean woman, they focused on one breed or mix of animals and sought them out. They considered themselves to be rescuers. Lorenzo was convinced that these people had some sort of mental illness. Mark said it was a form of agoraphobia, and when Lorenzo had asked him what that was, Mark said, "Fear of the marketplace. You know, from the Greek."

"From the Greek?" said Lorenzo. "*What* Greek?"

"The Greek language," said Mark. "The market, as in the *agora*."

"So, like, these hoarders, they afraid of goin' out to the Safeway, that's what you're saying?"

"In a way," said Mark. "More like they're afraid of seeing *people* at the Safeway."

"But if they was to see a bunch of dogs, up on two legs, pushing those shopping carts around the supermarket, they'd be all right with that."

"Precisely," said Mark.

Precisely. Mark talked funny, all that extra schooling he'd had. But Mark was all right.

On the way back to the office, Lorenzo stopped at a residence on Kennedy Street, in Northwest, at 6th and Longfellow. The old woman there had been leaving messages on his machine about her cat.

He entered the house and had a seat on the living-room couch while the woman, nearly bald and wearing a housedress, explained the situation to Lorenzo. As she did, an equally old man, wearing a sweater despite the heat, sat beside her, intently watching bare-knuckled Tibetan fistfights on the cable channel that was playing on the Sony. The curtains had all been drawn, shutting out the afternoon light. A fan blew warm air and dust across the room.

"I figured it was time to do this," said the woman. "Queen been slippin' out in the alley and visiting her boyfriends again."

"Past time," said the man, his eyes focused on the fights.

"Now, John," said the lady. "That little girl is just frisky."

Lorenzo looked through the screen of the travel box at the green-eyed cat. "She's a calico, right?"

"Through and through," said the old lady. "I appreciate you pickin' her up. I don't have a car and if I did I couldn't see to drive it."

"I'll take her to the spay clinic," said Lorenzo. "It's right next door to my office. They'll do it tonight, and you can have her tomorrow morning."

"Will you bring her back?"

"Someone will."

"I want *you* to bring her back, young man."

"Yes, ma'am. I'm gonna need a twenty-five-dollar check for the procedure."

"Shoulda done this a while back," said the old man. "Way that cat likes to spread her love around."

"John," said the old lady, reaching into her purse for her checkbook.

Five minutes later, Lorenzo went out the door, crossed the concrete porch, and headed down the steps of the row house with the travel box in his hand. He heard two old men on an adjoining porch discussing his presence.

"Why Miss Roberts got police calling on her for? Her great-grandson done somethin' wrong again?"

"That boy already payin' his debt. Anyway, that's no police. That's the dog man, come to take her cat."

"Take it for what?"

"To fix its privates."

"'Bout time."

"You should have it done your own self."

"You should too."

"I'd be disappointin' a lot of women."

"Not as many as me."

Lorenzo placed the box in the back of the van.

• • •

AFTER DROPPING THE CALICO off at the clinic, Lorenzo entered the lobby of the Humane Society office, greeting a couple of his coworkers, Jamie, attractive and gay, and Luanne, plain and straight. A tough white girl, Cindy, sat behind the dispatch desk, radioing a call to a field operative, an ever-present cup of Starbucks before her. Lorenzo rubbed the head of the latest house pet, a previously abused border collie mix named Tulip, who had gotten up out of her bed to greet him.

Down in the basement kennel, Lorenzo checked on the dogs he had brought in recently. All of them had been impounded, taken away from unacceptable living conditions. Most would make good house pets, with retraining and care. For various reasons, some could not live with children, and some could not live with cats or other dogs. A few were beyond rehabilitation. They could never coexist with humans or other animals and would have to be destroyed.

He feared this was the case with Lincoln, a pit he had brought in weeks ago. Lincoln had lived year-round in the paved backyard of a storefront church on 14th Street, between Quincy and Randolph. Lorenzo wondered how someone who preached the word of God could abuse an animal. But the live-in priest at the *iglesia* had done just that to this dog. Lincoln had been beaten and chained by his owner, and taunted and stoned by neighborhood kids his entire life. He was mercurial, aggressive, and unpredictable. He was a victim, and he could never be socialized.

Lorenzo whistled softly, made a fist, and put it up to the cage. Lincoln came forward, his jaws working furiously, and snapped at Lorenzo's knuckles. Then he retreated to the back of the cage. He looked at Lorenzo shyly, almost apologetically. He seemed to remember Lorenzo as the one who'd taken him away from his hellish existence, but he could not keep himself from trying to bite his hand.

"I ain't mad at you, boy," said Lorenzo.

Lorenzo took the two flights of stairs to the top floor. He went directly to the office of Irena Tovar, his boss, and dropped into the chair before her desk. Irena was in her late thirties, wore glasses, and had extremely long hair, which she always wore in a single ropy braid. The end of the braid touched the small of her back. She was of Venezuelan descent. Her eyes were almost black and long of lash. Lorenzo loved her like he loved Rachel Lopez. Both had done their part in helping to save his life.

"She did what I asked her to do," said Lorenzo, speaking of the Korean woman on Mount Olivet.

"Twenty-five dogs is a lot of dogs," said Irena.

"I heard *that*. Hard for me to care for one. Least she cleaned the place up. Right now, we got no grounds for abuse charges."

"Keep checking on her."

"I plan to."

Mark Christianson knocked on the frame of the open door.

"Sorry to break in," he said. Mark was tall and clean shaven, with longish curly black hair and hillbilly sideburns. His rolled-back sleeves revealed wood-hard, tattooed forearms.

"What is it?" said Irena.

"Got a call from a citizen east of the river," said Mark. "Man says there's something going on in the woods behind his house. Lotta players, tricked-out cars, like that. Guys walking pit bulls into the woods. Guys carrying coolers and pieces of wood."

"Did he call MPD?"

"He called us first."

"Go ahead and alert the police," said Irena, "and get down there. Stay in radio contact."

"You in, Lorenzo?" said Mark, wiggling his eyebrows the way he did when things began to jump.

Lorenzo was already out of his seat.

SEVEN

ELVIN LEE DROVE a 3-Series BMW slowly down an alley bordered by the backs of houses on one side and a large community garden of vegetables and flowers on the other. Past the garden were the deep woods of Fort Dupont Park. Lee and Rico Miller were off E Street and 32nd, between the Anacostia Freeway and Minnesota Avenue, east of the Anacostia River. Up ahead, where the alley came to a dead end, at least a dozen freshly detailed late-model imports were parked on the grass. Also in the group were several vans, SUVs, and high-ton pickups.

"The Way You Move," that Outkast in heavy summer rotation, was coming from the in-dash. Lee was into it, and the way Rico was moving his head to those bursts of horns, looked like he was into it too. But you couldn't tell if the boy had any joy in him. Only time he smiled was when he was thinking about putting the hurt on someone. Rico was one of those, seemed like he had gone from being a little kid straight to a man, skipped the fun parts in between.

"This alley don't connect to nothin'," said Miller, who noticed such things. "Onlyest way out is the way you came in."

"Police ain't gonna lock you up for *watchin'* no fights."

"Old people live in these houses, you know they ain't got nothin' better to do than look out their windows all day long. They gonna see all these cars, they gonna call the law."

Instinctively, Lee reached for the joint in Miller's hand, then thought better of it and drew his hand back.

"You can't?" said Miller.

"I'm about due to drop a urine. I drop a positive, I'm gonna be violated like a motherfucker."

"Your PO is on you?"

"On me *hard*," said Lee.

Lee swung the BMW into a space beside a Lexus SUV. Stepping out of the car, they could hear the thump of bass coming from down in the woods. Lee saw a boy, couldn't have been more than eight or nine, standing around the vehicles, a neighborhood kid, most likely, paid by someone to keep an eye out for the law. Lee handed him five dollars and told him to look after his ride. The boy positioned himself beside the car.

Lee and Miller entered the woods. Almost immediately, the land graded off and dropped to a steep pitch. Down below, they could see a clearing, and then the ground rose up again. In the clearing there was much activity and many men.

"There they go," said Lee. "Down in that valley."

"That's a valley?" said Miller, who had never been in the woods, outside of driving through Rock Creek Park, in his life.

"A ravine, then," said Lee, who was nearly as inexperienced and uncomfortable in this setting as Miller, but wouldn't admit it. "Somethin' like that."

They came into the clearing. Gamblers and spectators stood around drinking, smoking weed, and discussing past and upcoming matches. A bookie sitting in a folding portable camping chair took bets and cash, and wrote the wagers in a notebook. Another man sold beer, malt liquor, and wine concoctions from out of a cooler. A boom box played bomb-squad-style hip-hop. There were few women in the crowd.

On the fringes, dogfighters handled their animals, pit bulls with game-cropped ears, all leashed or in cages. Many were being scrubbed down with soap solutions, as was required, since dogs were sometimes sent into the ring with nausea-inducing chemicals on their coats. A card table had been set up to the side; laid out on it were first aid supplies: IV kits, sutures, alcohol preps, and sponges. Syringes, to be used for injectable antibiotics brought along by the handlers, were available as a courtesy as well. Also complimentary were vitamins and supplements: B12, and liver and iron extracts. Beside the table were a couple of scales.

The ring itself was constructed of wood and had been transported in sections and assembled in the clearing. It was twenty feet square, thirty-six inches high, and had hinged gates in two of its opposing corners. Its floor was covered in green outdoor carpet stained with blood.

Lee and Miller moved through the crowd. Lee nodded at those he knew and made minimal eye contact with those he did not recognize. Residents of all four quadrants of the city were welcome here regardless of gang or business affiliation. This event was for profit and relaxation. The settling of beefs or the initiation of any kind of conflict was discouraged. But things happened when gazes lingered too long.

Lee bought a couple of malt liquors for him and his boy. He then placed a bet with the bookie after examining the dogs that were next up on the unofficial card. Lee put fifty dollars on a black pit named Mamba, due to fight a tan-and-white named Lucy. He was advised to do so by an obese man he'd seen around the clubs, had a copy of the *Scratch Line* in his hand. Fat Tony seemed like he knew his stuff. Plus, Lee liked the way that dog looked, black and strong. Also, Lee liked its name.

The music was turned off, a signal that the fight was about to begin. The spectators and players gathered around the perimeter of the ring. In the pen, both dogs had been placed in their corners by their handlers.

A referee, dressed casually, the same as everyone else, stepped in and ordered the cornermen out of the pit. Both got out of the fighting area but held their dogs fast by their collars from outside the gates. The referee instructed them to face their dogs.

The dogs were released. They ran to the center of the ring and clashed. The crowd was loud and intense. They laughed and called out for murder and blood. The dogs were virtually silent. They fought methodically, battling for position and dominance. Both were taken down and both sprang back up. Both had been conditioned for strength and endurance with cat mills, carpet mills, and spring poles. Both wanted to please their owners and defeat their opponent. Only one could emerge victorious.

It was Lucy, in the end, who won, her jaw furiously clamped onto Mamba's face. Finally, after a word from the referee, Lucy's handler used parting sticks, which were nothing but ax handles, to force his dog off the other. Lucy drew back. Mamba's right eye had been ripped from its socket; it hung by nerves, just barely connected, halfway down his cheek.

Lee was angry for listening to the fat man, and for picking the dog because of its name, an amateur play. Miller, for his part, had enjoyed the fight. His dick had got hard in his South Pole sweats when that tan dog had bit right down on that other dog's face.

Mamba, confused and in agony, rubbed his snout on the bloody carpet, trying to do something about his useless, dangling eye. Mamba's handler stood over the dog, berating him, calling him names. Then he picked the dog up and cradled him in his arms. He walked from the ring and headed toward the first aid table.

"You ready to book on out?" said Miller.

"Not yet," said Lee, looking with contempt at the owner holding his crippled animal. "I'm gonna win my money back first."

"Mamba wasn't shit," said Rico Miller.

Lee nodded, thinking, Fuck that animal. Let it suffer some. Cur deserves to suffer for showing no heart.

• • •

LORENZO BROWN AND MARK Christianson took the Tahoe, the newest vehicle in the Humane fleet, across town, because it had the best ride and also because of the CD player in its dash. Lorenzo was a radio man, strictly PGC or KYS, but Mark liked a kind of rock that could rarely be found on the airwaves anymore. Mark called it "punk before punk." When they paired up, Lorenzo deferred to Mark's seniority and allowed him to drive and control the music. Mark had put *Fun House* into the player and turned it up.

Lorenzo looked over at Mark, normally easy mannered and genial, his face now set, his jaw tight. Mark got that way when they were making calls like this one. More than Lorenzo, he was totally committed to, some would say obsessed with, protecting animals. His dislike of animal abusers in general and dogfighters in particular bordered on hate.

But Lorenzo could understand it. Mark had been through the worst of it, had patrolled these streets during the most violent phase of the fight-dog fad, and had seen some very bad things. All while Lorenzo had been serving his time.

Mark had first worked for PETA, straight out of college, but quickly grew tired of meetings, fund-raising, and desk duty. He then took a job at the shelter, picking up strays and biters, working the 3 p.m. to 1 a.m. shift, going alone at night into some of the most run-down sections of the city. It wasn't long before he became a Humane officer, wanting to take his mission to the next level.

This was the midnineties, when the fight-dog craze was at its peak. Having a pit or a rottweiler had become a symbol of power and fashion, a hip-hop accessory, like having the platinum chains or the nicest car. Pit bulls, in particular, seemed to be everywhere. Never mind that few of their owners knew how to care for them or had the desire to learn. Dogs, especially those who had lost fights, were disposable, like a shirt friends ridiculed because it had gone out of style. Mark found dogs shot in alleys, lying curbside with broken necks, thrown off roofs, and disposed of in Dumpsters with the trash.

To do his policing, he went into neighborhoods, apartment complexes, and Section Eight housing projects where his was the only white face for miles around. Places like First Terrace, around M and North Capitol, where the theft of dogs was common, and Simple City, at the time a legendary breeding ground for violent crime. Worst of all was 50th Place in Lincoln Heights, in Far Northeast. There the most serious dogfighters resided and held their matches. Dogs were flown in from Florida, with thousands invested in the animals, many paid for by drug money. The owners had much to protect. Back in that cul-de-sac, Mark encountered some of the scariest people he had ever seen.

He was physically threatened, ridiculed, and called, alternately, a faggot, a punk, and a bitch. The threats of violence bothered him, but not the names. He knew he was on the right side. He had suffered from stress-related weight loss and sleeplessness during this period, but he hung with the job.

And then time eased the situation. The culture began to change. It became less fashionable to own a fighting dog. Some handlers became sickened at the injuries and death. Others just grew old. The gangster romance thing had its window, and that window stayed open, it seemed, only for the young. Mark knew dogfighters who had quit because they'd started families, or because their women had insisted they get out of the game, or simply because they knew they couldn't jail.

The laws changed too. Failure to provide veterinary

care to an injured animal was now a misdemeanor. More important, there was a new felony dogfighting law on the books. One judge in particular, down at the District Courthouse, was known to give offenders actual jail time. The law was often invoked to help put violent multi-offenders — domestic abusers, rapists, and the like — behind bars when other charges had failed. Its implementation had made a dent in the dogfighting in the city.

Some offenders had gone on to related but less risky ventures. Many bred and sold pit bull puppies. Others trained and engaged dogs in professional weight pulls, a different kind of wagering activity that did not involve violence. Some dogs trained and bred for weight pulls even wore harnesses lined with sheepskin so the pressure would not cut their coats. Lorenzo Brown was not opposed to such contests, as the dogs, though powered up on steroids, were treated with relative care. Mark, predictably, was passionately opposed to animal exploitation of any kind.

The two of them were mostly on the same page, though. Their outlooks were different, but only by degree. There was still plenty of dogfighting and animal abuse in the city to keep them mutually focused.

Mark Christianson took the Benning Bridge over the Anacostia River and turned left on Minnesota Avenue. Lorenzo reached for the CD player and turned down the volume. They were nearing their destination. He radioed in to the office and asked for the whereabouts of the police. The MPD had been called, but Cindy at the dispatch desk did not know if officers had arrived.

Mark hooked a right onto the residential block of E Street and drove east. He went back into the alley and slowed the truck. Up ahead, where the alley dead-ended at a field, they saw many cars. A boy stood beside a silver 330i. He straightened as he caught sight of their blue uniforms through the windshield of their truck.

"It's goin' on," said Mark.

"They got a lookout too."

Mark and Lorenzo were unarmed. They had a choke pole, a wire noose mounted on a stick to control the heads of extremely aggressive dogs, in the back of the Tahoe. They had canisters of pepper spray that they never carried on their persons and rarely used. Once sprayed on an impounded animal, the annoying, burning toxin was difficult to get out of the vans and trucks.

Pepper spray was just one reason that Mark and Lorenzo preferred to work without police. Police were quick to use the spray, then leave the Humane officers to deal with the aftereffects. Some police, especially those who did not own dogs themselves, were also quick to use their sidearms. Recently, Lorenzo had seen a 6D officer empty his magazine into a teeth-baring, saliva-dripping rottie that, with patience, could have been subdued. Lorenzo had the impression that this particular police just wanted to shoot his gun.

Lack of police was fine, long as you didn't need them. But as Mark and Lorenzo went down the alley, counting the cars up ahead, they both realized they could use some help today.

"Pull over," said Lorenzo. "I want to talk to that kid."

"How do you want to do this?" said Mark, sweat on his forehead, though the air conditioning was blowing full force on his face.

"Your call," said Lorenzo.

"I'll go in."

"Figured you would. You got your binos?"

"My camera too."

"I'll get a record of these license plates," said Lorenzo, grabbing his clipboard and pen.

"Right," said Mark, parking the Tahoe, putting the tree up in park.

"You get burned, you come on back. You need help, you holler."

"I will."

"Or we could both stay up here," said Lorenzo. "Wait for the law."

Mark, reaching for his binoculars and camera in a pack behind his seat, did not answer. Both of them got out of the truck.

"You," said Lorenzo, pointing at the kid, who was still standing beside the silver BMW.

The kid stepped away from the car. Lorenzo went to him.

"Take off," said Lorenzo. "Police on their way, and you don't want to be here for that. You did what you got paid to do. Now leave, hear?"

The kid gave him a tough shoulder roll before he walked off, a slight dip in his stride.

Lorenzo watched Mark enter the woods, stepping with care. When he looked back to check on the kid, he saw him booking down the dirt alley. Lorenzo knew that the kid would cut into the woods as soon as he was out of Lorenzo's sight. He'd go down there and warn the players that the dog man was here, which meant the police were on the way. That's what *he* would have done at this boy's age. Lorenzo didn't blame him. They all had to play their roles. Besides, the object was to break up the fights and, for now at least, spare those animals some misery. The kid, no matter his intent, was going to get it done.

Lorenzo walked the alley, quickly recording the license plate numbers of the attendees, and the makes and models of the cars. The way that kid was running, he and Mark didn't have much time.

EIGHT

MUST BE SOME OLD HEADS runnin' this thing, thought Melvin Lee, 'cause they're spinning that old-time stuff out the box. *Amerikkka's Most Wanted*, Ice Cube strong and proud, with that production, sounded like Public Enemy and them, behind it. The record had come out back around '90, when Melvin Lee was first getting into the game. That was some good times back then, like everything was waiting for him up ahead. He'd had some dreams.

If he was up on some blunt right now, this day here would be about perfect. Since he'd come out, though, he couldn't even get his head up, for fear they'd put him back in. Truth was, he wasn't supposed to be fraternizing with these kinds of people either. But what'd they expect, that a man was supposed to stop having fun?

Least the boy, Rico, looked like he was enjoying his

self for a change. He wasn't a laugh a minute, but Melvin Lee liked having him around. The way Rico looked up to him, he had to admit, it made Melvin feel important, like all this bullshit he'd done in his life had been worth something.

Lee had fathered two children of his own, what they called beef babies, with a couple of different women, when he'd gone to the mattresses, Corleone-style, all because of some violent conflicts he'd got himself in. He had no contact with those kids at all. He had no idea where they stayed at and didn't want to know.

But hanging with Rico, it was like he was a father to the boy, in a way. Rico was devoted to him, as any son would be. Too devoted, sometimes. Once in a while, when someone would look at Lee the wrong way, Rico was all too ready to step in, take it to the next level. When that happened, Lee had to hold him back. Wasn't no reason to hurt someone, you didn't have to. That was something you learned with age. Nice to know that the boy was ready, though. No-fear motherfucker like Rico, it was good to have him on your side.

"You goin' with that brown girl?" said Miller. He meant the brown pit with the white face, being led by her handler to her corner of the ring.

"She gonna change my luck," said Lee. He had picked her over her opponent because her name was Sheila. For a while, he was fucking this redbone who had the same name. Lee had already lost the two fights he'd bet.

The man controlling the box stopped the music. Both dogs got settled in their corners. The referee ordered the cornermen out of the pit.

A kid came into the clearing, went directly to the ring, and yelled, "Hold up!" The referee put his hand up, signaling the cornermen to pause while he found out what this was about. The kid, who Lee recognized as the boy guarding the cars, was short of breath. He said something to the referee that was hard to make out but that put a reaction on the man's face.

"All right, everybody," said the ref, loudly so that all could hear. "We got to clear out. Dog men are here, and the police are on their way. Move!"

Lee turned around and looked up at the rise. He saw a white boy in a blue uniform, standing beside a tree. The sun flashed for a moment off something in the white boy's hand. Wasn't no chrome, 'cause the dog men weren't allowed to carry weapons. Had to be a camera or binoculars, something like that.

Around them, supplies were boxed, tables were folded, and the ring began to be disassembled. Dogs were led away. Men were cursing, killing their beverages, and taking last hits off their smokes. Others were crowded around the bookie, collecting their bets. Lee went there, waited his turn, and got his money. When he was done counting it, he head-motioned Rico. The two of them went up into the woods, climbing the grade the way they had come.

• • •

MARK CHRISTIANSON STOOD beside an oak on the rise, taking photos through his digital camera, its lens zoomed to the maximum. He was focusing on the dog handlers, the referee, and the bookmaker rather than the spectators, though he caught many of them in the frame.

Mark had found his vantage point and remained hidden behind the wide trunk of the oak for as long as possible. He had first looked through his binoculars, more powerful than the lens of his camera, to familiarize himself with the people and the scene.

Immediately he had recognized Fat Tony Jamison, a former dogfighter turned oddsmaker and consultant, moving his 350-pound frame slowly through the area, working the crowd. Fat Tony had been around way too long. Then Mark saw Antoine Loomis, who had a pit on a leash and was apparently still in the trade. For a three-month stretch back in '97, "Twan" Loomis had run fights out of a condemned apartment building at 49th and A, in Southeast. He had always been one step ahead of the law. When a determined Mark finally did gain entrance to the apartment house, after Loomis had abandoned the site, he had found the cinder-block-and-concrete basement where the fights had been staged. Damp, mildewed copies of *Your Friend and Mine*, *The Pit Bull Chronicle*, *Face Your Dogs*, and other publications were spread about the floor. Also on the floor were broken malt liquor bottles, cigarette butts, feces, matches, bottle caps, and syringes. Blood was streaked on the walls.

Mark took a photograph of Loomis and his pit, checking the digital image for clarity. He wanted to be sure he had him on record. Loomis was one of the bad, stupid ones who had been responsible for the abuse and murder of many dogs. He had also been charged as an accessory to a homicide, but the charges had not stuck. The federal prosecutor with whom Mark worked was building a case against Loomis. The photograph taken here was not a revelation, but it would help, someday, in rounding out the file that would eventually get Loomis off the street.

When the boy came into the clearing, Mark stepped out fully from behind the tree and took as many photographs as possible in the time he had left. The camp was breaking quickly, and the participants began to come toward him up the wooded rise. He stayed where he was for a few more minutes, even as they passed by him, even as they began to comment on his presence, taunt him, and call him names. He wasn't frightened. He was used to this. But he figured he better get to the Tahoe and back up Lorenzo. He was worried for Lorenzo's safety, but, more than that, he was concerned that Lorenzo might lose his temper.

Lorenzo was a good worker. Mark wanted to make sure that he stayed on the job. Indeed, Irena Tovar had charged Mark with the responsibility of keeping Lorenzo straight.

Mark climbed the rise.

• • •

LORENZO BROWN, STANDING BY a silver BMW, watched the men coming out of the woods, players and participants alike, walking dogs to vans and SUVs, carrying equipment, sections of ring, and folding tables and chairs. Some dipped casually and a few moved hurriedly. Some walked right through the community garden that the neighborhood residents had planted. None ran. The dog players and handlers had seen the white Humane officer in the woods and saw Lorenzo in uniform now. They knew that both officers had limited power and that they were not police.

Soon Mark appeared at the tree line, followed by many others, some of whom were making derogatory comments in Mark's direction. Mark, as usual, seemed unfazed. He stepped around the community garden and met Lorenzo.

"You okay?"

"I got some pictures," said Mark, sweaty, pink-faced, jacked on adrenaline.

Lorenzo looked around the field. Cars and trucks were pulling out, heading down the dirt alley. Mark was staring at Antoine Loomis, who was letting his animal into the backseat of a large black Mercedes sedan.

"You need to leave him be," said Lorenzo, recognizing the look in Mark's eye. "He don't like lectures."

"I'm just gonna have a few words with him."

"You ain't gonna convert Twan, that's what you're thinking. Some judge gonna do that eventually."

"Just going talk to him, is all."

"It's not on you," said Lorenzo, but Mark was already off, heading toward Loomis.

Lorenzo was intending to go to the Tahoe, radio in, and check on the status of the MPD, when he saw a man and a young man coming toward him. He recognized the older of the two and tried to place him. As he was doing this, Lorenzo realized that he had been leaning against the silver BMW. He moved off the car.

The two got nearer, and it came to Lorenzo who the older one was: Melvin Lee. Lee and Lorenzo had both come up in Park View. Lee had worked for Deacon Taylor, done time, come uptown, and was rumored to be working for Deacon again. Lee had made himself a rep when he was young. But looking at him now, Lorenzo realized that prison had broken him, even if Lee did not know this himself. Lee and his running partner stopped a few feet shy of Lorenzo.

Lee was all arms and legs, with a small torso, as if God had run out of the right size the day he'd made him. Lee's head was tiny, and his eyes bulged slightly. He looked like something that crawled up a wall. He wore a baseball cap cocked sideways on his head. He wore the oversize jeans. He was trying for that youth thing, but it was never going to work for him again. Man his age, to be dressed that way, it was just pathetic. He was going for down, but the vibe he put out was defeat.

The boy standing beside Lee had slack posture and nothing eyes.

"Dog man." Lee looked Lorenzo over. "What, you done lost your mind or somethin'?"

Lorenzo did not cut his eyes away, nor did he stare with any sort of malice at Lee.

Lee stepped in. His breath smelled of alcohol and onions. "Someone give you permission to touch my whip?"

Your whip? What'd you do to get it? You ain't never worked an honest day in your life.

"Didn't realize I was touchin' it," said Lorenzo. Then he said something he never would have said, to anyone he was not close to, in his youth: "I apologize."

Lee looked over his shoulder at the boy, then back at Lorenzo. "Now he gonna 'pologize. You hear that, Rico? After he done rubbed his dog-smellin' self against my shit."

The boy smiled, revealing teeth and gums that no dentist had ever touched. It reminded Lorenzo of the way an animal might smile, when it was hunting another animal, in a cartoon. Maybe it was the boy's face. Thin, long, and lightly bearded. Only thing missing was the sheep's clothes.

"You remember me?" said Lee.

Sure. I punked your ass out once in a club. You thought you could step to me, and I put you down with my eyes. You weren't shit then. You less than shit now. So you just keep talking, if it makes you look tall and strong to this boy.

Lorenzo nodded, still showing no emotion.

Lee looked him over. "What *happened* to you? They turn you out in there?"

Lorenzo did not answer.

"What, you forget how to speak?"

I don't need to. You don't mean nothin' to me.

Lorenzo looked past Lee, at Loomis's Benz. Loomis was out of the car, up in Mark's face, his chest almost touching Mark's. One of Loomis's partners had come around the car and was heading toward Mark too.

"Look at *me*, motherfucker," said Lee. "I'm talkin' to you."

No need for this, little man. You only get one chance to break bad on a man, and you had yours.

"I got to get goin'," said Lorenzo.

"We ain't done here."

"Excuse me," said Lorenzo, stepping around Lee. He couldn't help brushing the boy's shoulder as he passed. The way it felt, rigid, it was like he was touching a corpse.

"I'm gonna see you again," said Lee to Lorenzo's back.

Lorenzo crossed the field to Loomis's car.

Now Loomis and his partner were both tight in on Mark, who was holding his ground. Mark was keeping his pleasant half smile, that game face he used when he talked to everyone on the job, no matter what he was saying. Loomis's partner, big boy with lineman guns coming out his T-shirt, and Loomis himself, looked like they were both ready to kick Mark's ass. Their dog, in the back of the Benz, had its head out the rear window. It was barking, growling, and baring its teeth.

"How's everyone doin' today?" said Lorenzo, stepping close to the group, speaking in a friendly, even tone.

Loomis studied Lorenzo, then stood back and took a calming breath.

"Your boy just talkin' *too* much shit," said Loomis. "I'm fixin' to introduce him to my right fist."

"Ain't no need for that," said Lorenzo, pulling on the sleeve of Mark's shirt, moving him out of reach of Loomis's partner.

"That's what I'm sayin'," said Loomis. "He ain't got no call to talk to me with that kind of disrespect. Askin' me, Are you aware of this, and, Are you aware of that. Yeah, I'm *aware*, motherfucker. And you about to be aware that you fucked with the wrong man."

"He don't mean nothin' personal," said Lorenzo. "He's just doin' his job. Just like you and your friend here, and me. We're all just looking to get along."

Loomis, the rage gone out of him, lowered his voice to a mumble. "I got enough stress without this *bull*shit."

"I heard *that*," said Lorenzo.

The BMW drove by them, Lee and the one called Rico smiling at Lorenzo as they passed. The rest of the cars began to pass them too. Loomis and the big man got into the Benz without further incident, the pit bull still barking itself crazy in the backseat, and left as well. Soon it was just Lorenzo and Mark standing in the alley, with only their Tahoe left in the clearing. A couple of elderly men had come out the back of their houses and were surveying the scene.

"We do anything here?" said Lorenzo.

"We hit the pause button," said Mark, wiping sweat off his forehead with a damp sleeve. "Maybe stopped a couple of animals from getting torn up."

"Today."

A Seventh District cruiser came down the alley toward them. The driver was taking his time.

"Here comes the cavalry," said Mark.

Lorenzo shook his head and smiled. "What you say to Twan to get him so riled?"

"I was just telling him about the dogfighting law we got in this city. It's a felony now, you know?"

"For real?"

"I was enlightening him."

"Looked like he was responding in a real positive way."

"You hadn't stepped in, I would have brought him around to my way of thinking. I mean, he was practically eating out of my hand."

"Looked to me, way both of those boys were crowded around you, that the two of them was gettin' ready to hand you your ass."

"That was a group hug."

Two officers, a black and a white, got out of the cruiser. They walked toward Mark and Lorenzo.

"You want to talk to them?" said Mark.

"You do it," said Lorenzo, handing Mark the clipboard. "I got a little problem interfacing with the police."

NINE

RACHEL LOPEZ SAT ON a living-room sofa in a home in Landover, Maryland, with a woman named Nardine Carlson. It was late in the afternoon, but Nardine, puffy eyed and disheveled, looked as if she had just woken up.

Nardine Carlson lived with her children and grandmother in Kent Village, a development of houses and apartments in various configurations and conditions. Nardine's place was on a trash-littered street of duplexes, where the cars outside the houses were much nicer than the houses themselves.

When Rachel had pulled her Honda up to the front of Nardine's house, she recognized a fat, unattractive man leaning against a new German import, talking to a cute younger girl wearing shorts that laced crisscross style up the front. The fat man, Dennis Palmer, went by the name of Big Boy on the street. He wore a wife-beater and was rolling out of it in all directions.

"Hey, Dennis," said Rachel as she walked past him and the girl, Nardine's file in her hand.

"Miss Lopez," said Dennis.

"Everything okay?" said Rachel, still walking.

"Don't worry, I'm still up at the Friendly's."

"That's good. You must be doing all right, what with that new car and all."

"Yeah, well," said Dennis, "you know."

Rachel did not stop to talk to him. She didn't have to, as he was no longer on paper. His supervision period had ended six months earlier, and her involvement with him was done. Also, she didn't like him. He had a history of abuse toward women and, though he still held a job at an ice cream parlor, was probably re-involved in the sale of drugs. When she saw him, Big Boy Palmer always seemed to be around young, pretty girls. At a glance, it was unexplainable, as he was about as ugly as a man could be. But Rachel knew that certain kinds of women went for the players over the squares every time.

"I'll see you again, Miss Lopez," called Palmer.

Yes, thought Rachel. Me or someone like me, for sure.

In the duplex, Nardine's grandmother, tired and light of bone, offered Rachel some iced tea. Rachel declined. The grandmother left Rachel in the living room in the company of Nardine and her two children, a six-year-old girl she was just now getting acquainted with and an eight-year-old boy. She was closer to the boy because she had spent more time with him than she had with the girl. Nardine had known her daughter for only a month before going off to do her time.

The children sat on a shag carpet before a television

set, playing PS2. There were snack wrappers strewn around them, along with empty bottles of orange soda and Sierra Mist. The girl had her hand in a tube of Pringles now. Her other hand worked a controller. The kids were playing a game involving criminals, prostitutes, and guns. Points were given for shooting a police officer. The sound track to the game included music from *Scarface*.

"It's sunny out," said Rachel, saying it to Nardine as if she were giving her some news. The curtains had been drawn, and it was dark in the room.

"They don't wanna go outside," said Nardine, reading Rachel's implication correctly. "They just wanna play that game."

Rachel nodded, not pushing the issue, knowing it would do no good. It wasn't her job to raise other people's kids. Nardine didn't look like she had seen much daylight herself.

"How's the job search going?"

"It's hard."

"I know it is. But you still have to do it."

"I went up to the *Mac*Donald's like you told me to. Saw that manager, Mr. Andrews?"

"And?"

"They ain't have but one shift open. I can't work those morning hours. Kids be goin' back to school next month, and I need to be here to see them off. That's important, right?"

"What's important now is that you find a job," said Rachel. "Your grandmother can see the kids off to school."

Nardine looked blankly at the carpet and breathed through her open mouth.

"Did Mr. Andrews offer you the position?" said Rachel.

"He said that if I could do those morning hours, then he would give me a chance."

"Well then, you need to get back over there and tell him you'd like to take the job."

"I'm sorry, Miss Lopez. I am just not a morning kinda person —"

"Neither am I. But I still get up and go to work."

"That's you, all right? I ain't never claim to be perfect or nothin' like it." Nardine balled her fist and rabbit-punched her own thigh. "Why you gotta *press* me like this?"

Rachel stared at her a bit harder now. Nardine looked away. She was too thin and had bad color and foul breath. She was irritable. These were signs that she was back on drugs.

"It's hard," said Nardine, her voice trailing off.

"I know it is," said Rachel.

I fall down too. I fail, just like you.

"Miss Lopez, I don't know if I can do this."

"You can try. Now, you need to get yourself to work. And there's something else."

"What?"

"You have to get over to the clinic."

"Again?"

"You have to drop urines regularly. You *know* this. You haven't done it for a while."

Nardine lowered her head and began to cry. Her shoulders shook and tears dropped into her lap. Rachel allowed her to cry without comment. It could have been an act or it could have been real. It made no difference, really, in the end.

"Mommy, why you sad?" said the daughter.

"Just play your game, girl," said Nardine with an angry slashing motion of her hand.

Rachel had fewer female offenders than she did males, but her female cases tended to take up a disproportionate amount of her time. Women were the most difficult offenders to reform. They often had children and leaned toward relationships with nonproductive men. In terms of their pasts, they came with the most baggage. Most of Rachel's female offenders had been sexually abused, either by family members or the boyfriends of their mothers, in their childhood and early-teen years. This, and their environment, had led them to drugs and drug addiction. They turned to scams, shoplifting, and prostitution to finance their habits, and graduated to crimes like armed robbery. Since the mideighties, at the acceleration point of the urban drug epidemic, the female prison population had more than tripled. The negative effects of this rippled out; two-thirds of incarcerated women had at least one minor child on the outside.

In prison, many of these women received drug addiction treatment, and got clean, for the first time in their adult lives. But when they came out, the situation for females was even more harrowing than it was for males. Few had held jobs in the past, and some were simply unemployable. A federal law enacted in 1996 imposed a lifetime ban on female offenders from receiving family welfare benefits and food stamps. No wonder many of these women believed they were better off behind bars.

Rachel thought there was some truth to this, for women and for men. Certainly for those who were beyond reform, or for those who were simply unprepared to deal with the straight world ever again, prison was a "better place." No question, it was easier to jail, for some, than it was to live on the street. Many offenders she had known, those who were clearly not going to make it, had spoken almost wistfully about going back to prison. In a couple of cases, she had told these offenders to violate themselves, go back to jail, get fat and recharged, and then come out and try it again. Many, of course, never did come out.

What she wouldn't do, what she could never do, was believe that supervision and reform did not work just because they did not work for everyone. If she lost faith in the possibility of redemption, then what she did on a daily basis made no sense.

"I'm gonna try to get over to that clinic next week, Miss Lopez," said Nardine.

"Tomorrow would be better," said Rachel. "Okay?"

* * *

LORENZO BROWN AND MARK Christianson sat in the Tahoe, idling on M Street, Northeast, off 3rd, looking at a used-car lot surrounded by a high fence topped with concertina wire. Nearby stood the husk of the old Washington Coliseum, its arched roofline rising above the landscape. A pack of kids rode their bikes down the street, turning to cool-eye the uniformed men in the truck.

Mark pulled the case report on the car lot's owner, Patricio Martinez, and studied it.

"Man still got Cujo back in there?" said Lorenzo.

"You mean Lucky."

"How many Spanish you figure call their dogs Lucky?"

"They do like that name." Mark closed the file. "C'mon."

They locked the truck and walked across the street, entering the open gates of the lot. The business sold old cars, none guaranteed, all with available financing at an exorbitant rate. Ford Tempos, low-end Nissans, Pontiac Fieros, Geos, and Chrysler products from the eighties and early nineties were parked in rows, some unwashed, all with prices soaped on their windshields. Most went for under a thousand dollars.

A young Hispanic man came out of the garage beside the lot office and eyed the men in uniform as he rubbed his greasy hands on a shop rag. The man was dark and small.

"Patricio around?" said Mark, that pleasant smile on his face.

"Offi'," said the young man.

"Can you get him for me?"

The man made no move to do a thing. They all stood there for a minute or so, Mark smiling and the young guy rubbing his hands on the rag and staring implacably at Mark and sometimes Lorenzo. Then a rotund middle-aged Hispanic wearing a gold chain decorating his neck and hairy chest, visible through an almost completely unbuttoned sport shirt, came out of the office to greet them.

"Mark Christianson," said Mark, extending his hand, which the rotund man, Patricio Martinez, shook. "From the Humane Society."

"I remember you, sure."

"Here to check up on Lucky. You mind if we get a look at him?"

"Yeah," said Patricio Martinez in a jovial way, "sure, sure."

Patricio made a come-on gesture with his hand and moved his bulk between the rows of cars. Lorenzo and Mark followed.

Lorenzo could see Mark's jaw tightening behind his smile. The keeping of guard dogs got Mark's back up.

Animals kept in auto parts graveyards, used-car lots, warehouses, and retail establishments had no care or companionship after business hours. On the days that those places were closed, or during act-of-god weather events, many had none at all. During big snowstorms, Mark went out while the rest of the city was at a standstill and fed, watered, and checked on dogs like Lucky. In fact, Mark had ripped his pants climbing over the concertina wire of this very lot to check on Lucky during the blizzard of 2003.

They turned a corner and came upon a cage, the back of which gave to an open bay door. Lucky smelled their presence. He came out, galloping like a horse, and began to bark, stopping in front of the links, baring his teeth at Mark and Lorenzo. It was a deep, booming bark, fitting for the dog's size. Lucky was the biggest rottweiler Lorenzo had ever seen.

"Looks like he remembers you, man," said Lorenzo. "From that time you came down here in the snow. They say once you feed 'em, they love you for life."

Mark ignored him and whistled softly, the way he liked to do when he approached an animal, making a loose fist and putting his knuckles close to the links. The dog snapped at his fist and continued to bark. Mark kept his hand in place and looked around the cage, checking for water and cleanliness. Brown streaks, left from recently shoveled feces, were visible on the asphalt. Greenhead flies had lit on the streaks. Flies, in bunches, were parked on Lucky's gnarled ears as well.

"That's a boy," said Patricio Martinez, looking fondly at the beast. "Goddamn Lucky, he's good."

"You see those feces?" said Mark.

"He no got fleas!"

"Feces," said Mark. "Dog shit."

"Dog shit, sure. I clean it up."

"But you didn't clean it up good enough. After you shovel it, you have to hose it away completely. Otherwise you get all those flies. And then the flies get on Lucky's ears. They get *inside* Lucky's ears, you understand?"

"Sure, sure."

Mark withdrew his hand, knowing the dog would not quiet down in the presence of his master, Lucky being Lucky, doing his job. Then Mark gave instructions to Martinez as to what could be done about the fly problem and the dog's ears. Mark said he would drop by a solution to rub on Lucky's ears in the next few days, to get him started on the treatment. Mark wrote out another Official Notification report so that Martinez would know he was serious.

"And you need to get that dog neutered," said Mark.

"Eh?"

Mark made a scissoring motion with his fingers down by his own crotch.

Martinez pursed his lips in distaste. "I'm not gonna do *that* to Lucky."

Having those big balls on him, thought Lorenzo, that's what keeps old Lucky angry. Unlike Mark, Brown wasn't going to put his hand anywhere near that animal. Pit bulls got all the negative press, and they could do some serious damage, but in Lorenzo's experience, unneutered male rotties were the least trustworthy, most aggressive dogs of any type. This one here had a head the size of a buffalo's too.

Mark truly believed that there was no such thing as a bad animal. Lorenzo had to remind him that they *were* animals. Mark just trusted them too much sometimes.

"Get him fixed," said Mark, finishing off the form and

handing it to Martinez. "We don't need any more un-
wanted animals in this city."

"Lucky's good," said Martinez, wiping at a tear in the
corner of his eye that was not there.

"I'll be seeing you again," said Mark.

Lorenzo and Mark walked out of the lot and crossed
the street to the truck.

"Lucky was really feelin' your love vibe back there,"
said Lorenzo.

"You lived like that, you'd be angry too."

"I bet no one steals none of those hoopties out of that
lot, though."

"Why would they?" said Mark. "I wouldn't take one
of those cars if Martinez was gonna give it to me for free."

"True."

"Lucky's just lonely."

"Maybe you ought to come down one night, crawl into
that cage, and lie down beside him. Sing him a lullaby,
somethin' like that."

"You think?"

"Show him that scissor sign while you're at it," said
Lorenzo. "The one that says, I'm about to cut off your nut
sack."

Mark chuckled. "Maybe I will."

"See how old Lucky responds to that."

•   •   •

NIXON VELASCO HAD BEEN working as a day laborer for the
past three weeks at a construction site on North Capitol
Street, south of New York Avenue. Rachel Lopez had told
him she was going to visit him on the job sometime during
the week and that she would be speaking to his foreman
about his performance. She had known which day she

would do this, but she had purposely not given him the exact information. She wanted the threat of her visit to be his incentive to show up for work daily and on time.

"*Como te va?*" said Rachel, using her Spanish, knowing he would answer in any English he could muster, a game the two of them played.

"Good," said Velasco, a short, barrel-chested man with native features and night black hair. His skin, already dark, had been deeply coppered by the sun. "Is okay."

They were off to the side of the site, by a trailer. Some of the other men had blown kisses at Rachel as she'd arrived, but Velasco had silenced them with his eyes. Later on, Velasco would tell them that Rachel was his probation officer. On future visits, the men would keep their eyes on their work and make no comments as she passed through the site.

"*Esta trabajando duro*, eh?" said Rachel.

A thin smile came to Velasco's lips. His face carried a film of dirt. His tan T-shirt was brown with sweat. He stank of perspiration and last night's beer. She could see the answer to her question in front of her. But he didn't take offense. It was pleasant to look at her, and he felt that she truly was watching out for his best interests. Besides, she was only doing her job.

"Yes," said Velasco, preferring to answer her, mostly, in English, telling her in his own way that he knew of the mixture in her blood. "I work har'."

"*Esta estable tu trabajo?*"

Velasco nodded. "I come every day."

"Very good," said Rachel. "*Recibi los resultados de tu prueba de drogras.*"

"The clinic?"

Rachel nodded. "You dropped a negative. *Esta limpio.*"

"I no use the drug."

"Keep it up. You're doing fine."

Maybe, thought Rachel Lopez, you'll make it this time. Velasco, named Nixon by his father in honor of the man revered by many Hispanics, had seen plenty of trouble in his youth. A member of the old Brown Union gang in Columbia Heights, he had done a stretch for multiple drug offenses, been paroled, and gone back in on an aggravated assault conviction, which had been pled down. By the time he had returned to the street, his former gang members were gone, erased by death, prison, or deportation. Newer, more violent Hispanic gangs like 1-5 Amigos, STC, La Raza, MS-13, La Mara R, and Vatos Locos had since come to prominence around the city and made headlines for their brazen, murderous acts. At thirty-one, Nixon Velasco was too old to survive the new game. Age and maturity, more than jail time, remorse, or conscience, had reformed him. He knew he could not compete, and he was too tired to try.

"*Donde este tu jefe?*"

Velasco pointed at the trailer. "Ramos in the offi'."

"Until next time, Nixon." Rachel looked him in the eye and shook his hand.

On the way to the trailer, Rachel passed another of her offenders, Rafael Salamanca, also out after back-to-back jolts. Rachel had used Salamanca as a contact to help find Nixon this job. Rachel greeted him in Spanish, but he only nodded grimly in return and kept his eyes on the hole into which he was thrusting his shovel.

She knew Salamanca was having problems with the straight life. Stress in his home environment, not pressure from old peers, was the main cause. A veteran of a defunct Latino gang himself, Salamanca had returned from prison to find that his daughter, a recent high school dropout, had joined Vatos Locos at sixteen years of age. In that particular gang, one of the initiation rites for females was submission to group rape. Salamanca, normally a quiet, brooding man, had recently confessed to Rachel that he craved drugs as a means of escape from the harsh reality of what his life had become. During that conversation, he had also called his wife a *puta* and a drunk, and her mother, who lived with them in their apartment, a "filthy old pig." Rachel was awaiting the report from Salamanca's latest urine test and was not optimistic about the results.

Rachel handled forty cases at any given time. Of those offenders, the majority worked in day labor, construction, landscaping, and house painting jobs. They found these jobs through other offenders and through employers who were sympathetic to the problems facing ex-cons, either because they had relatives who had been incarcerated or because they had done time themselves. Still others actively sought out offenders for employment, from shelters, halfway houses, and bulletin boards, because they felt it was the Christian thing to do. Every day, hopeful offenders stood before dawn at pickup points like University Boulevard and Piney Branch Road in Maryland, and Georgia and Eastern avenues in the District. If they did good work, and if they were dependable, this day-to-day struggle could often lead to steady employment.

In the air-conditioned trailer, Rachel found Nixon's boss, a good-looking, gray-templed man named Ramos, who had done a federal jolt in Lewisburg many years ago, behind a desk. He told her that Nixon Velasco was a good worker and, in his opinion, on the straight. This particular job would probably last for another three months. Ramos planned to keep Velasco on the payroll, if possible, for the duration of the build. After that, he couldn't be sure. If Nixon kept working the way he was now, maybe he'd take him along to the next job.

"How about Rafael Salamanca?" said Rachel. "How's he doing?"

"Okay."

"Just okay?"

"He's missed a few days. He needs a little encouragement sometimes."

"Let me know if you need me to jump in."

"How will I get in touch with you?"

"What's that?"

"Do I have your number?"

"You have it. I gave you my card the last time I came through."

"But that's just the work number, eh?"

Ramos tented his hands and smiled. The muscles in his tan forearms bunched with the action. He looked Rachel over in a manner that was not about business, and he smiled.

"You ever go out for a beer, something, when the day's done?"

"No." Rachel shook her head and tried to keep his eyes. "I guess I'm all about work."

"You should enjoy yourself more. Good-looking woman like you."

Rachel glanced at her wristwatch.

"Even with no makeup," said Ramos.

"I've got to get going."

"Okay," said Ramos, amusement in his eyes. "You go ahead."

In her car, Rachel smoked a cigarette, her hand out the open window. She thought no further of Ramos, but rather of Nixon Velasco and Rafael Salamanca. It looked as if Nixon was going to make it and Rafael was not. No matter what she did, no matter how diligent and tough she was, she felt she had little control. That was during the day. It could be different at night.

She had a few more stops on her schedule: Eddie, whom she always enjoyed visiting, and a couple of others, whom she did not. She could put all of these appointments off until tomorrow, she supposed. It would set her back at the office in terms of her paperwork, but the field visits needed to be done.

She didn't have to meet with those offenders now. She was ready for a drink, and something else.

TEN

DERIC GREEN COULDN'T DECIDE between small DVD
screens in the headrests or one big screen in the
dash. That way, he could look at movies and videos himself as he was driving his Cadillac. Why should he care if
his passengers had their own screens? They wanted them,
they could do their own cars that way.

The other thing was, he didn't want to mess up his
ride now that he had it the way he wanted, customized and
personalized. He had paid this woman good money to em-
broider his name on every headrest in the truck. She had
done it in cursive and used gold thread. Against the black
leather, the gold looked real nice.

Maybe he could skip the dash thing and do something
else. He'd seen this video, had to be Ludacris, where Luda
or whoever it was had installed a DVD screen right smack

in the middle of the steering wheel. That was cool too. Only, if you turned the wheel while you was driving, and you *had* to turn it to drive the car, how the fuck could you see what was going on?

Green pushed his fingers under his Raiders cap and scratched at his head. He did this unconsciously when his thoughts went deep.

"Pull over, D," said Michael Butler, sitting in the leather bucket beside him, pointing to a Giant supermarket on Georgia Avenue. "I wanna get Nigel's moms some ice cream."

"Nigel told you she ain't need nothin'."

"She love that mint-chocolate Breyers, though."

"I know it," said Green, thinking, She love it like a dog loves a steak bone. Why she fatter than a motherfucker too.

"We got to go by there anyway, drop off the count. Thought we'd bring her a surprise."

DeEric Green turned the Escalade into the lot of the Giant without further comment. He parked in a handicapped space and watched Michael Butler walk into the store. Boy wanted to bring Nigel's mother a surprise, he wasn't gonna fight it.

A 4D cruiser came into the lot and drove through it slowly. Green reached down and pushed the butt of his chrome full under the seat.

So now Butler was gonna get another gold star for being thoughtful to Nigel's mother. Green guessed that Butler felt the need to kiss on Nigel's ass, make a place for himself as some kind of house cat, 'cause he sure wasn't gonna shine out on the street.

Green wondered why Butler wanted to be in the life at all. He didn't buy expensive things with the money he made. He took no pleasure in being hard. He didn't talk about football, fucking dudes up, killing bitches in the bed, or none of that. Instead, Butler could point out foreign countries, like Canada, on a map. He could tell you about star constellations and stuff like that. He read books, newspapers, and magazines. Butler was different.

Still, odd and soft as Butler was, Nigel was moving the kid up little by little. Green couldn't deny that it bothered him some. You could even say it hurt him, 'cause he had been loyal to Nigel for a couple of years now. He had even put some work in for Nigel, back when he first came on.

And what, exactly, had Michael Butler done to get his self on that fast track? He'd never smoked anyone. He'd never, far as Green knew, handled a gun. Nigel had taken a liking to Butler, was all, and now he was getting ready to promote him. All right, so the kid was smart, maybe even smarter than DeEric, if you measured it by books and shit like that. But didn't being fearless out here count for nothing no more?

Truth was, and hard as it was for Green to admit it, he could see why Nigel liked Butler. Butler had an easy manner about him. He was gentle, steady, and quiet. Even when he was drinking alcohol and smoking weed, his personality stayed the same. Green didn't feel like Butler was suited for the game, but what else was a young man in his situation going to do? Butler didn't have no man at home to guide him right, and even if he did, coming from the house where he came from, living with a no-ass straight-up fiend of a mother, Butler wouldn't know how to act in the square world. Wasn't like he was gonna go to Howard or Maryland U and blend in with them fraternity boys. College wasn't in the boy's future, anyway. He'd already dropped out of high school.

So Butler had made his choices. Same way Green had made his, early on.

Green had followed the path of his older brother, James, a midlevel dealer in Columbia Heights. James had done all right for a while, but he had died from a bullet to the back of his head five years back. James sold drugs, but he wasn't about beefing with no one. It had happened over some girl.

James was just crazy behind that ass. He saw it, he liked it, he had to go and hit it. Didn't matter if some other motherfucker held the deed on the bitch's pussy. DeEric had told James that this hunger was gonna kill him some-day, and it did. Their mother, she had cried like a mad-woman at the graveside. DeEric had kept his face set tight at the funeral, 'cause you had to in front of your boys. But when he got to their house on Lamont Street, up in his room? He'd cried his eyes out too. He still missed James fierce. Worst thing was, he couldn't avenge him. By the time DeEric found out who'd done the thing, the killer was dead his own self by another man's hand.

The new Bone Crusher came on the radio. Green turned it up.

It settled on Green that Butler was taking the elevator to the top floors no matter what, and he, DeEric, was gonna be staying down in the lobby. He wasn't going to complain about it or anything else to Nigel. Nigel was why he was driving this Escalade right here. Nigel was why he was wearing these platinum chains. The preacher at his mother's church called them slave chains, but that Bama was driving a Ford Taurus with duct tape on the bumper, so what could he know? Green liked what this life gave him. He wasn't ashamed of one thing.

Anyway, Green was a soldier, not an officer. He knew this. Maybe he'd be taking orders from Butler someday too. That would be fine, long as he kept getting paid.

He sensed that Nigel didn't want no bad to come to the kid. Green would make certain that none did.

Green looked in the rearview and side-views. The police was gone. He didn't notice the silver BMW that had followed them into the lot. Green took a half-smoked joint out of the ashtray and struck a match.

As Green was hitting the weed, Michael Butler came out of the supermarket and got back in the Caddy. He reached into the bag where the ice cream was and pulled out a roll of Sweet Tarts.

"This you, D," said Butler, handing Green the roll. Sweet Tarts were DeEric's favorite candy, especially when he was high.

"Thank you, cuz," said Green, passing the joint over to Butler, who took it and drew on it hard.

Green thinking, Ain't nothin' wrong with this kid, when you get down to it. The boy's just nice.

*　*　*

RICO MILLER WAS UNDER the wheel of his 330i, sitting low, as Melvin Lee, in the passenger bucket, scanned the radio for a song he liked. Miller had let Lee drive the car for most of the day, but now it was time for Miller to take back what was his.

Lee had this hoop, an old Camry, the kind of car a white man in the suburbs bought when he thought he'd made it. It was the car to go with the relaxed jeans and the goatee and the wife with the long T-shirts trying to cover her fat ass. Funny to see Melvin driving a car like that, much as he loved nice things, but that was part of his strategy for layin' low and staying free. Show no flash, hold a job up at the car wash, watch the weed intake, report steady to the correctional officer, pee in the cup when they asked you to, all that. Melvin carried no gun, either, 'cause a felon like him, he got caught with one, that was a mandatory ten-to-fifteen right there. What they called the Reno law. Melvin did *not* want to go back to prison.

So Rico Miller let him drive his whip. Not all the time, but some. Even let Melvin pretend it was his, like when he was talking mad shit to that dog man back at Dupont, saying, "You leanin' against my car." Dog man playin' Melvin off, not using his words but his eyes to let Melvin know that he didn't give a good fuck about Melvin or what he had to say. Anyway, if it made Melvin feel better about his circumstances to call the car his own, Miller had no problem with it. Melvin knew whose car it was.

Rico Miller hit the hydro he was smoking and smiled about nothing. The weed was starting to blow kisses to his head.

"I like this right here," said Melvin Lee, his NY baseball cap sitting loose on his tiny head, taking his hand off the radio's scan.

"Alicia?"

"Joint is tight. She tight too."

It was the one where the coffee shop waitress at "39th and Lenox" calls up a customer, this dude she's been noticing, and leaves him a message on his answering machine, right in the middle of the song. She tells him how she's been slipping milk and cream into his hot chocolate, even though the manager wouldn't like her doing it, because she, the waitress, finds him "sweet." Rico would never listen to this kind of bitch music on his own, but

Melvin was an old head who was into that old-type thing. Rico didn't ask him to turn it off.

"I'd give that girl a whole *bucket* of cream," said Miller, who felt he had to say something.

Lee swigged from a bottle of malt liquor he had in a paper bag and wiped his chin. "They turnin' up there."

"I got eyes."

"They turnin', is all I'm sayin'."

Miller and Lee had followed DeEric Green and the Butler boy in the black Escalade through Petworth and into Park View. It was early in the evening, not yet close to dark. The sun was low and throwing gold on the street. People were walking on Georgia, going in and out of markets, Laundromats, liquor stores, check-cashing operations, and bars, their shadows long on the sidewalks. The activity would pick up soon. On the side streets both east and west of Georgia, open-air drug sales would intensify as the night progressed.

The Escalade turned left onto Otis and went up its grade. It cut a right on 6th. Rico Miller kept his distance, going slowly up Otis and pulling over to the curb before the turn. He didn't want to get burned, and from where he'd parked, he could see just fine down 6th. Also, he was being mindful of the territory into which he'd crossed.

This was Nigel Johnson's turf, from Otis to Park Road. Deacon Taylor had the south section of the neighborhood, from Lamont through Kenyon, down to Irving. They shared Morton, and the Park Morton Section Eights. What got confusing sometimes, what caused trouble, was some of those corners in between.

Neither Nigel nor Deacon worked the area west of Georgia Avenue anymore. Way the Spanish were acting back in Columbia Heights, with their gangs, La Raza and especially that STC mob, just goin' wild back in there, there wasn't any upside to it anymore.

Miller cut the engine. He and Lee watched DeEric Green and Michael Butler get out of the Escalade. Green had a shoe box in his hand and Butler had a bag.

"What they doin'?" said Miller.

"That's where Nigel's mother stay at," said Lee. "Most likely, they be droppin' off the count."

"Lotta cash to go to his moms."

"She get some every day. She be bankin' it for Nigel."

"Both of them carryin' money?"

"The bag the kid be carryin'? I expect he got some food in that motherfucker. 'Cause you know that fat-ass heifer do like to eat."

Miller stared at the house. "We gonna brace 'em when they come out?"

"Not in front of Nigel's mother's place," said Lee. There were some things you did not do.

They sat there for a while, Rico Miller enjoying his high, fingering the knife in his pocket as violent images moved like swift dark clouds behind his eyes. Melvin Lee drank methodically, staring at the run-down stretch of 6th. His mind was on simpler things.

"I fucked a girl on that street," said Lee, seeing her in his head.

"Which house?" said Miller.

"I'm tellin' you, I fucked her *on* the street. We was walkin' back from the Black Hole one night, and she couldn't wait. I bottomed her ass right there on the asphalt."

"What her name was?"

"What difference does that make?"

"Make the story better," said Miller, "if you know her name."

"How am I supposed to remember her name, all the girls I done had?" Lee grinned. "I can tell you one thing about her, though."

"What?"

"She *looked* like your little sister."

"Hmm."

"Matter of fact," said Lee, getting into it now, "it might could have *been* your sister. Dark as it was that night, I couldn't tell."

"Did she scream?"

"Like I was murderin' it, son."

"Then it wasn't my sister."

"Why you say that?"

"My sister don't scream when you fuck her," said Miller.

"That's 'cause you ain't doin' it right," said Lee. Only Lee laughed.

Not much later, DeEric Green and Michael Butler came out of the row house and got into the Escalade. When they pulled off the curb, Rico Miller fired up the BMW and followed the Cadillac north, back to NJ Enterprises, Nigel Johnson's storefront on Georgia Avenue.

ELEVEN

LORENZO BROWN WENT through his voice mail and got his paperwork up to date before clocking out of the office. He said good night to Mark, Irena, and his other coworkers, and patted the heads and stroked the bellies of his favorite animals, those who ran free and those caged in the basement kennel. Many were not pleased to be in cages, but all were better off than they were before they had been impounded. The lucky ones would be adopted and get second lives in good homes.

Out on the sidewalk, Lorenzo went two doors down to the spay clinic to check on Queen, the old lady's cat from over near Kennedy Street. The calico was shaking in the back of her cage.

"You all right," said Lorenzo, putting his index finger

through the links. Queen edged forward and rubbed her face against his skin. "You gonna feel different, is all, when this is done. More calm."

The Humane employees parked their work trucks and personal cars on Floral Place, a residential court behind the office alley, accessible through a break in a narrow stand of trash trees and brush. Parking stickers for that particular zone were available to residents only, so the employees were constantly dodging tickets from traffic control. The court folks were cool; the residents back there did not complain, knowing they could call on the dog people and get a quick response if they had a problem on their street.

Lorenzo got into his Pontiac Ventura, a 1974 he had bought on the cheap from the brother of a man he'd befriended in prison. The man had tipped him to the car and given him his brother's address, over in Far Northeast. The Ventura, GM's sister car to the Chevy Nova, was a green-over-green two-door and held that strong 350 engine, highly regarded in its time, under the hood. It had been in poor but serviceable shape when Lorenzo bought it, but at eight hundred dollars the price was right. After he turned it over to his boy Joe Carver, who had always been good with cars, the vehicle was more than right. Joe had installed new belts, hoses, plugs and wires, ball joints, and shocks. He'd replaced the muffler and the dual pipes, injected Freon into the cooling system, and reupholstered the back and front bench seats. Once that was done, Lorenzo had washed and detailed the Pontiac under an oak on Otis and stepped back to admire it. The Ventura had nice, clean lines.

The Pontiac was old and needed a paint job and new

chrome, but it was a runner. Young men driving drug cars, who knew only of German luxury automobiles and upscale rice burners, laughed at him at streetlights, but he got compliments occasionally from men older than he was. They called it "that *Seven-Ups* car," and when he asked them what they meant, they said, "The *movie*, youngun." If it was a movie, it was before his time, but Lorenzo said politely that he'd have to check it out someday. He'd never been one to watch movies, but it was something he was meaning to get around to. He *had* gotten into books in lockdown some, for the first time in his life. The prison librarian, a pale man named Ray Mitchell, had turned him on to street stories by writers like Donald Goines, Chester Himes, and this dude Gary Phillips, had his picture on the dust jackets, big man with Chinese eyes, looked like the real. So movies, yeah, maybe he would start to check out some of those. He'd like to read more books too. He sure did have time.

Lorenzo drove south on Georgia, into the city. Dusk had fallen on the streets.

Down near Fort Stevens, in the retail strip between Brightwood and Manor Park, he parked and entered the Arrow Cleaners. Lorenzo had his uniform shirts cleaned and pressed there. It was an extra expense, but he felt that a man needed to look right, like he cared about what he was doing, when he was on the job. This place here always gave him good service. The owner-operator, a Greek named Billy Caludis, showed him respect. Caludis had hung a Dick Gregory poster up on the wall, another reason for Lorenzo to patronize the shop. Lorenzo had read *Nigger* in prison too.

"No starch, on hangers," said Caludis, handing Lorenzo his order across the counter. "Right, Mr. Brown?"

"Right," said Lorenzo. "You have a good one."

Coming out of the store with his shirts in hand, he saw Nigel standing on the sidewalk with two of his people out front of his place, NJ Enterprises, on the other side of Georgia. Lorenzo opened the back door of the Ventura and laid his shirts flat on the seat. Those hooks they put in most cars were long gone from this one.

"Hey, Renzo!" said the booming voice of Nigel Johnson. "Hey, man, what you doin'?"

Lorenzo turned, stayed where he was, shouted across the lanes of north and southbound traffic to his friend. "Just got off work. 'Bout to head home."

Nigel put his hands on his hips and bugged his eyes theatrically. "And you just gonna, what, drive that race car away without stoppin' to say hello to your old boy?"

Lorenzo hesitated, then locked down his car. Nigel was right. Wasn't any harm in visiting now and again. It sure wasn't like Nigel was gonna try and make him re-enlist. It had been a while since they'd spoke. Lorenzo waited for a break in traffic before crossing the street.

They hugged briefly and patted each other's backs. Lorenzo stood back and had a look at Nigel. He seemed fit.

"You pay rent on this place," said Lorenzo, "and you out here standing on the sidewalk."

Nigel's eyes went to the live cigar in his hand, a Cuban, no doubt. "Just stepped out to have a smoke. I don't like the smell settlin' in my office."

"Nice hookup," said Lorenzo. The powder blue Sean John warm-up was draped exactly right on Nigel's large frame.

"Had it tailored," said Nigel, "to accommodate these extra el-bees I been carryin'."

"Nah, you lookin' all right."

Nigel nodded. "You too. But then, you always did keep your physical self together."

"I'm tryin'."

"How's Joe? You see him much?"

"All the time. He's got steady work, layin' bricks. Joe's doin' good."

Lorenzo looked at Nigel's employees, over by a black Escalade curbed in front of the office. The older of the two, wearing the same Raiders cap and bright orange FUBU shirt he'd seen him wearing that morning, the one who'd laughed at him as he was walking Jasmine, was slouched against the truck. The younger one, no more than a boy, had gentle eyes. Both looked like they were high.

"Meet Lorenzo Brown," said Nigel. "This here's DeEric Green."

"Been hearin' about you a long time," said Green, who did not move off the truck. It was meant to be a compliment, Lorenzo supposed, but Green's dull look said he was unimpressed.

"And this young man here is Michael Butler," said Nigel, a hint of pride in his voice.

Butler stepped forward and shook Lorenzo's hand. "How you doin'?"

"I'm good," said Lorenzo.

This Michael Butler looked like one of Nigel's personal projects. Nigel liked to pick the most promising, most intelligent ones out and take them under his wing. It never did work out. None who stayed on came to a good end. This was the one definite of the game. Still, Nigel kept trying to promote the ones he felt had promise. He was an optimist that way.

"Your job goin' all right?" said Nigel.

"Everything's good," said Lorenzo.

"You need anything?"

"I'm straight," said Lorenzo, looking at Nigel deep, telling him that he would never need anything from him again.

There was no animosity in their eyes, no bad blood between them. They were friends and would always be friends, but nothing would ever be as it was. Both had fulfilled their end of the bargain, and now that part of their lives, the part where they'd been together in business and as running boys, was done.

In the interrogation rooms at the time of his last arrest, and in court at his trial, Lorenzo had stood tall. He had not flipped on Nigel, as they had tried to get him to do, and had in fact refused to speak Nigel's name. He had given up no one, not even enemies. He'd made no deals and done his time.

For his part, Nigel had staked Lorenzo with a package as soon as he'd come out of prison, a common practice for those who had fallen and returned. It was a relatively small amount of heroin, which would finance Lorenzo's reentry into the world. The package was delivered to Lorenzo by one of Nigel's boys without a word. Lorenzo accepted it, knowing what it was without having to open it. He moved it quickly and quietly, took the proceeds, and used the money to cover the first month's rent on his apartment and to buy his car. He never thought about getting back into the life again. Between Lorenzo and Nigel, all of this remained unspoken.

"How's your little girl?" said Nigel.

"All right, I guess."

"You ain't seen her?"

"Not to speak to."

"That woman ain't right," said Nigel, meaning Sherelle, the mother of Lorenzo's child.

"Time gonna fix it," said Lorenzo, roughly echoing the words of Miss Lopez.

Nigel dragged on his cigar. "You still follow ball?"

"I watch it when I can."

"At MCI?"

"Not on my salary."

"I got club seats for the season."

"What, you can't afford the floor?"

"Go on, man. You know they got Gilbert, right?"

"He can play."

"Boy's *sick*. You and me should check out his game this winter."

"Yeah," said Lorenzo, "we should do that."

"We *damn* sure should."

"Look, Nigel . . ."

"What?"

"I gotta see to my dog. She been inside all day."

"Go ahead, then," said Nigel. "Don't be a stranger."

Lorenzo and Nigel executed their old handshake, as natural as putting one foot in front of the other, then went forearm to chest. Lorenzo nodded at the two employees and crossed Georgia to his car.

"That your boy, huh," said DeEric Green.

"Yes," said Nigel, watching him go. He turned to Green and Butler. "Y'all headin' out?"

"You got somethin' special you need us to do?" said Green.

"Just check on the troops and pick up the count. Tell the soldiers I realize they runnin' low, but I got a package comin' in later this week." Nigel turned to Butler. "Mind

DeEric. Man's a veteran. You watch close, you gonna learn."

Butler nodded. DeEric Green, energized by the compliment, got off the truck and stood straight.

"By the way," said Nigel. "My mother called me, said you brought her some of that Breyers. That was real nice." Nigel looked from one to the other. "Watch yourselves out there, you hear?"

Nigel went up the steps and entered his storefront door. DeEric Green and Michael Butler got in the Escalade.

Across the street, Lorenzo Brown pulled away from the curb and hit the gas. Through the intersection, parked just past Rittenhouse Street, he saw the same silver BMW from the dogfights over in Fort Dupont, and the two he'd encountered, Melvin Lee and his shadow, in the front seat. They turned their heads to stare straight ahead as he passed.

Lorenzo understood the codes of respect and disrespect, and the consequences of breaking same, but their minor confrontation at the dogfight hadn't seemed like it was all that big an incident. Not enough to warrant them tracking him down. Maybe they were there to watch Nigel and them. Lee did work for Deacon Taylor; leastways that's what Joe Carver had told him. Anyway, it was no business of Lorenzo's.

He kept on driving. He thought of his daughter, Shay. Down by the Fourth District Police Station, at Quackenbos, he hung a left.

．．．

IN THE BMW, Melvin Lee and Rico Miller watched the black Escalade come off the curb and head south.

"Let's go," said Lee.

Miller ignitioned the 330i and drove north, then swung a U in the middle of Georgia and got in, four or five car lengths back, behind the Cadillac.

"What you suppose the dog man be doin' over there with Nigel?" said Miller.

"Brown worked with Nigel," said Lee. "Brown was Nigel's boy."

"He comin' back?"

"He too soft to come back," said Lee. "You saw how he acted today."

Yeah, I saw, thought Miller.

"Prison broke that motherfucker," said Lee.

Same way it broke me.

"They bookin'," said Miller.

"Get up ahead of 'em. You know they gonna be goin' up Otis. We'll block 'em there, have our talk."

"They gonna run that light," said Miller as the Escalade accelerated toward the next traffic signal, gone yellow.

"Then you gonna need to run it too."

Miller blew the red.

• • •

SHERELLE STAYED ON 9th Street, around the corner from the police station and the tall radio towers, in one of a series of boxy brick apartment buildings grouped back from the street. The apartments had back porches, many of whose screens were ripped and hanging from their wooden frames. Between the buildings there was plenty of green grass, worn grass, dirt, and open space for kids to run. Though dusk had gone to dark, kids were out there now.

Lorenzo Brown parked his Pontiac on the street in front of Sherelle's unit. He knew Sherelle's schedule.

She worked a noon-to-eight shift at a makeup-and-hair shop over on Riggs Road. After Sherelle got off, she picked up Shay from her mother's duplex near Riggs, on Oneida Street. Sherelle and Shay got back to the apartment on 9th Street every evening at about this hour. Lorenzo knew because he'd watched them many times.

Soon they arrived in Sherelle's new-style Altima. Too much car for that girl to be carrying on her budget, but then Sherelle always did spend beyond her limit. Lorenzo could see his little girl in the backseat, Sherelle behind the wheel, and a big man beside her in the passenger bucket. That would be Sherelle's new George.

The three of them got out of the car and walked up onto the sidewalk. Sherelle, always on the full-figured side, looked like she had put on weight. She kept her style fresh, though, the way those hair girls liked to do. Shay, in a sleeveless shirt and shorts, looked plain pretty and sweet. She skipped along the sidewalk and reached for her mother's hand.

Lorenzo, seeing Shay, got out of his car without thinking on it. He was just a half dozen automobiles away from Sherelle's. The sound of his door made them stop and turn.

Sherelle's face hardened. She pulled Shay along. Shay looked back at Lorenzo and then up at her mother.

"Who's that, Momma?" said Shay.

"Nobody," said Sherelle. "You come along."

The big man, heavy and tall, wearing khakis and a loose silk shirt, stayed behind. He wore a crucifix outside his shirt. He stood on the sidewalk under a street lamp, staring at Lorenzo, waiting for his girlfriend and her daughter to get inside their place.

"I don't want no trouble," said Lorenzo.

"Ain't gonna be none," said the man.

"I'm her father."

"I know who you are."

Lorenzo shifted his feet. "I just want to talk to her."

"That's not gonna happen," said the man. "You already made your choice. You care about Shay, you got to let her be."

Lorenzo did not challenge the man or what he said.

"Go home," said the man, his eyes softening. "Your little girl is loved; you don't need to worry about that. She gonna be all right."

Lorenzo walked back to his car. He sat behind the wheel and watched the hulking silhouette of the man cross the grounds and head toward Sherelle's apartment. Time was, he would have stepped to that man for being so bold. But Lorenzo had come to a point in his life, he was old enough to know, and admit to himself, that the man was right.

"Who's that, Momma?"

"Nobody."

Lorenzo started his car.

That's right. I ain't shit.

TWELVE

RACHEL LOPEZ HAD BATHED, and the water in the tub, drawn very hot, was now warm. The candles she had set on the tub ledges were lit and were the sole source of illumination in the room. Beside one of the candles was a goblet of California merlot. It was her third glass.

Rachel's shadow danced on the bathroom wall. Freddy Fender sang "The Wild Side of Life" in Spanish from a portable stereo she had placed on the floor. Rachel sat naked on the edge of the tub, one foot on the tiled floor, one up on a step stool she had placed nearby. An electric fan whirred under the music, blowing air on her knees, thighs, fingers, and cleanly shaved sex.

She closed her eyes. In the darkness, pictures ran through her mind. Briefly, the man in her head was the handsome construction boss Ramos. Then he was a stranger beneath her.

The cool of the porcelain beneath her buttocks, spread so that the surface touched her anus, was pleasant. The ligaments and veins inside her filled with blood, and she felt a wash rush forth. She caught her breath and her muscles contracted violently. Her head pitched forward and she was done.

Rachel cleaned herself with a warm wet washcloth. She put on a dark red lacy brassiere and then slipped into thong panties that matched. In the mirror, with the light of the bathroom now switched on, she applied eye shadow, eyeliner, and lipstick, all in deep colors. She bought the inexpensive brands, available at any drugstore, because she found their colors more dramatic. She unscrewed the cap of her night perfume, which was strong but not flowery, and shook some onto her fingers. She lightly rubbed her fingers on the muscles high inside her thighs, reached around and touched the very base of her back and the nape of her neck, and rubbed the remainder between her breasts. Finally she ran her perfumed fingers through her hair. She stepped back and looked in the mirror. The brown nipples of her small hard breasts showed through the lace of the bra. She was aroused, not by the sight of her own body, but by the preparation itself.

Rachel dressed in a black leather skirt that accentuated her hips and womanly ass. She wore no stockings; her shapely bare legs were already brown. She put on a red shirt and unbuttoned it so that the front clasp of her bra showed. She put on medium-heeled black pumps. She hung a necklace on her chest and let its silver pendant fall on the upcurve of her left breast. She brushed out her black hair.

Rachel had a fourth glass of wine, gathered up her purse and cigarettes, and left the apartment. She drove downtown.

• • •

THE BMW HAD SPED down to Park View ahead of the Escalade. It now faced west and idled in the middle of Otis Place between rows of parked cars. Through the windshield, Melvin Lee and Rico Miller waited and watched.

"Where they at?" said Miller.

"They gonna be along."

As if Lee had willed it, the Escalade turned off Georgia and started up Otis.

"What I tell you?" said Lee, a barely detectable catch in his voice.

The Escalade did not slow down as it approached them.

"We ain't got nothin' to back us," said Miller. He was not frightened, but stating a fact.

"We ain't gonna *need* nothin'," said Lee. "We're gonna talk, and they gonna listen."

By giving this strong response, Lee hoped to distract Miller from noticing the lack of confidence on his face. Lee had always been cocky in his youth. That natural, youthful swagger, along with an easy access to guns, had fueled his reckless courage. Age, and the experience of incarceration, had humbled him. Now, under supervision, he could not risk being around any kind of firearm. He felt vulnerable and defenseless without one, like in those dreams he had where he was walking naked among his enemies on his own streets. But Deacon had told him to go out and send a message, and that's what he was going to do. And then there was Rico. He had to be hard around the kid.

The Cadillac came up on them and braked just a few

feet from their grille. The headlights of the Caddy, on a higher platform than those of the BMW, nearly blinded Miller and Lee. But Miller did not reverse the car. It was a given that neither driver would back up or pull over to let the other pass.

DeEric Green, behind the wheel of the Escalade, landed on his horn. "C'mon, motherfucker. Move it."

"That's Deacon's people," said Michael Butler, recognizing the man in the passenger seat of the BMW and the animal-looking boy under its wheel.

"*I* know that," said Green. "Don't mean they got the right to block the street."

Green hit the horn again and kept his palm on it. A couple of lights went on in the nearby row house windows. The BMW did not move.

"Fuck this bullshit," said Green, reaching under his seat and finding the checkered rubber grip of his automatic. It was a stainless steel eight-shot .45 Colt. Green had bought it, a Gold Cup Trophy model, because it was the most expensive one the dealer had.

Green kept the gun low. He checked the safety and racked its slide. He thrust his pelvis out and slipped the gun under the front of his jeans so that the grip leaned toward his right hand. He put the tails of his FUBU shirt out so that they covered the gun.

"Let's go, Michael," said Green.

Butler hesitated. He was hoping for a quiet resolution to this. He had always managed to avoid violence.

"Let's *go*," said Green.

Green left the motor running and the headlights on as he and Butler stepped onto the street. Miller and Lee did the same. Melvin Lee stepped forward; so did DeEric

Green. Michael Butler stayed back behind Green and slightly to his left. Rico Miller hung by his car. He kept his eyes, heavy with contempt, on Butler.

"'Sup?" said Green, looking Lee over, looking down on him because he had the height advantage and could.

Lee waited a moment before speaking. It was a moment too long. It told Green that he was hesitant and maybe afraid.

"Somethin' you want to say to me?" said Green.

Lee nodded.

"Then say it."

"Heard you stepped to our boy Jujubee this morning," said Lee, finding his tongue.

"That ain't news."

"You told him to move on."

"So?"

"Boy was on *our* real estate."

Green took another step forward and got close to Lee's face. He spoke clearly and evenly. "I made a mistake. I already discussed it with the man I needed to discuss it with, and he gonna work it out with your man his own way."

"You —"

"What I *don't* need to do is discuss it with an itty-bitty motherfucker like you."

Green brushed his hand over the front of his shirt. Lee saw the lump there, right above the waistline. Lee, confused, looked over his shoulder at Miller. "You . . . you hear that, Rico?"

Miller did not answer. He kept his eyes on Michael Butler.

A Toyota drove up Otis and, blocked by the Cadillac, came to a stop. The driver gave a short, timid sound of his horn. He did not roll his window down or say anything to the men and young men standing in the street.

"You gonna be seein' me later on," said Lee in an unconvincing way. He clumsily pointed a finger at Green's face.

"I'm seeing you now," said Green. "What, you gonna act like a man *later on?*"

Green laughed. He knew he was showing off. But Melvin Lee was just making it too easy. He didn't even feel the need to prove to Lee that he was strapped.

"You had your say," said Green with a jerk of his head. "Now take your boy and get."

"Yeah," said Lee, nodding his head rapidly. "Yeah, okay." He was trying to maintain, searching for the right clever parting words. But nothing would come.

The driver of the Toyota hit his horn again. Another light came on in a nearby house.

Green grinned. "You ain't gone yet?"

Lee turned around. He saw Miller staring at Michael Butler, smiling at him in that way of his that was all about pain.

"Let's go, Rico," said Lee, unable to look in the eyes of the young man who worshipped him. Miller nodded, his smile frozen in place, and the two of them went to their car.

Miller backed his BMW up Otis and turned south on 6th.

Lee rubbed at his face and turned to Miller. "He was strapped, Rico. You saw it, right?"

Miller did not respond.

In the Escalade, Green and Butler settled in. Green put the transmission in drive, turned on the radio, and headed up the street.

"How you know to do that?" said Butler.

"Wasn't no thing," said Green, getting low in the

bucket, his wrist resting casually over the steering wheel, proud despite the nagging feeling that he'd pushed it and done wrong. "Alls you had to do was look in his eyes. His heart was pumpin' Kool-Aid."

"What you mean?"

"Melvin was scared. I could tell just by lookin' at him, 'cause I been knowin' him a long time. He used to run with my brother, James, back when." Green blinked away the image of his brother, playing basketball down by the courts, imitating MJ with his tongue out the side of his mouth, laughing about it, having fun. "Melvin don't belong out here no more."

"You punked him," said Butler with admiration.

"Wasn't me," said Green, a touch of regret in his voice. "Boy got his ass broke in the cut."

As the Cadillac went up Otis, it passed the home of Edwina Rollins, Joe Carver's aunt. Joe sat on the dark porch and nursed a beer. He had watched the conflict involving the occupants of the Cadillac and the BMW, and had listened to the muffled threats with only mild interest. He had been involved in countless confrontations just like that one in his old life. They bored him now.

Joe would have gone inside and caught a little ESPN, but it was all baseball this time of year, a sport that he had played growing up but that did not interest him on television, and anyway, he was waiting on his friend. Lorenzo would be out walking his dog right about now. Joe would just sit out here and wait for Renzo. Wouldn't be too long before his boy would be stopping by.

• • •

JASMINE MOVED JAUNTILY along, leading Lorenzo down Princeton Place. She had done her business in the ball field up by Park View Elementary and had the bounce of the unburdened in her step.

Coming upon his grandmother's house, Lorenzo noticed candlelight on the concrete porch of the row house to the south and the outline of a female figure sitting on a glider there. As he went up the sidewalk to his grandmother's, he heard a little girl's voice call out and saw her braided head, in silhouette, come up over the rails of the neighboring porch.

"That Jazz Man?" said the voice.

"Depends on who's asking," said Lorenzo, stopping, holding the leash and Jasmine fast. "Is that Lakeisha?"

"How you know my name?"

"Santa Claus told me."

"Santa?" said Lakeisha with delight.

"Yeah, he called me up," said Lorenzo, walking across the grass toward the house so that he didn't have to shout. "Told me about this pretty little girl named Lakeisha, lived in my neighborhood? He didn't have her phone number, so he asked me to find out what that little girl wanted for Christmas."

"I want Cinderella Dream Trunk!"

"Settle down, girl," said Rayne, Lakeisha's mother, getting up off the glider and coming to the edge of the covered porch. Lorenzo stopped at the foot of the stairs and looked up at her. Her face was barely lit by the votive candles she had placed about. There was music playing softly, probably from a portable stereo she had put somewhere up there. Lorenzo recognized the song.

"Evening," said Lorenzo.

"Evening to you," said Rayne.

"Can I pet Jazz Man, Mommy?" said Lakeisha.

"If Mr. Lorenzo says it's all right."

"She'd love you to pet her," said Lorenzo.

Lakeisha descended the steps and crouched down. Jasmine rubbed her snout in Lakeisha's outstretched hand and wagged her tail as Lakeisha patted her belly and then ran her fingers down her coat. Lorenzo leaned, with deliberate cool, against a brick post. Rayne had a seat on the top step, a glass of white wine in her hand. Now that she was out from under the roof of the porch and in the moonlight, Lorenzo could see her face and figure more clearly. Lorenzo thinking, as he always did when he ran into her, She is fine. Realizing that he was staring, he looked down at Lakcisha and Jasmine.

"She's a natural with my dog," said Lorenzo. "She'd be a good candidate —"

"Don't say it," said Rayne, smiling a little. "I got enough mouths to feed. Anyway, you off the clock, right? You don't need to be working that pet adoption thing all the time."

"What, you don't think about cutting hair when you're out the shop?"

"Please. After standing up for eight hours straight? I try to forget it when I'm not there. Trouble is, my feet won't let me." She looked him over. "How'd you know I was a stylist?"

"How'd *you* know I was dog police?"

Lorenzo and Rayne chuckled. She had a nice smile. Rayne was the first to look away. He liked the shyness of her too.

"This is pretty right here," said Lorenzo.

"What is?"

"This song."

"'Miss Black America'?" said Rayne. "Lakeisha likes it. It takes me back myself. My mother had the album when I was a little girl. She used to play it for me, right here in this house."

"That was the one with Mayfield on the cover, wearing that lemon yellow suit."

"You remember it?"

"Just called *Curtis*. A friend of mine's mother, she had it too."

Now it was Lorenzo's turn to cut his eyes from hers.

"You feel like goin' out sometime?" said Rayne.

"Huh?"

"For coffee or something."

"Sure," said Lorenzo, standing straight. "Or, you know, we could do something, like, all of us together. With Lakeisha, I mean. Go to, I don't know, Six Flags. Or go down to Hains Point and just walk around some. Somethin' like that."

"That would be good."

"But listen," said Lorenzo, the words coming freely from him now. "Before we go making plans, I got some things in my past that you need to know about."

"You're under supervision," said Rayne. "You were incarcerated on drug charges."

Lorenzo nodded slowly. "That's right."

"Seems to me like you got your head on straight now."

"I'm tryin'," said Lorenzo. "What else you know?"

"You got a little girl of your own, about Lakeisha's age. She stays up in Manor Park with her mother."

"Okay." Lorenzo stroked the hairs on his chin. "Question is, how you know so much?"

"How you think?" said Rayne, smiling again.

"The old girl been tellin' you everything, huh."

"She just being neighborly," said Rayne.

"Mama," said Lakeisha, moving her cheek off Jasmine's coat, where she had been trying to listen to her heart. "Can I keep her?"

"No, baby. That's Mr. Lorenzo's dog."

"Tell you what, little princess," said Lorenzo. "You can visit with her anytime you want."

"You gonna bring her back?"

"Are you?" said Rayne.

"I reckon," said Lorenzo, tugging on Jasmine's leash, walking toward his grandmother's house.

"Bye, Jazz Man," said Lakeisha.

Lorenzo turned his head and looked back at Rayne. "I'm gonna call you, girl."

Rayne sipped at her wine.

Lorenzo used his key to enter the row house next door. He removed Jasmine's leash and draped it over a jacket peg by the door. The house smelled of his grandmother's cooking.

Willetta Thompson came forward from back in the living room and hugged him roughly. She was a tall, strong woman with lively eyes, not yet sixty-five. A graduate of Strayer's Business College, she had worked as a HUD secretary, in the same office, for over thirty years. Her hair was shop styled and gray.

"Hello, son," she said.

"Mama," said Lorenzo.

They thought of each other that way.

"Saw you through the window, talking to Rayne."

"Uh-huh."

"That's a good woman right there. Responsible."

"You just about gave her my whole life story."

"Someone had to," said Willetta. "Didn't look to me like *you* were gonna do it."

"That chicken I smell?"

"I saved the thighs for you." Willetta pulled on his hand. "I put a little somethin' aside for your animal too."

"Dogs shouldn't be eatin' on chicken bones."

"This one's plenty big," said Willetta. "She won't choke on it."

Lorenzo and Willetta went toward the dining room, walking down a plastic runner Willetta had laid on the carpet to keep it new. Jasmine's tail wagged as she followed, sniffing at their heels.

THIRTEEN

RICO MILLER DROPPED Melvin Lee at his place on Sherman Avenue. They had barely spoken since the incident on Otis. For Lee, the silence had been excruciating.

Lee no longer communicated with his blood relatives. When he'd come out of prison, his siblings, who had never written or visited once during his stay, refused to speak to him. His mother had died long ago. He didn't know his children or where their mothers stayed. As for the friends he'd come up with, they were in the cut or dead. Only thing he had now was his work with Deacon Taylor. Closest thing to a son he'd ever have was Rico. And now he'd been punked right in front of him. He wondered if Rico Miller could ever look at him the same way again.

Lee walked down the sidewalk, his shoulders slumped. Miller drove away.

Miller went down Georgia. Past Howard University, at Florida Avenue, he drove east. Farther along, he crossed the Benning Bridge over the Anacostia River and took Minnesota Avenue to the Deanwood area of Northeast. He parked in front of a bungalow at 46th and Hayes.

His house was set on a fairly large plot of land. The block he lived on had many decent homes, but others were run-down, blighted by plywood doors, sagging roofs, and hanging gutters. Some had cardboard stuck in their window frames. A few had been recently abandoned or had stood unoccupied for years. Raccoons nested in their chimneys and rats moved freely beneath their porches. The shades were always drawn so that inspectors could not look inside. Long as the owners cut the grass on a fairly regular basis, these houses could not be condemned.

Miller had found this house, in fact, when he saw the owner outside it, mowing its weedy lawn. One wall of the house had been spray-painted with tags: a "46" and an "RIP Mike." This meant there was gang activity on the street. In areas such as this, neighbors were typically frightened or plain tired of calling police and so they minded their own. Miller had been driving slowly on this particular street because it looked like the kind of place where he needed to be. Didn't look like anybody gave a good fuck about it, and it wasn't near a major road crossing. It seemed like a smart spot to hide.

He offered the man a thousand dollars a month, cash up front, three months in advance, as is, to rent it. The money would cover utilities as well. For phone service, Miller would use his cell. Rico told the owner to leave the lawn mower and gas can, and he'd take care of the grass. The man took the deal.

Miller had another month, prepaid, on the house. He'd move on to someplace else, like he always did, after that.

He left no records. Even his car, the BMW, was a rental. He'd got it from this man, Calvin Duke, lived by the railroad tracks at 35th and Ames. It was known in certain circles that a young man like Rico could get damn near anything from Duke. The man had the rental business cornered in Northeast. Called his self Dukey Stick; Miller did not know why.

Except for the landlord and Calvin Duke, no one knew where Rico Miller lived. Not Melvin Lee and not Deacon Taylor. They wanted him, they could get him on his cell. Since he'd left Oak Hill, that juvenile facility they'd put him in, he'd been on his own. If anyone was looking for him, they hadn't caught up with him yet. He aimed to stay free.

Rico went into his house. It was a shithole to begin with, and he'd done nothing to improve it. Bare light bulbs dangled from damaged plaster ceilings. The walls, unadorned with pictures, were chipped and water stained. Wasn't any furniture to speak of, a sofa and some old broke chairs and a folding table, stuff he'd found around Dumpsters and the like. He'd bought a mattress and some sheets at the Goodwill store. The kitchen was of little use to him. Rico didn't eat all that much; it was KFC and Wendy's when he did.

Miller went back into the room where he slept. He turned on the light. He took his knife, secured in his personalized sheath, from his pocket and tossed it on his bed.

On the floor next to the mattress sat a lamp, a portable stereo, some CDs, and a couple of ass magazines he used for masturbation. In the other corner of the room was a nineteen-inch television set on which he sometimes watched videos but which he mostly used for PlayStation 2. In the closet, behind where he hung his shirts, was a false wall, a piece of particleboard that came away with a tug. He went to the closet, parted his shirts, and pulled the board free.

Behind the wall was a rack. The rack held a cut-down pump-action Winchester shotgun with a pistol grip, an S&W .38 revolver, and a 9 mm Glock 17. He had bought the 17, as did many young gun owners in the area, because it was the official sidearm of the MPD. Also on the rack were various holsters and a leather shoulder harness, popular with men who robbed drug dealers, designed to hold the Winchester steady under a raincoat.

Miller pulled the shotgun and the Glock off the rack. He found a brick of PMC ammo on the floor. He loaded the Winchester with low-recoil buckshot. He checked the Glock to see if it was ready, saw that it was, and palmed its magazine back into the grip.

Melvin was the only friend he had in this life. Melvin was his father.

Rico Miller heard the sound of his own teeth grinding.

• • •

THE BAR WAS in a boutique hotel on Massachusetts Avenue, down around 10th, in Northwest. It was away from the cluster of upscale chain hotels that were located downtown and in Georgetown and the West End. The amenities were not comparable in any way to those at the Ritz and the Four Seasons, but a certain kind of guest preferred the quiet charm of this hotel and its relative isolation. It was a particular favorite of closet drinkers, full-on drunks, couples engaged in extramarital affairs, and serial adulterers looking to score.

Rachel sat at the bar, located through a hallway past the circular lobby, drinking a scotch rocks. She had ordered a Johnnie Walker Red from the 'tender, a young man with long Jheri-curled hair that he wore pulled back and banded. The JW was in her price range, a step up from the rail, and fine. She sat erect and smoked a cigarette.

Rachel drank exclusively in hotel bars. In hotels, she was unlikely to run into police, private investigators, attorneys, coworkers, or anyone else she knew in her daytime life. These people drank at the FOP or in their favorite locals. Similarly, though some of her offenders worked in privately owned restaurants, most had trouble securing kitchen employment with the hotel chains, which tended to do exhaustive background checks. Also, she simply liked the drinking atmosphere of hotels better than she did freestanding watering holes. The crowds were past their twenties, behaved more maturely behind their alcohol, and contained fewer boisterous regulars. The customers were often in town for only a couple of days. Many would never return to D.C.

Here, the single guests ranged from midlevel managers, conventioneers, filmmakers in town for festivals, and route salesmen to men who had temporarily left their families for two-day benders. The staff played jazz on the sound system, and on weekends a live combo appeared on the small house stage, performing mostly standards. Rachel was not a jazz or pop fan, but she was not here to listen to music.

The room was large and oddly configured, with many tables and booths hidden behind thick posts and in dimly lit semiprivate alcoves. The bar itself was half full. Two

couples occupied stools along with a group of three busi-
nessmen, techies by the looks of their dress, ready-wear
pants and cotton-poly-mix shirts. All wore marriage bands.
The discussion, what Rachel could hear of it, centered on
mortgage rates and Honda Accords. To the right of them
sat a single middle-aged man, staring at a glass that was
holding something amber, content with his solitude and
his drink. His gut drooped over his belt line. Another single man, midthirties by the looks of him, also sat alone at
the end of the bar. He had entered earlier, and Rachel had
watched him walk in and take his seat. He was short to
medium height, had a chest and an ass, and stretched his
cotton shirt across the shoulders and back. She stared at
him, and he held her gaze and smiled. By default, he was
the one.

She waited. He picked up his drink and walked down
along the bar and stood next to Rachel.

"Hey," he said, showing her his teeth.

"Hey," said Rachel, her mouth turning up on one side,
half a smile, an opening.

"Mind if I join you?"

"Why?"

"Might as well close the gap. You haven't taken your
eyes off me all night."

He chuckled in a self-deprecating way, a smart tactic.
If he was off base, he was just kidding. If not, he was in. He
was kind of good-looking in a nonpretty way, with dark
eyebrows and dark, curly, tightly cut hair. Laugh lines
framed his eyes and parenthesized his large mouth. He
had a large nose as well. This was a turnoff to some women,
but in Rachel's experience, it was a plus.

"Have a seat," said Rachel, nodding at the empty
stool beside her. "So I don't strain my eyes."

His name was Aris O'Leary, and when Rachel said, "Harris?" he said, "No, *Aris*. It's short for Aristotle." He was the son of a Greek American woman, second generation, and an Irish American father, third. "It means I like good food *and* this." Aris held up his glass of Jameson neat. She wondered how many times he had said that to women in bars.

"What's your name?" he asked.

"Don't be so bold," she said, and he laughed.

Aris was a sales rep for a major appliance manufacturer out of "Saint Joe's." Aris was in D.C., his first time, for the Home Improvement Expo at the new convention center. Aris had wrestled at Michigan State, but "that was twenty pounds ago." Aris had hoped to check out some of the museums and the monuments while he was in town, but he would have to do it on another visit, as he was leaving in the morning. Aris was thirty-four years old.

Rachel nodded, her eyes on his, seemingly attentive but barely seeing him or registering his words. She was thinking of Eddie, her offender who cut hair and was about to get off paper. She was sorry she had not had time for him today and was looking forward to seeing him in the morning. Eddie was a good one, a genuine success.

"I guess I picked Michigan State 'cause they were the Spartans," said Aris. "You know, with my mom and all. Plus the in-state tuition. You can't beat the price, you know what I mean?"

Rachel crossed one leg over the other, deliberately flexing her thigh, making sure he saw the cut. She leaned forward a little to give Aris a look at her lacy bra, her breasts loose inside it, the aureole of one brown nipple edging above the lace. It was humid in the bar, and the warmth was around her and on her chest.

"You okay?" said Aris, his eyes bright.

"A little hot, is all. You?"

"Yes."

They ordered two more drinks. Aris signaled the bartender for the check as Rachel lit another cigarette. The room doubled for a moment as she looked around it, trails coming off the men and women at the bar. Not surprising, with the red wine and now the scotch.

"Don't mix the grain and the grape, little girl."

"Who has time, Popi? You know I work too hard."

"You play too hard too. I see it on your face."

Aris wrote his room number on the check. She noticed the sun line on his ring finger as he scratched out his signature. At his age, he probably had a child as well. She guessed he had been married for seven years or so. "Seven Year Ache." She loved that song.

"Something funny?" said Aris.

"Was I smiling? I guess I'm happy, is what it is."

"So," said Aris, "you gonna make me beg you for your name?"

"Rachel Lopez," she said. "I'm a mutt, just like you."

"Rachel, like in the Old Testament."

"My mother was Jewish."

"But Lopez isn't Jewish. Your father was what?"

"Latino, born in west Texas."

"Your folks still around?"

"Deceased."

"Sorry."

Both had passed within months of each other. If there was a blessing, it was that her father had gone first. He could not have handled seeing her mother, a husk of bones and loose gray flesh, in her last days.

"So you're half Jewish and half Spanish," said Aris.

"Latina."

Aris smiled rakishly. "Which half is Latina?"

Rachel dragged on her cigarette. "You stop acting so fresh, you'll find out."

"Okay," said Aris, squaring his shoulders, cocky, knowing he was in. "But listen, I need to use the head."

"Pass the front desk and go down the stairs."

"Don't go anywhere," said Aris, pointing at her before getting off his stool.

Don't tell me what to do. I'm in charge, not you.

Rachel killed her drink and crushed out her cigarette in the ashtray. She walked through the bar and out into the circular lobby, nodding and smiling at the two Middle Easterners behind the reception desk, and went down a stairway to the carpeted lower level. It was empty of people and, as in all the times she'd been here, virtually soundless. She passed by the women's bathroom, pushed on the door of the men's bathroom, and stepped inside.

Aris was facing the urinal, shaking himself off. He glanced over his shoulder as he heard her heels slapping on the tiled floor. His face pinkened with embarrassment. Also, he looked scared.

"What, you lost?"

"Ladies' bathroom's too crowded," she said, walking quickly toward him.

"No it isn't." He chuckled nervously. "It's quiet as a church down here."

Rachel came to him and pressed her breasts against his back and kissed him behind his ear. She reached around him, pushed his arm away, and wrapped her hand around his meat. It was warm and thick and already hard.

She ran her thumb and forefinger down his shaft like she was squeezing toothpaste from a tube, and it grew harder still.

"Holy . . . *shit*."

"Shut up," she said very softly.

She stroked him and talked to him. His breath got short. Her touch was expert, and he came with a shudder and voluminously against the porcelain.

"Now you're ready," she said.

Docile and relaxed.

Up in his room, he offered her a drink from the mini-bar. She refused. She found the local country station on the clock radio while Aris took off his shoes as she had instructed him to do. The station was playing George Strait. She went to Aris, standing motionless as a statue in his socks, still off-balance from her bold act in the restroom, and further undressed him. She took off his button-down and pulled his T-shirt over his head as a mother would her little boy's, then unzipped his pants and eased him back onto the edge of the bed so that she could pull the pants free. He was there on his elbows, watching her as she unhooked her skirt and unbuttoned her blouse and let both drop to the floor. She came to him in her bra and thong, and she pulled his boxers off and leaned in and kissed him deep.

As her tongue slid over his, she took his hand and guided it inside the cup of her bra. He found her nipple, and as it began to swell she put her hand over his fingers and squeezed.

"Like that, *Aris*," she said.

He moved back to the pillows, in a heap at the head-board, and she followed him on all fours. She let him remove her panties and she let him stroke her. He tried to turn her over, but she would not allow it. She took his bull cock and rubbed its helmet on her thighs and clit and then between her breasts and full on her breasts until she was wet. She straddled him, impaled herself upon him, and fucked him, her hips jacked and moving fluidly. She listened to the music from the radio, thinking of the raw sensation, remembering her father and how he sang Tejano and Texas country in their house when she was a child, and her mother in her blue print dress and how she hummed along. The blood welled up inside her and rushed forward. It felt like childhood, uncluttered, when they were all under one roof, alive. She could bring them back like this, only like this, when she was in control.

Rachel's body stiffened; she came furiously, saliva dripping from her open mouth.

She washed herself in the bathroom. When she returned, the man from Saint Joseph, Michigan, was asleep on his stomach and snoring into the sheets. Rachel got dressed.

FOURTEEN

YOU WANT ANOTHER?" said Joe Carver, reaching for the small red cooler at his feet.

"Sure," said Lorenzo Brown. "Long as you're buyin'."

Joe withdrew two Miller Genuines from the cooler and handed one to Lorenzo. Lorenzo ran his hand over the bottle to remove the water and bits of ice. He and Joe hand-turned the caps, tapped bottles, and drank. Both had worked full days in the summer heat. The beer was cold and went down straight.

The porch was unlit and absent of moonlight beneath the cover of its roof. Joe and Lorenzo sat on cushioned chairs that faced the street, Joe's feet up on the rail. Jasmine lay on her belly, also watching the street, blinking her eyes slowly, her snout hanging over the porch's first step.

Joe liked to sit out here most nights, from spring well into the autumn. He had fallen before Lorenzo and done longer time. Ten years in Kentucky after his third conviction, a federal rap. He had refused to testify against Nigel or anyone else, and suspected that because he'd stood tall, he had been penalized with a harsher sentence. It was a story as old as history: The soldiers fell on their swords and the kings survived.

In prison, Joe hadn't boasted on plans or unattainable goals like some of the talkers he knew. He had dreamed of getting a job, breathing fresh air, and, when the workday was done, finding a comfortable place to sit where there were no walls. Now he was doing just that.

"So you gonna date this woman?" said Joe. He meant Rayne. Lorenzo had described her and their encounter.

"I don't know about date," said Lorenzo. "I plan to do something with her and her little girl, like a daytime thing. See how we all get along."

"She know about you?"

"Yeah. She fine with it. Least she claims to be."

"Be careful."

"She don't look all that dangerous to me."

"I'm sayin', you got your own little girl to think of."

"Shay doin' fine," said Lorenzo. "I saw her this evening. Her mama wouldn't let me talk to her or nothin' like that, but she looked great. *Happy*. Looks like Sherelle got herself a good man this time."

"You met him?"

"In a way. He seems all right."

"My boy's got a man looking after him too. He stay in the same place with my boy's mama. He ain't the father, but . . . long as they loved, right?"

"Yeah."

"You and me, we fucked up. But that don't mean our kids got to be fucked up because of it."

"For real."

Joe looked out at the night, picturing his son. "Whole lot of ways to make a family."

They drank some more and listened to the crickets, the dogs barking in the alleys, and the swish of tires on asphalt from down on Georgia Avenue. The sounds were familiar and comforting. Jasmine sighed and closed her eyes.

"Your truck running all right?" said Lorenzo, looking at it, a '95 Ford, the pre–jelly bean body style, parked under a street lamp.

"Long as I change the oil regular," said Joe. "What about your runner?"

"Fine, thanks to you."

"You miss them pretty whips we used to drive?"

"Not really."

"Neither do I. They weren't ours *no* way."

That's right, thought Lorenzo. None of it was real.

Joe's chair creaked under his weight. He was a big man who'd gained forty pounds since his release. His slowing metabolism, his aunt's cooking, and his nightly intake of beer had gotten the better of him, despite his hard daily labor as a bricklayer.

"I was thinkin' on us and those whips earlier tonight," said Joe.

"Why's that?"

"I saw some boys out here earlier, jawin' in the street. Couple of 'em was Nigel's. I seen their car before, a black Escalade with spinners, over there on Sixth, where Nigel like to rally the troops."

"I know who those two are," said Lorenzo.

"Yeah?"

"I saw Nigel and them earlier, up near his office on Georgia. I stopped to visit."

"How Nigel look?"

"Fit," said Lorenzo. "What happened with his boys?"

"They was just talkin' mad shit with these other two boys who had blocked the street. All of 'em got out the cars and showed their teeth. Then Nigel's got back in their Escalade and the others got back in their BMW and all of 'em went on their way."

"Other car was a BMW?"

"Three-Series. Silver or blue, hard to tell, way the headlights was on it."

Lorenzo stroked the whiskers of his chin. "Describe the two came out the BMW."

"I couldn't make much out."

"Don't make no difference. I'm pretty sure it was Melvin Lee. Him and some hard kid named Rico."

"How you know that?"

"I had a call today, some dogfights down around Fort Dupont. Lee was there, and we had some words. You remember Melvin, right?"

"I'm the one told you he came back uptown. People I know say he workin' for Deacon again. Got a front job, up at the car wash on Georgia, 'cause he's still on paper."

"Right."

"Melvin ain't shit. Never was."

"I know it."

"Why you interested?"

"I'm not. Only . . ."

"What?"

"Melvin and his shadow were watching Nigel when me and Nigel was talkin'."

"So he watchin' Nigel and them. It's his job to scout the other team. That ain't got nothin' to do with you."

"You're right."

"Anyway," said Joe, "it just reminded me, seein' them out there, how it was for us."

"Ain't nothin' changed."

"Look around you. Why *would* it change?"

"But if these kids knew how it has to end . . . I mean, if you could only tell 'em."

"But you can't tell 'em shit. They ain't gonna listen to no old heads, that's for damn sure. Same way we didn't listen. We knew it all." Joe chuckled. "Now I got to pee in a bottle to remind myself of all the ways I failed."

"You're doin' fine."

"Tell it to my PO."

"He on you?"

"Like a motherfucker," said Joe. "Yours?"

"Mine's on me too. She good, though."

"Yeah?"

"Yeah," said Lorenzo. "She's good."

Lorenzo and Joe finished their beers.

"Well," said Joe, getting up laboriously out of his seat, "let me get on inside. I got to be on that construction site at seven."

"I'm on early shift myself."

"It works if you work it."

"No doubt."

Lorenzo and Joe shook hands and patted each other's backs. Joe went inside the house, moving quietly so as not to wake his aunt, as Lorenzo leashed Jasmine and walked her down the steps. The two of them headed for their apartment, a short way down the dark street.

• • •

MORTON STREET AT NIGHT, east of Georgia and back toward
Park Morton, was alive with traffic. Touts, runners, fiends,
drive-through customers with Virginia plates, and neighborhood residents walking to their row houses and apartments crowded the strip.

A couple of times every night, Fourth District cruisers
would slowly make a pass down Morton and through the
Section Eight apartment complex, their uniformed occupants shouting from the open windows of their Crown
Vics, telling the dealers and users to move on. Less frequently, in the wake of a publicized fatality or a *Washington
Post* investigative piece, a special unit would descend on
the area and do jump-out busts. This would result in some
arrests and a few convictions, but it did not in any way stop
the flow of business. Drug sales of one kind or another
had been ongoing in this area, and west into Columbia
Heights, for over thirty years.

DeEric Green drove the Escalade down Morton,
Michael Butler by his side. They had just picked up the
count from a boy named Ricky Young. Young had handed
the money, stashed in a T-MAC 3 Adidas shoe box, to
Green, who had in turn handed it to Butler. The money, in
various denominations, now sat in the shoe box on the carpeted floor of the backseat. Green had put a Rare Essence
PA mix, recorded on May 15 at the Tradewinds, into the
CD player and was rocking it loud.

"Busy," said Butler.

"Summertime," said Green.

On a hot corner up ahead, they could see some of their
people, all in street clothes. On another corner stood Dea-

con's, wearing long white T-shirts and loose-fitting jeans. A bandanna worn around the neck meant the seller had heroin. Around the leg, it meant coke. This type of coding, in variation, had become common in the East Coast urban trade. Deacon insisted his people use the bandanna system and made it mandatory that they wear the T-shirts. He liked the idea of them in uniform. Also, it differentiated them from the competition. Nigel let his soldiers wear whatever they pleased.

Butler hit a joint as they neared the end of Morton.

"Boy," said Green, "you actin' like you the only one in this car like to get high."

"Here," said Butler. He passed the weed, tamped into a White Owl wrapper, to Green.

The circle at the end of the block had been the gateway to the Park Morton complex until recently, when yellow concrete pillars had been erected, blocking the entrance to an asphalt road that ringed the apartments. The pillars kept dealers and killers from doing their dirt where mothers walked and children played, but they hampered the police from driving back there too. Now it was an avenue of escape for those who wanted to book out on foot. Nothing worked back here. No one was going to stop a thing.

Green swung the Cadillac around the circle and headed west, back toward Georgia.

"I got to pick up the count again, one more time, before the night's out," said Green. "You worked a full day. You want, I could take you home."

Butler thought of what he would find at his apartment. If his mother wasn't hitting it, she was looking to. Wasn't unusual for him to come in and find her giving up her face to a strange man for the price of a high. She had no ass and few teeth, and her hair was never combed. If Butler stayed out late enough, she might be asleep. He wouldn't have to look at her when he got home.

"I'll hang with you," said Butler, "if that's all right."

"Sure," said Green, who was getting used to having the boy around. "This hydro's got my hunger up, though."

"Mine too."

"Let's get us somethin'," said Green. He turned right on Georgia Avenue and headed north.

Rico Miller, idling in the convenience store lot on the corner, saw them through the windshield of his BMW. He had been cruising the neighborhood, hoping to spot Green and Butler, and had stopped here, at one of the city's many fake 7-Elevens, to get a Sierra Mist. Miller put the car in drive.

Up at Kennedy Street, outside the Wings n Things, Green parked the Caddy near a row of brightly colored racing bikes, Ducatis and such, that always seemed to be out front in the warmer months. Butler listened to music while Green went inside and returned with a large bag. He wasn't in there long; he had called in the order from his cell.

"Dag, DeEric," said Butler, wide-eyeing the bag. "You got a whole *rack* of wings."

"All drums."

"You get the extra hot sauce?"

"What you think?" said Green. "Let's find us a quiet place to eat 'em. Smoke up the rest of this funk before we do."

A short way down Kennedy, Green turned southeast onto Illinois Avenue. He reached Sherman Circle and a quarter way around it veered off on Crittenden Street. Behind a side street off Crittenden, down near Bernard Elementary, he parked the Cadillac in an alley. He had fucked a girl in this alley not long ago and knew it to be quiet. Lot of folks in the city kept dogs in their backyards at night, would bark at damn near everything. But this alley here, for some reason, was dog free.

They left the windows down, kept the music low, and smoked the rest of the blunt. Their appetites sufficiently whetted, they started in on the drums.

DeEric Green, tripping hard on the highly potent hydroponic weed, was focused on the food before him. His thoughts were happy and not complex.

Michael Butler was also at the peak of his high. But his thoughts went deeper than Green's. The percussion and call-and-response of the go-go mix were hypnotic and almost too much for his head. He didn't mind feeling this way. He could never get too high.

When he was up like this, Butler didn't think on his mother sucking some stranger's dick. When he was up like this, he didn't wonder who his father was or why he'd left. Instead, he dreamed of traveling to places he'd never been before and seeing things he'd only read about in books. Like the Eiffel Tower, and that big arch they had over there in the same city. He guessed he could see that tower and that arch if he wanted to. Why couldn't he? He knew where they were. He could point to that country on a map. Alls he needed to do was get one of them passports, buy a plane ticket, and go. But how did you get a passport? How did you buy a plane ticket? He could find out somehow, he guessed.

When these thoughts got too complicated, he'd just stare up at the night sky. He'd look at the stars and imagine what it would be like to fly in one of them spaceships.

To look out the window when you were right there in the middle of space, with all them big rocks, them *asteroids*, going by. He wondered what you had to do to become one of those astronauts. Did you have to go to an astronaut school or something special like that? How did you get picked? He would like to be an astronaut someday.

He dreamed about these things. But he never did anything but dream about them, because most of the time he was high.

"These drums is tight," said DeEric Green. He stared at the chicken he held in both hands. The hot sauce was shiny on his lips and stained his face.

Butler had many questions, but he didn't know where to go to find the answers. He used to be able to ask his teachers, but that was before he'd dropped out of school. He had no family, except for his mother. Nigel and DeEric and them, they were his family now. But they weren't the kind of people you could ask.

One time, he'd told his mother that he'd like to go up in space.

"So now you gonna be an astro-not," she said. "You can't even spell it, boy."

"Yes, I can," said Butler, and to show her that he could, he did.

"Smart little motherfucker," she said, "actin' all superior. You ain't goin' no goddamn where but where you at now. The last place you be goin' is space."

Michael Butler stared out the windshield. From the depths of the alley, out of the darkness, he saw a tall figure walking toward them with a strange dip in his gait. He was wearing gloves. Looked like he was wearing a long raincoat or something too. But it wasn't raining.

"Someone comin' toward us," said Butler.

Green glanced out the windshield. "Yeah?" He closed his eyes and bit into a piece of chicken, tearing the meat away from the bone.

The figure came closer.

"I'm just sayin'," said Butler, a catch in his voice.

"Nigga takin' a walk, is all," said Green. "Ain't no law against it."

"Too hot to be wearin' gloves," said Butler.

"Fuck you talkin' about?" said Green.

The man walking toward them triggered a motion detector hung from the eave of a freestanding garage. As the light hit him, Butler saw that it was Melvin Lee's partner, the boy with the frightening smile. He was breaking into that smile now. Smiling wide as he pulled a sawed-off shotgun out from under the coat.

"Hey, D," said Butler.

Green looked through the glass. He dropped the chicken into his lap and reached for the butt of his Colt, protruding from under the driver's seat. His hand, slick with the grease of the chicken, slipped off the grip. He saw the boy rack the shotgun and heard it, and with his right hand, Green reached across the buckets and pushed down on Michael Butler's head. As he did this, he saw, for a brief moment, a shower of glass rush toward him. He was blinded by the glass and a ripping pain, and felt slickness on his neck and chest. The air was cool on his face, and then the air felt like fire. He wanted to scream. He tried to open his mouth, and then he tried to close it, but he could do neither.

Butler, staying low, opened the passenger door and rolled out into the alley.

Miller moved quickly to stand beside the open driver's-side window. In the bucket sat Green. His jaw was gone. Threads of blood and saliva, and shreds of white bone remained. Green was dead or dying. His feet kicked at the floorboards of the truck.

Miller had seen Butler exit the Escalade. He could hear Butler talking to himself. Praying or getting his courage up as he tried to scrabble along the other side. Miller walked behind the SUV and turned its corner. He found Butler on all fours. Butler looked up. He was crying, and it smelled like he'd shit his jeans.

"Stand up," said Miller.

Butler tried but couldn't do it.

Lights began to glow in the back of several houses. Percussion came through the open windows of the Cadillac. Behind the drums was the faint wail of a siren.

"Stand yourself *up*," said Miller.

Michael Butler willed himself to his feet and raised his hands. His hands shook. Tears ran dirty down his cheeks. Miller leveled the Winchester and rested its shortened stock on his forearm.

"I ain't *done* nothin' to you," said Butler, his lips trembling.

"So?" said Miller.

The alley flashed. It looks like lightning, thought Butler. It feels like the wind.

Michael Butler opened his eyes. He was on his back. His chest was warm. He coughed up a spray of blood. He looked at the night sky. He looked at the stars.

Miller came into his vision and stood over him. He held the shotgun loosely. Now there was a pistol in his other hand.

"I," said Butler. "I . . ."

I ain't ready, God.

Miller sighted down the barrel of the Glock and shot

Butler in the mouth. He rolled him over with his foot and shot him in the back of the head.

Miller holstered the Glock in the waistband of his jeans. He slipped the cut-down Winchester into the special harness he wore under the coat. Squinting his narrow eyes, he found both 9 mm casings and the shotgun shell near Butler's body. Still wearing his gloves, he managed to pick them up. He then found the first shell that had ejected in front of the Cadillac's grille and dropped it into the pocket of his raincoat along with the others.

He went to the open window and looked at Green's corpse. He looked inside the car. Opening the back door, he found the Adidas shoe box and examined its contents, then closed the lid and slipped the box under his arm. Wasn't no reason to leave it behind.

Miller walked down the alley. In his side vision, he saw lights on in the back rooms of some of the houses, but few curtains parted and no one came outside. He heard the siren grow louder. He didn't run.

Miller reached his BMW, parked near the alley's T, before the police arrived. He turned the ignition key and pulled away from the curb. He drove carefully and with his headlights full on. He was not nervous or frightened. He felt no remorse, or anything else.

Miller hit the power button on the radio. He found an Obie Trice he liked and turned it up.

• • •

RACHEL LOPEZ, the windows down in her Honda, listened to a Brooks and Dunn on the radio and smoked a cigarette as she drove up 7th Street.

She was careful to stay in her lane and she watched the speedometer as well. She glanced in the rearview and saw no police. Looking at her reflection, she noticed that her makeup had run in streaks from around her eyes. She was ugly. She supposed she had cried.

It didn't matter. Tomorrow she would be back on the job, sober and straight. This was Rachel at night.

FIFTEEN

LORENZO BROWN OPENED his eyes. He stared at the cracked plaster ceiling and cleared his head.

Jasmine's warm snout touched his fingers. Lorenzo rubbed behind her ears and breathed out slowly. It was time to go to work.

He did curls with forty-pound dumbbells while listening to Donnie Simpson on PGC. Simpson was playing an old EWF, "Keep Your Head to the Sky." It was a song released well before Lorenzo's time but one that he was familiar with and loved. The newsman came on and talked about the war and a helicopter downed by a rocket and the death of three young servicemen. He talked about some people who had been in charge of the local teachers' union and how they'd stolen from out the pension fund. He mentioned briefly a double murder in Northwest.

Lorenzo finished his workout. He showered, ate his breakfast, changed into his uniform, and walked Jasmine. He left food and water for her, directed the fan toward her bed, and got on his way.

Cindy, the dispatcher, was just settling in behind her desk as he entered the Humane Society office. He could hear the sound of one dog barking down in the kennel.

"Mark in yet?" said Lorenzo.

"Downstairs," said Cindy.

Lorenzo found Mark in the basement, wrapping a bandage around his hand. He was standing beside the cage of the pit bull rescued from behind the storefront church.

"Lincoln get you?" said Lorenzo.

Mark nodded, his face colored with embarrassment. "I didn't think he'd bite me."

"It's not your fault," said Lorenzo. "You can't trust him. I mean, he don't trust nobody himself, after what got done to him."

"I know it." Mark stared at the blood seeping through the gauze on his hand. "I was trying to get through, is all. Irena's getting ready to sign off on him."

"She *has* to. That dog's not adoptable. You see that, right?"

"Yes."

"Some animals just got to be put down, Mark. Not every one of 'em can be saved."

Lorenzo stepped over to Mark, unwrapped the gauze, and examined his hand.

"He didn't go deep."

"I'm fine."

Lincoln had backed himself to the rear of the cage. He looked up at Lorenzo shyly.

"What've you got today?" said Mark.

"Gonna check my answering machine first. Take a cat back to some old lady. Make some follow-up calls. I'm gonna try to catch a meeting round lunch time. You know, see how the day goes."

"I'll be out on calls too," said Mark. "You need me, you can get me on the radio."

"Leave me the Tahoe," said Lorenzo.

"Yeah, all right."

"I mean it, man. I know you like that CD player, but you can listen to the radio for a change. I'm tired of gettin' bounced around in that Astra."

"I said I would."

Mark went up to the lobby area. Lorenzo stayed behind and crouched in front of Lincoln's cage. He whistled softly and put his knuckles near the grid. Lincoln moved forward, snapped at Lorenzo's hand, growled for a few seconds, and stepped back. The other dogs in the kennel began to bark.

"You can't help who you are, *can* you, boy?" said Lorenzo, looking into Lincoln's eyes. "It's gonna be better soon."

Up in his office, Lorenzo sat at his desk and washed down two ibuprofens with house coffee while he checked his messages. A man named Felton Barnett had called the day before to complain about a dog barking in an apartment in his building. He had phoned Lorenzo directly because he had dealt with him on "another matter" and been satisfied with the service. Also, the old lady off Kennedy Street had called about her cat.

Jerry, a huge multitattooed Humane officer who had a desk nearby, dropped the Metro section of the *Post* on Lorenzo's desk without comment before walking heavily from the room. In the morning, Jerry left the newspaper for Lorenzo, section by section, as he finished it. Lorenzo automatically went to Metro's page 2, where they had the Crime and Justice feature, which many called the Roundup and some cynical types still called the Violent Negro Deaths. Lorenzo read this feature religiously, even in prison, back when it was just called Around the Region. There, under the heading The District, and then under the subheading Homicides, he read the following:

A twenty-four-year-old man and a seventeen-year-old youth were found fatally shot in an alley off the 500 block of Crittenden Street, N.W., late last night. Police said the man, DeEric Green, and the youth were both pronounced dead at the scene. The identity of the youth is being withheld until notification of relatives. Police are treating both fatalities as homicides.

Lorenzo dropped the paper on his desk. He reached for his coffee cup but did not lift it. He moved the cup in small circles.

He didn't have Nigel's number anymore. But he did still have his mother's memorized. Lorenzo picked up the phone and punched her number into the grid.

"Hello."

"Miss Deborah?"

"Yes."

"Lorenzo Brown here."

"Lorenzo! My goodness, it's nice to hear your voice."

"Yours too. I'm trying to reach Nigel. I was hoping you could give me his number."

"Nigel kinda funny about that, Lorenzo."

"I understand. Let me give you mine, then. Maybe he can get up with me, he has the time."

He gave her his cell number and listened to her chewing on something as she wrote it down. The woman loved to eat. She enjoyed feeding guests, especially kids, too. She'd filled him with plenty of good food in that warm kitchen of hers when he was a boy.

"Thank you, Miss Deborah."

"Come visit, Lorenzo."

"Yes, ma'am. I will."

Lorenzo gathered his files and accessories, put them in a backpack, and went downstairs. Queen, the old lady's calico, had been delivered by the spay clinic to the cat kennel, situated behind the lobby. The cat was docile, lying on her side in a cage. Lorenzo took her out and found a portable carrier.

"You ain't so frisky now, are you?" he said, placing her in the handled box. "Don't fret. You goin' home."

Passing the pegs by the back door, Lorenzo saw that the keys to the Tahoe were gone. He mumbled under his breath and took an Astra key off the peg. He stepped out into the alley with Queen in hand, going up the small hill to Floral Place. Mark was there in the court, standing in front of the Tahoe, grinning, swinging the keys from his bandaged hand.

"Looking for these?"

"You had me cursin' your name, Boy Scout."

Mark and Lorenzo exchanged keys. Lorenzo threw a soft right to Mark's head. Mark dodged the punch.

"You're not mad, are you?"

"Nah," said Lorenzo, "I'm straight."

Driving south on Georgia a few minutes later, Lorenzo thought of Green and Butler, and how Nigel was going to carry their deaths, and the waste. Lorenzo had a pretty good idea who was involved in the killings. He realized that he could have called the police with the information first thing. Instead, he had tried to call Nigel.

Straight.

I'm a long way from straight.

• • •

RACHEL LOPEZ HAD TWO assistants on staff charged solely with handling the paperwork related to her caseload. Rachel had planned on finishing her field calls but decided to drop by the office first to see how the assistants were coming along and to check her messages. It had been a struggle to get out of bed and out of her apartment. She could not even think of food and had not smoked her usual morning cigarette. A shower had revived her, but not by much.

Rachel had a door on her office, an undecorated room with nothing on the walls, and a window that gave to a view of the nearby garden apartments. This morning, after briefing her young assistants and listening to their complaints and concerns, she kept her door closed. She normally left it open, but she was trying to get her physical self together in private. A knock on the door and Moniqua Rogers's musical voice told her that her solitude would be short-lived.

"Come in."

Moniqua entered, bringing her strawberry perfume along with her. She was a correctional officer with almost as many years in as Rachel. Their styles could not have been more different. Moniqua dressed loudly in big-legged pantsuits, laughed easily and deeply, and never brought her job home to her husband and three kids. She wore plenty of makeup. She carried a gun. Rachel was her opposite in nearly every way. None of this stopped the two of them from liking each other. Because Moniqua had a family and Rachel did not, and because of their cultural differences, they rarely saw each other outside work. But they were friends.

"Damn, girl," said Moniqua. "Look what the cat thought twice about draggin' in."

"I didn't get much sleep last night."

"Were you tossin' or getting yourself tossed? The latter, I hope."

"Nothing that exciting. I couldn't sleep."

"Okay." Moniqua parked an ample ass cheek on the edge of Rachel's desk. "Look, I got a new offender coming in this afternoon for his initial consult. But my oldest is in some swim meet thing at the pool and she wants me to be there. Can you cover for me?"

"No."

"Didn't even have to think on it, huh?"

"I'm gonna be out in the field. I didn't finish my calls yesterday, and I can't get behind."

"Are they good calls or bad calls?" said Moniqua.

"A couple of gentlemen I could do without. But I'm gonna see Eddie Davis today, one of my success stories. That's always good."

"What about your boy, what's his name, the dog man —"

"Lorenzo Brown. I met with him yesterday."

"You like him, don't you?"

"He's got potential."

"I *know* he's one of your favorites. And don't try and act like you don't have favorites. Shoot, I like my baby boy more than I like his older sisters. I can admit it."

"Lorenzo's good. But you got to love 'em all, right? Even the bad ones."

Moniqua patted the .38 holstered in the belt clip on her hip. "You keep one of these on you, you don't never have to worry about the bad ones."

"I'd probably hurt myself," said Rachel. "Anyway, you pull that thing, you're gonna have to use it. I don't want to shoot anyone."

"I ain't never had to pull it, honey. They put their eyes on it, they mind their manners."

"I gotta get going," said Rachel, getting up out of her seat. "Sorry I couldn't cover for you."

Moniqua looked her over. "You sure you're not sick?"

"What if I am? Can I stay home from school, Mommy?"

"Go ahead, girl," said Moniqua. "You're long past school."

. . .

LORENZO BROWN FOUND DEANWOOD to be the most country of all neighborhoods in D.C. Many of the houses, though gone to seed, were on large plots of land holding vegetable gardens, tall trees, and all variety of vines. In the summer, older residents sat on open and screened-in porches and conversed in Deep South accents.

Because of their origins, some of the folks in Dean-wood still clung to country ways. A few kept goats, and more than a few had chickens and roosters caged or running about their yards. Owning livestock and fowl was illegal in D.C. After the standard warning, Brown would return to find the chickens gone. He assumed they were killed and eaten. He did not know or ask how the goats were disappeared.

Lorenzo was not checking on unusual violations today. He was following up on a caging call he had made the week before to a woman named Victoria Newman, who lived with her dog, a rottie named Winston.

Lorenzo parked in the alley and walked through Victoria Newman's yard. He passed Winston, standing in his cage beside his igloo-style doghouse, quietly eyeing Lorenzo. The cage was in the shade of a magnolia tree. Winston was healthy, well fed and watered, and had a clean, shiny coat that was fly free. There were minimal droppings on the cage's concrete floor.

Winston barked one time at Lorenzo and, having done his job, opened his mouth to let his tongue drop out the side.

Victoria Newman answered the door after parting the curtains on the ground floor. She wore a bathrobe over a low-cut nightgown; both barely contained her lush figure. She was light skinned, green eyed, and had big features that suited her. She leaned on the door frame as Lorenzo reintroduced himself.

"You again," she said in a not unfriendly way.

"Yes, ma'am," said Lorenzo. "Just doin' a follow-up on . . . It's Winston, right?"

"That's my boy. He lookin' good, isn't he?"

Her eyes were unfocused. That and the sound of her television and stereo system both playing at once told Lorenzo that she was high. But a blind man could have seen that, as she stank of weed. The cigarette burning between her fingers did not hide the smell.

"No doubt, he looks fine," said Lorenzo. "But we still got the same problem I spoke to you about last month. That space you got him in is too small. He needs to be in an enclosure that's at least eight by ten, not including the shelter within it."

"You mean the house where he sleep at?"

"Exactly."

"Eight by ten, that's the parameter."

"Yes," said Lorenzo, seeing no point in correcting her.

"Wasn't like I disregarded what you told me," said Victoria. "I'm in the process of takin' care of it right now."

"You need to do it."

"I been waitin' on this handyman I know to come over here to make the cage larger, only he been busy."

Lorenzo filled out an Official Notification form on his clipboard.

"Winston's healthy, though," said Victoria.

"Yes, he is."

She dragged on her cigarette. "You healthy too."

"I'm hangin' in there," said Lorenzo.

He held out the form. She touched his thumb and gave him a hungry smile as she took it.

"You must be thirsty, all this heat. I got some cold water inside."

"I got water in my truck," said Lorenzo.

But I'd love to loosen the belt on that robe of yours. You keep talkin', I might. I'm just a man.

"You sure?" said Victoria.

"Thank you for asking," said Lorenzo. "Take care of Winston for me, hear?"

Driving away, his dick semihard, his mind a mixture of relief and regret, Lorenzo thought about Victoria Newman, high at nine-thirty in the morning, alone in that house, not yet out of her bedclothes on a workday. All the people he met in the city on his daily runs, and all those he didn't know but saw, standing on corners, drinking out of paper bags, lighting their cigarettes, all of them with nothing, absolutely nothing, to do. He didn't know how folks like that got up in the morning and faced the day.

The speaker below the dash crackled. He listened to the voice on the other end. It was Cindy, from the dispatch desk, informing him of a call.

"A Felton Barnett, in Anacostia. Dog's been barking in one of the apartments he manages. Says it's been going on for the last two days."

"Congress Heights," said Lorenzo. "Man already left a message on my machine."

"You gonna take it or should I call Mark?"

"You can call Mark, you want to," said Lorenzo. "But I'm gonna take it. Matter of fact, I'm on my way now."

He replaced the mic in its cradle. He did not notice the silver BMW parked on the corner of 46th and Hayes as he passed.

Lorenzo squinted and reached for his shades. His headache had returned.

SIXTEEN

Rachel drove into town. She was looking for a man named Carlton Sims and a bottom feeder named Tyrone Meadows. Both stayed in the same facility, a halfway house in Northeast.

The halfway house was not a house, but rather a warehouse with a couple of trailers grouped around it, off New York Avenue in an area that was zoned for commercial as well as residential use. It was run by a private contractor based in Michigan and funded by the federal government through the Bureau of Prisons. Men and women just out of the joint used facilities like this one to get acclimated to the world for the first two or three months of their straight life.

The contractor had been under fire from neighborhood residents since the facility had opened, quietly, the previous year. The city had approved the site, and the mayor and the police chief had been briefed, as required by law, but no one had thought to consult the neighbors. Every day, kids walked by the halfway house, now referred to as a "community corrections center" by its contractor, on their way to school. They stood at the same bus stop and frequented the same corner market as the offenders, some of whom had rape and molestation charges in their jackets. A similar facility had been blocked in wealthy Ward 3, but in the relatively poorer sections of town, citizens had less power. Rachel Lopez understood the concern but also wondered where these people would stay, in the absence of family or friends, if programs such as this one went away.

Rachel entered the greeting area of the main facility, a former storage structure now sectioned into dorm-style sleeping quarters, cafeteria, lounge and recreation room, and administrative offices. She badged a security guard and asked to speak with Millie Gales, the facility's manager. As she waited, she watched the occupants milling about in the dim light of the cafeteria, talking guardedly, palming one another smokes, moving slowly. It reminded her of a prison dayroom.

Millie came out of her office in short order and met Rachel by the sign-in, sign-out counter. She was a big woman in her fifties, dark-skinned, high of hip, with strong arms and muscular legs. She was missing three fingers on her right hand. A large gold crucifix hung outside her dress.

"Hey, girl," said Millie.

"Millie."

They hugged. Millie's eyes lost a little light as she stepped back and studied Rachel. Rachel wondered if she looked as bad as she felt. Maybe she reeked of last night's alcohol.

"Who you here to see?" said Millie.

"Carlton Sims, for one," said Rachel.

Millie picked up the clipboard on the counter. "Carlton signed out of here at four forty-five a.m."

"For work, I hope."

"Oh, yeah. Carlton working most every day. He got hooked up with Darius Wood, has that landscaping business?"

"Darius Wood. Isn't he an ex-offender?"

"Uh-huh. I met him at my church originally. He comes by and picks up men now, around dawn. So far, Carlton's doing all right."

"What about Tyrone Meadows?" said Rachel. "He in?"

"Tyrone's most definitely in," said Millie. "He ain't even looked for work since he been here."

"Can I speak to him?"

"I'll get him," said Millie, then put her two-fingered hand on Rachel's arm. "You want some water, something? You look kinda pale."

"It's just the heat. Thanks, I'm all right."

Rachel Lopez and Tyrone Meadows sat outside at a picnic table so that Tyrone could smoke. Meadows was a hustler who lived off women and had a history of domestic abuse to go with his felony drug charges. He was thin and wiry, with Omega tattoos burned via hot wire into both biceps. He had a radiant smile that clashed with his cruel eyes.

They sat directly in the sun, among other offenders who had come out here to catch air and cigarettes. It was not yet noon, but the temperature had climbed to ninety degrees.

"So what you want to know?" said Meadows. He dragged hard on a live menthol and looked at her with smiling eyes.

"I want to know when you're going to start looking for work," said Rachel, meeting his stare. Her eyes were all business.

"Soon," he said. "Need to find me some presentable clothes, though, before I go out on that job search. Man like me, it's important I look good. I'd be disappointing a lot of ladies if I just stepped out in these old khakis, right?"

"You go down to that corner there at sunup, you're gonna find work. You don't need dress clothes for that."

"That's chain gang bullshit right there. I ain't accustomed to no common labor."

"You better get accustomed to it," said Rachel. "You need to find work. Any kind of gainful employment. The Seven-A form that you signed requires it."

"Oh, it *requires* it, huh?" Meadows hit his cigarette, let out some smoke, and French-inhaled the same smoke. "What y'all gonna do, send me back?"

"If you don't look for work —"

"Look, it don't make all that much difference to me. I'm a survivor, darling."

"It's Miss Lopez."

Meadows chuckled. "Okay. I'm a survivor, *Miss Lopez*. You can send me back if you feel the need to. I don't even like stayin' up in this motherfucker, see? The food's plain awful, for one. Least I had some privacy in the cut. Three-hots-and-a-cot is lookin' pretty good right now, you want the truth."

Keep talking, Slick, thought Rachel. I could arrange it for you, if that's what you want.

"But," said Meadows, "since it's you askin'—"

"I'm not asking."

"Damn, you *feisty*."

"You need to find work, Tyrone."

"Listen, I'm feelin' like you and me, we got a problem." Tyrone leaned forward, glanced at her chest, smiled, and looked back up into her eyes. "You know, they got a motel, walking distance from here, on New York Avenue? You and me could settle this right now."

"And I could violate you. Right now."

"Why you got to act like that?" said Meadows, genuine hurt appearing on his face.

"One more thing," said Rachel. "You need to get over to the clinic and drop a urine."

"*Damn.*"

"I'm gonna check back with you soon," said Rachel, getting up off the picnic bench and walking abruptly to her car. She felt dizzy and faint.

Rachel drove down the block. Out of sight of the half-way house, she pulled over to the curb and cut the engine. She smelled gas fumes, broke into a cool sweat, and dry-heaved into her lap. She rested her head back and closed her eyes. Sitting there in the Honda, with the passenger window barely open, she fell asleep in the August heat.

•   •   •

LORENZO BROWN GOT A CALL on his cell while climbing the hill toward Saint Elizabeth's, on Martin Luther King Jr. Avenue, in Anacostia, Southeast. He turned down the Tahoe's radio and picked up his phone from out of the console's cup holder.

"Brown here."

"Renzo. My mother said you called." Nigel Johnson's voice was hoarse. His tone was weary.

"Right," said Lorenzo. "I read in the newspaper about Green and the boy. That was Michael Butler, right?"

"Yeah," said Nigel.

"You okay?"

"You know how this go. It's all in the game." It was something they had said to each other many times in the past. Nigel did not sound as if he believed it anymore.

"This line safe?"

"I'm on a disposable. You can talk."

"After I left you yesterday, I passed by a silver BMW parked on Georgia, near your shop. The two inside the car were watching us — watching *you*, I expect. Last night, Joe said he saw the same ones from the BMW, havin' some kind of verbal confrontation with Green and Butler out in the middle of the street, right on Otis Place. Green drives that black Escalade, doesn't he?"

"He did. You know who was in the BMW?"

"Melvin Lee. Also, a hard-lookin' kid he ride with, name of Rico."

"How'd you recognize their car?" said Nigel.

"I had my own thing with them earlier in the day. Somethin' to do with my job."

"Lee works for Deacon. He been back with Deacon since he came uptown."

"What I heard," said Lorenzo. Passing between the brick walls of Saint E's, he continued driving south on MLK.

"None of this is no surprise," said Nigel after a long silence.

"You knew?"

"I knew DeEric fucked up."

"How so?"

"Green came up on some kid retailing on one of Deacon's corners. He told this kid to step off, thinking the corner was mine. Made a dumb mistake, is all. Deacon's people came back at him, I guess."

"Was Butler with Green when he made the mistake?"

"No. I only had him ridin' with DeEric to pick up the count, watch how we do. I wanted Michael to learn. That was *my* fuckup there. Michael wasn't cut out for that kind of drama."

"You think Deacon ordered the hit?" said Lorenzo, turning down Mississippi Avenue, going along the park known as Oxon Run.

"I don't know," said Nigel.

Lorenzo drove through the open gate of a fenced complex and parked the Tahoe in the lot of a group of squat brick apartment buildings on Mississippi.

"I got work to do, Nigel."

"So do I. But look here: This the last conversation we gonna have about this."

"No question."

"I don't want you involved."

"You don't have to worry about that."

"I mean it, Lorenzo."

"So do I."

"You need me again, for anything, you call me direct. Leave a message and I'll get back to you."

Nigel said his phone number; Lorenzo wrote it on the notepad clipped on the dash of the truck.

"You didn't tell my mother about the killing, did you? I don't like to upset the old girl."

"I didn't say a thing."

"Take care of yourself," said Nigel, and he cut the line.

Lorenzo radioed Cindy and told her he had arrived at the location of the complaint. He then got out of the Tahoe, leaving the motor running and the air conditioning on full, and locked the door with his spare key. He went up the hill toward the apartment building to make his call.

SEVENTEEN

NIGEL JOHNSON STARED AT the disposable cell phone, one of many he kept in the office. He leaned back in his leather chair and listened to it creak. His enforcer, Lawrence Graham, slight as a fourteen-year-old boy, sat on the edge of Nigel's desk.

"What your man say?" said Graham. It was always *your* man when he spoke of Lorenzo Brown. He resented the fact that Nigel still held Lorenzo in such high regard.

"Looks like it was two of Deacon's killed DeEric and Michael," said Nigel. "Melvin Lee and a boy name Rico."

"Rico Miller. I don't know where Rico stay at, but Lee work up at the car wash on Georgia. I could wait until he gets off his shift."

"I ain't ready to drop him yet."

"I'm just sayin'. You want me to do it, I will. I'll put work in on Miller too."

"It might come to that. But I want to talk to Deacon first. Give him a chance to tell me how he gonna carry this."

"I can get word out with Griff that you lookin' to talk."

"Do it. Set up a meet, someplace neutral, that's what he wants." Nigel slid the cell phone across his desk. "And get rid of this burner."

"You want me to leave outta here now?"

"Yeah. Homicide gonna be callin' on me soon, I expect. Better if I'm here alone."

"Anything else?"

"Have someone arrange the funeral home. Buy some T-shirts from that boy in Petworth. Get the flowers at the usual place. Send some to DeEric's mother too."

"What about Michael's mother?"

"Fuck that bitch."

Graham left the shop. Nigel sat heavily in his chair, staring through the plate glass window to the street.

. . .

LORENZO WALKED to the entrance of a squat brick apartment building that held four units. He was familiar with the layout of the complex and could describe the interior of the dwellings without having been in this actual structure. These kinds of apartments, minimally maintained and surrounded by black iron fences, were common in Southeast. In his early years, Lorenzo had lived in one just like these, here in Congress Heights.

Outside, kids were plentiful, cracking on one another, riding bikes, and making up games on the dirt-and-weed grounds. Mothers, most in their teens, stood around with one another, smoking, talking with men and young men who were not the fathers of their children. A couple of the older kids hard-eyed Lorenzo as he passed. He was not police, but he was some kind of official, which put him on the other side. A boy in a wife beater and loose pants, no older than fourteen, got on a cell phone as he watched Lorenzo enter the building.

Inside, the building smelled of fried food, with the faint tang of urine and feces in the mix. A dog barked from behind one of the two apartment doors on the second floor. Lorenzo went directly to the first-floor dwelling of Felton Barnett, the man who had left the message on his machine.

Barnett answered Lorenzo's knock. His eyes carried the baggage of repeated late-night alcohol consumption. He was small, middle-aged, and fastidiously dressed.

"Remember me?" said Barnett.

"Yes," said Lorenzo. It was not a pleasant memory. For some reason, Barnett reminded Lorenzo of a rodent in man's clothes.

Barnett had contacted the office months ago with what turned out to have been a nuisance call. Lorenzo had responded, been polite, and shown him respect, something Barnett was apparently not used to. Now Lorenzo was Barnett's personal officer. When he phoned the Humane Society, he dialed Lorenzo's direct number.

"I got a problem, a *very* serious problem up in two-B. Dog been up there barking for two days straight." Barnett, who smelled of beer and cigarettes, pointed a thin finger at Lorenzo. "Y'all need to respond quicker than you do."

"I just got the message this morning. If you had called the main number —"

"I did call it, this morning."

"If you had called it originally, they would've sent someone out yesterday."

"I don't want *someone*," said Barnett, standing ramrod straight. "You're my man. When I call, I want you."

"You got a key to the apartment?"

"I'm the resident manager," said Barnett. It was like he was telling Lorenzo that he was the king of New York.

"Let's go check it out."

They went up the stairs and approached 2B. On the landing, the barking was incessant and loud. The smell of feces was strong. Lorenzo's headache was back full-on.

"You tried contacting the resident?"

"Boy who rents this place don't reside here. You want to know what I think?"

Lorenzo began to knock on the door.

"He keeps drugs and money up in here," said Barnett, tired of waiting for Lorenzo to reply.

"Go ahead and open it," said Lorenzo.

Barnett used his key to unlock the door, then stepped behind Lorenzo. Lorenzo pushed on the door and opened it enough to look inside.

A cream pit bull with a brown eye patch stood in the corner of the living room, baring its teeth, barking maniacally at Lorenzo. The room was bare, the floor nearly covered in feces. The dog's coat carried several deep lesions, some of which appeared to be infected. The dog's ribs were highly defined in its coat, and its eyes bulged in their sunken sockets. Flies nested in one prominent lesion and were bunched in clumps on the dog's ears. Flies buzzed about the room. There were blood streaks on the wall where the animal had tried to rub at the cuts. There was an empty aluminum bowl, pocked with teeth marks, on the floor.

Lorenzo backed onto the landing and closed the door.

"Go back to your place," he said to Barnett. "Write down the name of the man who rents this apartment and any other information you have on him from his lease."

"What are you going to do?"

Lorenzo took the stairs without answering and went directly to the Tahoe. He got Cindy on the radio and told her of the situation, and when she asked if he would like MPD assistance, he told her that he could handle it himself. He got the choke pole out of the truck and headed back into the building. As he went through the door, he heard comments and laughter from the young men gathered outside.

In the apartment, Lorenzo breathed through his mouth to avoid the stench. He looked carefully at the barking dog. He whistled to it softly.

"You all right," he said, like he was talking to a baby in a crib. He walked toward it.

The dog showed its teeth, growled, and backed up until its hindquarters touched the wall. Lorenzo kept walking through the feces, step by careful step, flies buzzing around him, one hand out, the other holding the wooden pole with the wire noose on its end. He looked at the dog's eyes, desperate and afraid. He reached out and put the noose near the dog's head, and the dog lunged at him and backed up again.

"You all right. *You all right.*"

Lorenzo dropped the noose over the dog's head. The dog moved in his direction. Lorenzo put slight pressure on the pole to let the dog know that he could control it now at will. But the dog was not coming toward him with aggression. It had stopped barking. Its nub of a tail wiggled weakly on its rump.

Lorenzo felt his heart rate slow. He realized how very hot it was in the room, and that his shirt was damp with sweat.

"Come on," he said. "Let's get you some cool water."

Using the pole and noose as a leash and collar, he walked the dog down the stairs. The dog went calmly with him.

"Everything all right?" said Barnett, standing behind the door, open just a crack.

"Fine. You write down that information I asked for?"

"Right here," said Barnett, handing Lorenzo a slip of paper. Lorenzo read the name written on the paper, put it in his breast pocket, and walked out of the building into the bright sunlight.

A small crowd had gathered outside the building, mostly kids and some adults. He heard some positive things said by the adults. Some of the kids looked away at the sight of the sick, injured, dehydrated dog. Others laughed. The boy with the cell phone said, "Man who own that dog on his way," and "He gonna fuck someone up too." Lorenzo did not look at any of them. He went directly to the truck.

He got the dog up into the back of the Tahoe and re-leased it from the choke pole. He poured a small amount of bottled water into a bowl and let the animal lap it up. He poured a little bit more and placed the bowl in a large cage. The dog went into the cage without being prodded. Lorenzo closed the cage door and then the rear hatch on the Tahoe. He heard a car come into the lot, bass thumping from its windows, and he heard some boys talking and laughing with excitement and a car door slam, but he did not look at the source of the sounds. He locked the hatch and went to the driver's side of his vehicle.

"Fuck you think you doin'?" said a voice. Lorenzo turned around and faced the man standing behind him.

The man was as tall as Lorenzo, and younger. He had good size. He wore a four-finger ring that spelled LEON. His shirt was a genuine football jerscy that went for one hundred and seventy dollars. He had stepped out of a fifty-thousand-dollar car.

"I'm impounding this dog," said Lorenzo, rubbing his finger on the spare key in his right hand.

"You mean you takin' her."

"That's right," said Lorenzo, keeping his gaze steady on the swinish eyes of the man. "Are you the owner?"

"Yeah, I'm the owner. What the fuck you think?"

Lorenzo removed the piece of paper from his shirt, looked at it, and replaced it. "Leon Skiles?"

"Why you need to know?"

"Just want to make sure I got it straight. It'll help me identify you when we prosecute."

"Oh," said Skiles, "so now you gonna *prosecute*. Motherfucker, you ain't even police. Standin' there with that fake-ass uniform and shit."

Some people in the crowd laughed.

"Look here," said Skiles, stepping forward, getting close to Lorenzo's face. "You ain't takin' a *got*damn thing from me."

A boy cackled and another one whooped. Lorenzo did not step back or cut his eyes away. He could feel his blood pulsing through his veins.

"You think I'm gonna let you just drive on out of here with my personal property?"

Lorenzo did not answer.

"What," said Skiles, "you fixin' to stare me to death?"

Lorenzo made a loose fist and moved the key so that its tip came out between his middle and index fingers.

"Play the bitch, you want to," said Skiles. "I'm about to drop your bitch ass too."

"Do it," said Lorenzo, hearing something in his voice he had not heard in a long while. Knowing the code, knowing, as he said it, that Skiles could not back down.

Skiles put his weight on his back foot.

Now you gonna throw your right.

Skiles swung his fist. Lorenzo sidestepped it and came with an uppercut, bringing his shoulder and chest full into it. The blow landed squarely under Skiles's jaw; the key stabbed him there.

Skiles staggered and tried to keep his feet. Lorenzo rushed forward, pushed Skiles up against the Tahoe, and pinned his left forearm to Skiles's neck. Lorenzo put the tip of the key to Skiles's right eye. The sun winked off the metal.

"Smart-mouth boy like you came at me in the cut," said Lorenzo, keeping his voice low. "I stuck him in the eye with a little old file. Wasn't no bigger than this key I got in my hand."

"I ain't . . . I ain't want no more trouble," said Skiles, gasping as he spoke.

"You gonna relax now, right?"

Skiles nodded slightly under the pressure of Lorenzo's arm. "I'm straight."

"Straight," said Lorenzo, chuckling quietly. He released Skiles and stepped back.

Skiles, blood trickling down his neck from where he'd been cut, looked away. There were only mumbles from the crowd. The air had gone out of it. The wrong man had won.

Lorenzo got into the Tahoe and drove away, his hands

tight on the wheel. His headache was gone. In the rear-view, he saw that his eyes were alive. He felt like getting high.

He punched the gas. First thing he had to do was drop this dog at the kennel. Get her situated and get her some care. Then, if he could, get to someplace he should be.

* * *

RACHEL LOPEZ WOKE UP in her car at a little past noon. Her shirt was soaked with sweat. The Honda stank of perspiration, alcohol, and nicotine. She rolled the window down and breathed clean air.

Rachel drove to the nearest gas station. There, in a filthy bathroom, she washed herself as best she could. She stared at her reflection in the mirror, then looked at her watch. She still had time to get to the meeting on East Capitol. She needed it today.

EIGHTEEN

LEFT MY BABY a little present this morning," said Shirley, the small young woman with the almond eyes and smooth chocolate skin. "Put it right there on the doorstep of my grandmother's place, where my little girl stay."

"What'd you get her?" said a dark-skinned woman sitting in Shirley's row.

"What you call a playwear set. Got it up there at the Hecht's company, thirty percent off. With the coupons, it was next to nothin'."

"Hecht's havin' a sale this weekend," said a man.

"They *always* be havin' a sale," said another.

"The shirt part of the outfit had a drawing of these four young white dudes on it," said Shirley. "I don't know who they are, but the lady at the Hecht's told me the kids are into 'em."

"The Wiggles," said the dark-skinned woman help-fully.

"That's who it was," said Shirley. "So I was walkin' away from the house and I heard the door open, and I turned around? And there my little girl was, standing with my grandmother. And my little girl took that outfit out of the bag, looked at it, and smiled. 'This for me?' she said to my grandmother. You could see she liked it, 'cause she was all happy. And my grandmother said to my little girl, 'That's a present for you from your mother.' My little girl looked at me, said, 'That my mother right there?' It sunk my heart that she forgot me, but she wasn't no more than a baby when I left. My grandmother says, 'Yes, sweetheart, that's your mother. Tell her thank you, child.'"

Shirley cocked her head. "She couldn't say it. She was scared, or too shy. But the look she gave me . . . That look is gonna keep me sober. I'm gonna carry that look with me for a long time." Shirley wiped at her eyes. "Thank you for letting me share."

"Thank you for sharing."

Rachel Lopez leaned back in her folding chair. Her nausea was gone, and color had returned to her skin.

The hard middle-aged man named Sarge, wearing a T-shirt and the same dirty Redskins hat he always wore, raised his hand and was acknowledged by the guest host.

"Sarge here . . ."

"Hey, Sarge."

". . . and I'm a straight-up addict. Now, I had a little episode last night, over at my efficiency. I was goin' through this drawer in this old dresser I got, lookin' for a knife. This one drawer, I keep all this stuff inside it from when I was little. Got an old baseball I kept from when my team won the city championship, under the lights in

Turkey Thicket, back in seventy-three. A Zippo lighter and some firecrackers and shit. You know, boys' stuff. There's this badge in there too, like a sheriff's badge. I used to pin it on my shirt when I was a boy."

A man chuckled. He stopped abruptly when Sarge gave him a cool look.

"So I was lookin' for this knife," said Sarge. "Not to cut no one or nothin' like that. I had some dirt under my fingernails, and I wanted to clean 'em out, see? I remembered I had this pocketknife, with a pretty pearl handle and a sharp little blade that could do the trick. But I couldn't find it. I guess I lost it somewhere or it got took. What I did find, though, inside this cuff link box, was a joint of weed I forgot I had. I mean, it could have been five years old, sumshit like that. I musta hid it in that box, either from someone I was stayin' with at the time or from my *own* self.

"So I'm standin' there, staring at this old joint. I had some music playin' in the room at the time, comin' out this box I have. That song 'Rock Creek Park,' by the Black-byrds. Donald Byrd and them? 'Doin' it in the park, doin' it after dark' . . . Y'all remember that one. It just reminded me of, you know, *summer* and shit. Bein' with this one girl I knew, the way the park smelled all green and nice, and how this girl smelled nice too. Kids ridin' their bikes in packs down Beach Drive, blowin' on them whistles like they used to do. Cookin' some chicken or whatever on the grill, having a cold beer. Gettin' your head up good."

"*Yes,*" said a man in a far corner of the room.

"I needed to speak to someone," said Sarge, "before I went ahead and put some fire to that stale-ass joint." Sarge made a head motion toward Shirley but did not look in her direction. "And I remembered that young lady over there, she said at yesterday's meeting it would be all right to call her. So I did. We talked for a long while. And by the time we was done talkin', I had decided to flush that weed down the toilet. It hurt me to do it, but that's what I did."

"You did right," said the dark-skinned woman in Shirley's row.

"Understand, I didn't call that woman up because she was female," said Sarge. "I don't want to get with no females right now, anyway. I don't *act* right with 'em when I do."

"Hmph," said a man.

"But I just wanted to tell y'all about my experience," said Sarge. "It don't mean nothin', really. It's just a story."

"We all in the same lifeboat," said Shirley. "Ain't no one here deserve to get throwed out before no one else."

Sarge tightened his hat over his graying hair and lowered his voice to a mumble. "So thank you for letting me share."

"Thank you for sharing."

Lorenzo Brown raised his hand. Rachel looked down the row to where Lorenzo sat, at the far end of the horseshoe-shaped aisle. She had seen him enter the meeting room at the same time she had but had not approached him. She wanted to respect his privacy and leave him to his spiritual time. He was under no obligation to talk to her, after all.

The host nodded in Lorenzo's direction. "Go ahead."

"My name is Lorenzo . . ."

"Hey, Lorenzo."

". . . and I'm a substance abuser. Something happened to me today, on my job."

"You some kind of police?" said Shirley, looking him up and down with interest.

"Dog police," said Lorenzo. "This morning, some man got up in my face over an animal he'd been abusing. I retaliated in a physical way, which I shouldn't have done. But the thing is, it felt good. I get these headaches most all the time now. After this man tried to take me for bad and I went right back at him, my headache went away. But something else came over me too. I wanted to get high. Doin' violence, getting my head up . . . it's all part of the same package for me, I guess."

Lorenzo glanced around the room. "Most of y'all, you made a decision to try and stop what you was doin' on your own. Me, I had it decided for me. I'm comin' off an incarceration, see? I caught a charge for dealing drugs."

"You ain't alone," said a man.

"All respect," said Lorenzo, "that don't make it any easier. You can't always be at these meetings or get someone on the phone. One thing I learned, this here's not a team sport. It also ain't no sprint. The more you walk this road, the longer the road seems to be."

"I heard *that*," said the same man.

"*Long* road," said Lorenzo. "Shoot, I started sellin' marijuana when I was twelve years old. Started smokin' it around that time too. By then, I had already lost my mother to drugs. She got to the point, she was selling herself for money. Later, she did this grand-larceny thing and got put away. She came out eventually, but she couldn't make it. She had to violate herself to save her life. My mother's behind walls to this day."

Lorenzo shifted in his seat. "I never did have a father. I ain't cryin' about it. That's just the way it was.

"I moved in with my grandmother early on. I loved her, but she couldn't contain me. Y'all know how that is. I ran with some boys, one in particular, and when those boys and my main boy went down to the corner, I went with 'em. They were my people, the closest thing I ever had to male kin. I dropped out of high school and moved up to dealin' heroin and cocaine. I was arrested for it and did a couple of stays in juvenile. It didn't teach me a thing. Matter of fact, I was further down the hole when I came out. I impregnated a girl. I did other bad things. Finally, when I was an adult, the jump-out squad got me on a corner in my own neighborhood, doin' hand-to-hands. I was up on some good hydro when they did. I had a whole rack of foil in my pocket, and I took a felony charge. They wanted me to flip on my number one boy. I wouldn't do it. I was just arrogant, the way I handled it. Between my priors and me showin' no kind of remorse, the judge came down hard on me. I did eight on a six to eighteen.

"Prison was prison; y'all know what that's about. When the time came, I didn't even show for my first probation hearing, 'cause I knew I wasn't ready to come up town. Thing of it is, you never are ready. It's harder in some ways to do your straight time than it is to jail.

"I came out the cut and got on a bus. I had thirty-some dollars in my khakis and a blue shirt on my back. I was wearing sneaks had Velcro on 'em 'stead of laces. Prison gear, and I looked it too. Rolled into D.C. at night, went straight to a drugstore near the bus station, and bought some cologne, 'cause I felt like I had the smell of jail on my skin. I get up to the register, and people be runnin' cards through some machine they got on the counter. No one was pullin' out cash. Everyone be talkin' on their cells, everyone be wearin' new fashions. I realized, I am an old head now and I am lost. I do not know what the fuck is goin' on out here anymore. Right there, in the drugstore, realizing what I was up against, that's when I got scared for the first time in my life. Standin' right there in that store, I felt that ache come to my head.

"When I come out that drugstore, I spent the last of my money on a taxi and went to my grandmother's place in Park View. She was waitin' for me. She looked good. Her house smelled like her cooking. She had tied balloons to the banister, right there in the entranceway. She hugged me soon as I came through the door, and I hugged her back. 'Welcome home, son,' she said. 'Welcome to your new life.' Both of us just stood there and held each other. My grandmother cried. I ain't ashamed to admit it, I cried some, too."

A chair creaked in the room.

"It just takes one person to believe in you," said Lorenzo. "When I hugged that woman, I knew I was gonna try to do right. And that's all I can claim. I'm *tryin'* out here. I don't mean to bore you, but I needed to talk to someone today, and you people came to mind. So thank you for listening, all a y'all. Thank you for letting me share."

"Thank you for sharing."

"Anyone else?" said the guest host.

"My name is Rachel Lopez . . ." said Rachel, speaking quickly, not planning to speak at all, not knowing what she was going to say.

"Hey, Rachel."

". . . and I'm an alcoholic."

Lorenzo leaned forward in his chair.

"I don't have the right to be here," said Rachel. "I haven't even tried to get sober. I was drunk last night. I was still drunk when I woke up this morning."

"I remember those mornings," said a woman.

"It's not just that I haven't tried to get straight," said

Rachel. "I'm a probation officer. I make my living telling other people that they need to stay on track. And that makes me a hypocrite. Because I jumped the tracks myself a long time ago."

"I recognized you the first time you came to these meetings," said a male voice behind her. "You used to come to my mother's house to call on my brother. You always showed my mother respect. You got the right to be here, same as anyone else."

Rachel did not turn around to match a face to the voice. She laced her fingers together and rested her hands in her lap.

"I've been drinking a long time. I started when I was about fourteen, down in Texas. . . ."

Rachel Lopez spoke of high school, then college. She spoke of being the last one standing in the bars at the end of the night. Her friends said she handled alcohol well. She didn't change while under its influence. While drinking, she seemed to have control.

"I got a degree in criminology at the local college. I don't know why I chose law enforcement, exactly. It seemed exciting, I guess, and I had a vague notion that I was going to help people. After graduation I took an internship at a halfway house near my parents' place. I didn't like the work, and I felt stifled, living at home. . . ."

She had entered into no romantic relationships. She had continued to drink.

"I wasn't happy. I sent in an application to become a probation officer in Maryland. The EEO was on my side. They needed Spanish-speaking POs at the time. Still do, I guess. Anyway, I got the gig.

"My father . . ."

Rachel closed her eyes and saw him, in bed, on his last

day. He was going to die and yet he was not thinking of himself. He wanted to talk about her. He was worried about *her*:

"My father got sick," said Rachel. "My mother got sick too. I took a leave of absence from my job and went back to Texas to stay with them. You know, to help. But I couldn't help. I couldn't control what was happening to them. They both had inoperable cancer. The doctor called it an unfortunate coincidence. My father passed, and then my mom."

"They're together now," said a voice in the room.

"Yes," said Rachel. "And here I am, still drinking. Still trying to control things I can't control. I don't even know why I'm telling you all of this today. It's not like I've got a plan or anything like it. Anyway." Rachel cleared her throat. "Thank you for letting me share."

"Thank you for sharing."

The basket was passed around. The group gathered in a circle, their arms resting on one another's shoulders, and said the Serenity Prayer and afterward, the Lord's Prayer. An older gentleman extolled the virtues of Narcotics Anonymous. The meeting dispersed, and its participants went on their way.

Out in the parking area of the church, facing East Capitol, Rachel Lopez lit a cigarette. Some members of the group went to their cars, alone or in twos and threes. Others went to the bus shelter and sat on a bench protected from the sun. Lorenzo Brown walked across the grounds of the church and stopped beside Rachel.

"Hey, Miss Lopez."

"Hey, Lorenzo." She exhaled a stream of smoke. "What about that incident you described in there? The physical-retaliation thing. We gonna have a problem with that?"

"The man I stepped to, I don't think he'll report it. That's how it goes in the street. Callin' the police is the last thing he's gonna do."

"I'd hate to see you violated over something as trivial as that."

Lorenzo chuckled. "You ever stop working?"

"When I stop working I get in trouble." Rachel's eyes softened. "You know . . ."

"What?"

"I'm sorry you had to hear all that."

"You're human, is all."

"I appreciate it."

"We all just tryin' out here."

"Yes."

"You ever want to talk about any of this, you can call me. Doesn't need to be about me all the time. You hear me, Miss Lopez?"

"Sure. But when it's on that level, it's Rachel."

"Okay, then. Rachel it'll be."

Shirley, walking with the quickness of the short and compact, came from the church and joined them.

"Hey," said Shirley.

"Hey," said Rachel.

"Can I get a Marlboro, Rachel?"

"Sure."

As Rachel retrieved the pack from her purse, Shirley looked Lorenzo over with blatant interest.

"You *tall*," said Shirley.

"Everyone is to you," said Lorenzo, and Shirley smiled.

Rachel shook out the filtered ends of a few cigarettes,

and Shirley drew one from the pack. Rachel handed her a matchbook from the hotel she'd been at the night before and told her to keep it. Shirley lodged the cigarette behind her ear as Sarge passed them on foot.

"Hey, Sarge," said Shirley. "Where you headed?"

"Back to my efficiency," said Sarge, not breaking stride. "What you think?"

"You need someone to walk with you?"

"I don't need it," said Sarge, still moving, but slowing down. "But if you got a mind to, I ain't gonna try and stop you."

"He ain't all that tough," said Shirley. She looked at Rachel and then at Lorenzo. "You two have a blessed day."

"You also," said Rachel.

Shirley joined Sarge by the shelter.

"I need to get back to work," said Rachel.

"I do too," said Lorenzo.

"You been to the clinic yet?"

"I haven't had the chance."

"Better do it."

"I will."

Rachel touched his arm. "Thank you, Lorenzo."

"Ain't no thing."

Rachel walked to her vehicle; Lorenzo went to his.

NINETEEN

"THAT WAS DEACON," said Melvin Lee. He closed the cover of his Samsung cell and placed the phone on the table by his chair.

"Figured it was," said Rico Miller. "He ain't happy, huh?"

Lee did not answer. Instead he rubbed at his face.

They were in the living area of Melvin Lee's apartment, on the third floor of a row house on Sherman Avenue, near Irving Street, in Columbia Heights. The house had been subdivided into six apartments, two on each floor. It was not far from where Lee had been raised.

The apartment's decor reflected Lee's solitary lifestyle. The few pieces of furniture were secondhand. Only the electronics, a thirty-six-inch high-definition Sony television with theater sound and an Xbox video game system, were new. Lee rarely watched movies or programs, not even sports, on television. He preferred to sit on his threadbare couch for hours on end, playing Counter-Strike, Brute Force, and Project Gotham. Anything with guns or cars.

"Homicide already done visited Deacon," said Lee. "They got them gang-task-force people, know all the players. You know how they do."

"That means they been to see Nigel too."

"That's a bet."

"Nigel ain't gonna say a thing to the police. He gonna want to handle this his own way."

"I expect."

"Nigel and his want more blood, we gonna give 'em some. We soldiers, right?"

Lee looked across the room at Miller, who stood by the big picture window fronting the street. Miller had been pacing the room like an animal who'd got up on two legs for the first time. He'd been unsettled ever since he'd shown up at the apartment and described the murders in detail. Miller had expected Lee to be pleased. He was perplexed at Lee's reaction.

"*Why?*" Lee had said upon hearing the news.

"Why I kill 'em?" said Miller. "Shit, they was gonna go at you, wasn't they?"

"DeEric was just talkin', Rico. He was doin' his job. I been knowin' DeEric since he was a boy. He was *bold* like that."

"Too bold, you ask me."

"And that kid. He wasn't gonna hurt *no* goddamn one."

"You right about that. That boy was a straight bitch."

"You missin' my point. Deacon say the kid was special to Nigel."

"Nigel gone faggot now, huh?"

"*Listen* to me," said Lee, desperation and anger in his voice. "You ain't hearin' me, Rico. We got a problem here. We got to find a way to work this out."

"Thought you'd be happy," said Miller, lowering his head. "I did this thing for you."

Lee had left the conversation lying there, like something dead in the room you stepped over on the way to somewhere else. There wasn't any use in going on with this. Miller seemed to have no remorse for what he'd done. For the first time, Lee feared him. He'd heard about this kind of thing, had always thought of it as street bullshit passing for wisdom. But now he saw that it was true: Came a time in every relationship like this, you traded places. The father became the son.

And now the call had come from Deacon, a call Lee had expected and dreaded all morning long.

"What Deacon say to do?" said Miller.

"He wants you to sit tight right here. He don't want you to go nowhere, 'cause if he wants to pull up on you personal, he need to know where you at."

"He can get me on my cell."

"That ain't good enough. Since you don't want to tell no one where you stay at, you gonna have to be within physical reach for now."

"Where you gonna be?"

"I got to get my ass into work," said Miller.

"What I'm gonna do here all day?"

"Play Xbox, you want to."

"I don't even *like* Xbox. I roll with PS2."

"You gonna have to deal with that, Rico."

Lee got up out of his chair, gathered his cell and keys, and went to the front door. He looked at Rico Miller, standing there with nothing but some peach fuzz on his face, slouched and gangly, deadlier than most men but really no older than a kid.

"Don't be standin' by that window," said Lee.

"I ain't stupid."

"I'm just sayin'. Po-lice could put me together with them bodies somehow, might come calling on me."

"I wouldn't let no police fuck with you, Melvin."

"I'm sayin' . . . Shit, Rico, I'm thinkin' of *you* right now. Any law shows up here, you leave out the fire escape, through my bedroom window. It'll lead you back to the alley. That ladder drops the way it supposed to. I know, 'cause I tried it out." Lee put his hand on the doorknob, then thought of something else.

"You ain't bring no gun in here, right?"

"What you think?"

"That's a mandatory right there. I can't be gettin' violated."

"Guns I used are put away."

"You need to get rid of 'em. They dig the lead up out of those bodies, I'm talkin' about the pistol lead, they can match it to that gun."

"They won't find the guns. Anyway, I picked up the casings off the street."

"Anyone see you last night?"

"I don't think so." Miller cocked his head in a birdlike way. "You ain't mad at me, right?"

Lee looked away. "We gonna work this out."

Melvin Lee took the stairs down to the street and found his faded Camry, parked on Sherman behind Rico Miller's shiny BMW. Driving up Georgia toward the car wash, he looked at the people out on the sidewalks and breathed the warm summer air rushing through his open window. He wanted to enjoy the sights and smells. He had the sick feeling that these things would be taken away from him again all too soon.

He could drive out of town right now, but he knew that someone would catch up to him eventually. He'd been running on a wheel, in a cage, his whole life.

He drove to work.

· · ·

DEACON TAYLOR CLOSED his disposable cell and settled himself in the driver's seat of his S Series Benz. He had parked on Luray Place in Park View and was waiting for Griff to roll up and report on his meet with Nigel's enforcer, Lawrence Graham. Looked like Griff was coming his way now. Griff favored fast Japanese sedans, and drove a 260-horsepower midnight blue Infiniti G35.

Deacon had already had an eventful day. A Homicide team had come by his place and interviewed him about the murders. He had told them he knew nothing, and they had gone on their way. He had spoken to Melvin Lee and conveyed his extreme displeasure over the murders of Green and Butler. Then, on his personal cell, he had made a call to an officer in 4D he had been friendly with for some time.

Officer Muller was a careful man. He refused to finger informants, rough Taylor's enemies, or make false arrests. He would not initiate anything that he felt would compromise his personal code. He did provide Taylor with information on occasion that he thought was of a harmless nature. Taylor, in turn, fed information to Muller that was equally benign. For this dialogue Muller accepted nothing in the way of cash or gifts. The first-name-basis familiarity with a drug dealer and the attendant camaraderie appealed to his self-image. Muller liked to think of himself as a cop who was hardwired to both sides of the street.

"What you hear about that double off Crittenden last night?" Deacon had said.

"Hold up, Deacon," said Muller. "You need to tell me why you're interested first." Always reminding Taylor that he, Muller, was in charge.

"Ain't no secret that it was two of Nigel Johnson's got themselves dead. I'm just tryin' to keep informed."

"That's all?"

"You and me don't play games like that, big man," said Deacon. In fact, he was playing Muller with every word.

"Just so we're clear," said Muller.

"We *crystal* clear."

"Victim one died of shotgun wounds inside his SUV. Victim two was killed in the street by the same shotgun. Vic two also took bullets to the mouth and head."

"Sounds like the shooter was angry about somethin'."

"Prob'ly just one of those misunderstood youths we got out here."

"Killer leave any prints?"

Muller did not reply. It was answer enough.

"No witnesses either, huh?" said Deacon.

Again, Muller said nothing.

"You keep me posted, hear?" said Deacon.

"I expect the same from you."

"You know I will. This kind of violence is bad for business. Pretty soon the neighborhood gonna be crawling with bad elements like yourself."

"You don't want that, dawg."

"Word," said Deacon. He hadn't used that expression to anyone but Muller in the last ten years.

Griff pulled his Infiniti up alongside the Mercedes and idled it in the street. They went nose to ass, the way police did, so they could speak.

Griff was serious, dependable, and strong of body and character. He dressed neatly and without show. He was Deacon's most fearsome employee. Only fault he had was he talked too much, and bragged, when his head was up on weed. Maturity would cure that. Someday the boy would become a man and learn how to handle his high.

"What's up, soldier?" said Deacon.

"I got up with Graham," said Griff.

"Talk about it."

"Nigel want to parley with you about this problem. Says he'll do it somewhere neutral, just the two of y'all."

"I'll meet him," said Deacon. "But I ain't ready just yet. Need to think things out before we talk."

"You got a plan?"

"I don't plan," said Deacon. "I look for opportunities."

"You want to do this tonight?"

"Tonight's good."

"I'll go back to Larry."

"Don't call him Larry to his face," said Deacon. "I heard his mother named him after the bass player, and I heard he don't like it."

"What bass player?"

"Larry Graham," said Deacon.

Griff shrugged and looked blankly at Deacon.

"Awright then," said Deacon. "Go talk to Graham and set it up. Say, eight o'clock at the fort?"

"I'm on it," said Griff.

"No doubt," said Deacon. Griff pulled away in his car.

Deacon thinking, Boy don't know who Larry Graham

is, at least he should have pretended like he did. Tryin' to make me feel all ancient out here.

. . .

LORENZO BROWN CAUGHT a quick tuna sub at his Subway and got back to work. He radioed in to Cindy, still on the desk, to see if there were any calls he needed to take. She told him about a chaining complaint over in Columbia Heights. He told her he would pass by the address on his way back to the office. She didn't mention anything about the incident in Southeast. Leon Skiles had followed street code, as Lorenzo had expected, and not reported the assault.

Lorenzo started up the Tahoe and headed for Columbia Heights.

. . .

EDDIE DAVIS WAS A CUTTER in a styling shop on Florida Avenue, in Trinidad, near Gallaudet. He was a slim man in his midfifties, quiet and gentle, with a trim mustache and kind eyes. Nothing about him suggested that he was the same person who in 1977 had stabbed a man repeatedly for looking at his girlfriend the wrong way in a Petworth bar. Eddie Davis, up on PCP, had left an Italian switchblade in the man's neck after burying it to the hilt, and then resumed his drinking. No one had come near him until the police arrived. When he was smoking that boat, Eddie felt as if he had the strength of ten men and, feeling that way, he did. In fact, it took four police to subdue him that night.

The murder charge bought him a twenty-five-year sentence. He had fathered two sons before he went inside. As teenagers, without a strong male figure to keep them in line, both young men became involved in the crack cocaine trade, which hit Washington like a plague in the summer of '86. As adults, Eddie's sons eventually caught drug charges and were incarcerated for most of the nineties. Eddie himself was released and was promptly violated on possession-with-intent-to-distribute offenses. He returned to prison, where the one-two punch of Jesus and drug rehabilitation finally found traction with a man who realized he was both too old to play the game and lucky to be alive. As for Eddie's sons, they were CSOSA cases: Transferred from Lorton to federal facilities, they had served out the rest of their terms far away from D.C. and now were out on paper, trying, like their father, to stay on the straight.

Rachel Lopez entered the styling shop, a unisex affair owned by an ex-offender named Rock Williams who aggressively employed men and women who had done time. The shop was full-service, with stylists, barbers, manicurists, and pedicurists, and specialized in hair coloring and extensions. Williams had a loyal clientele. Most of the customers had family members either in incarceration or on paper and were behind the concept of redemption through hard work.

"Mr. Williams," said Rachel Lopez, approaching the broad-chested owner standing behind the register counter.

"Miss Lopez." He extended his hand and she shook it. "You lookin' for Eddie?"

"I am."

"He's around here somewhere. I'll get him for you."

Williams went past the styling area and through curtains to a back room. Rachel listened to the soft soul and jazz of the Howard University radio station, WHUR, coming from the house system. She got nods and eye contact from a couple of the cutters and a wink from a female man-icurist working close to the counter. All had been told by Eddie Davis and Williams that Miss Lopez was a PO and that she was all right. She had never once caught attitude in the Rock Williams House of Style.

Davis emerged from the back room smiling. He met her at the counter and shook her hand. She drew him into her arms impulsively. He hugged her as he would a daughter.

"How do I look?" he said, stepping back.

Davis wore a black barber's smock with "Eddie" stitched in cursive across the chest. Above his name was an embroidered tableau of crossed scissors over a barber pole. His hard life had aged him prematurely and considerably, but Rachel could still see the handsome man he once had been. Everything about him she needed to know was in his eyes. There was nothing bad there; it was impossible that there would be evil in him again.

"You look great," she said.

"Do I look like a man who's about to come off paper?"

"I wrote the termination letter a few days ago. I'm ready to send it in."

"That don't mean we gotta stop seein' each other, right?"

"I'll be around," said Rachel. "And I'm gonna expect that Christmas card too."

"You're family, Miss Lopez. I ain't never gonna take you off that list."

They looked at each other for a few moments. She hoped that what he said was true. It was with mixed feelings that she let go of certain offenders. The fact that an Eddie Davis was going to make it validated her life's work. That he was walking out of her world caused her sadness too.

"How are your sons?" she said.

"Good. Charles and Michael both cuttin' heads in separate barbershops." Eddie looked around to make sure that Williams was not within earshot. "Plan is, I'm gonna start up my own shop. Get my sons under my wing. I'm lookin' at this little space over there on Good Hope Road. It's close to my apartment. Want a place I can walk to every morning, turn that key."

"Don't worry about Rock hearing you," said Rachel. "He'd be happy if you went out on your own."

"I'm gonna do it, Miss Lopez. I am going to *do* it."

"I believe you. Your sons are in Anacostia as well?"

"Yeah. Both of 'em bought little houses over there in Southeast. I helped 'em out with the down payments. I had a, what do you call that, *motive* for it. I want to be close to my grandchildren."

"It's all about family."

"Yes," said Eddie. He looked her over. "You look nice today, you don't mind my sayin' so."

"I was feeling poorly this morning. But I'm better now."

"You gonna be able to come by that barbecue this weekend? My sons and their kids are gonna be there. They'd love to see you."

"I'll try."

Eddie pointed a gnarled finger in her direction. "I'm not gonna let you lose touch."

"I promise. We've come too far together, you and me."

"God is good," said Eddie Davis.

He can be, thought Rachel. They hugged again before she left the shop.

Out in her Honda, Rachel looked through her files. She had one more stop to make before returning to the office. The offender had given her his work schedule, by her request. He was a person she needed to stay on top of, a career criminal who up to this point had been unable to leave the drug game behind.

Rachel wanted to interview the offender at his place of employment whenever possible, to verify that he was there consistently. It looked as if she had missed that opportunity when she had failed to make all of her calls the day before. She'd have to visit him at his residence on Sherman Avenue.

According to her records, that's where the offender, a man named Melvin Lee, stayed.

TWENTY

R ICO MILLER SAT on a folding chair by the big front window of the apartment, watching the street. Melvin had told him not to stay there, but he was bored. He had tried playing Counter-Strike on Xbox, but he was used to the PS2 controller and grew frustrated using one he didn't know nothing about. He had thought getting high might help him master the system, but that didn't educate him either. The fat joint he'd smoked had only made him more confused. And that had sent him to where he was at right now, staring out the window. Wasn't much skill you needed for that.

Down on Sherman, a white woman with stuff in her hands got out of her car, some square-back hooptie. Looked like she was carrying a file or something like that. A cell too, and some kind of little leather case.

She didn't look all white. She might have been Span-ish or something; he couldn't tell. She was wearing jeans and a shirt had no style. She didn't belong on this street. It wasn't her color. There were a few whites and plenty of browns down here. It was the way she carried herself, walking down the sidewalk, aware of where she was, trying to act like this was her neighborhood when it was not. Miller had this talent. He could smell police.

Soon as this entered his mind, a 4D patrol car, heading east on Irving, turned up Sherman. It slowed near where the woman was walking and pulled over to the curb. The woman hesitated, seemed to recognize the driver, and went to the open window. He couldn't see the woman's face as she bent forward.

That woman's talking to one of her own, thought Miller. She's conspiring with the police in the car.

The uniform police spoke to the woman police for a couple of minutes, and then the uniform took off. The Crown Vic's tires caught rubber on the street. The woman got back up on the sidewalk, went down it some, and turned toward Melvin's row house. As she made her way to it, she looked up at the third-floor window. Miller leaned back in his chair.

She seen me, he thought. I fucked up. Police coming up here looking for Melvin. I should do what Melvin say to do and go out the fire escape and run.

He went back to the bedroom and opened the window. He looked down at the mesh platform outside the window and the ladder below it. What good would it do Melvin if he, Rico, was to book on out? If the police was looking at Melvin for the murders, they would get him up there at the car wash just the same. What Rico needed to do was to stop them from looking. Leastways, hold them off until he and Melvin could leave out of town. Besides, to run on out of here, from a woman? That didn't work for him.

High like he was, it was hard to know what to do. He closed the window and stood stupidly in the center of the room.

Miller put his hand in his pocket and touched leather. He touched the rough part of the leather where the letter *C* was at. He ran his finger down to touch the *R*. Then the *E*, and then the other *E*. And then the *P*.

Miller heard a grinding sound.

. . .

RACHEL PARKED on Sherman, gathered her badge case, her cell, and her file on Melvin Lee, and got out of her car. She locked the Honda and went down the sidewalk toward Lee's address. It was a row house like all the others on the block. The file said he lived on the third floor.

An MPD patrol car came off Irving and up Sherman. Rachel clocked the Fourth District designation and identification numbers on the Crown Vic. It came to a stop curbside. As the window slid down, she saw that it was Donald Peterson, one of the many cops she had worked with over the years, behind the wheel. Peterson was a sergeant, black, and somewhere on the good side of forty. He was well built, close to handsome, and, like many cops, divorced.

She liked him; he had a confident cool. He had flirted with her when they'd first met, down at the District Courthouse, and asked her out. It was a respectful, non-aggressive flirtation, and she had been flattered. But she had politely declined, explaining that she had just come through a rough stretch, dealing with the illness of her parents, and wasn't ready to date. Of course, it had nothing to do with her parents. She had never been in an equal relationship, one where she was not in complete control. The thought of it frightened her.

"Hey, Donald," she said, leaning on the lip of his window, feeling the bite of the ice-cold air-conditioning blowing in the car.

"Miss Lopez. Making a house call?"

"A Melvin Lee."

"Spidery-lookin' gentleman," said Sergeant Peterson, who had been working the Fourth for over fifteen years. "Toiled under Deacon Taylor, if I recall."

"If you say so."

"Don't tell me: You missionary types are interested in their futures, not their pasts."

"Can't do anything about their pasts."

"What's he doing now? Pediatric surgeon, somethin' like that?"

"He works in a car wash."

"Another productive member of society."

"Somebody's gotta keep the cars clean."

"Send him up to the station. Mine could use a bath."

"You guys are always looking for a handout."

A call came over the radio, something about a man driving erratically down Georgia Avenue. Peterson keyed the mic and told the dispatcher that he'd respond, then replaced the mic in its cradle.

"I was wonderin' . . ."

"What?"

"You like seafood?"

"Love it."

"Ever been to Crisfields?"

"No."

"You gonna make me work for this, aren't you?"

"I've never been to Crisfields and I'd like to go."

"When?"

"Give me a call."

"You still in that same office?"

"Yes."

"Okay." Peterson pulled down on the transmission arm. "Let me get on over to Georgia. See what this guy's malfunction is." He looked Rachel over, then looked directly into her eyes. "Be safe."

"You too, Donald."

Rachel backed off the window and Peterson drove away. His tires squealed, leaving rubber on the asphalt, as he took off.

They can't help themselves, thought Rachel. They're all boys at heart.

She went up the walkway to the row house where Melvin Lee stayed. As she walked, she smiled and shook her head. All this impulsive behavior in one afternoon. Sergeant Peterson had tried one time, a while back. Turning his car up Sherman as she was making a house call, maybe it was just his lucky day. Could be it was hers too.

Rachel entered the row house and took the steps up to the third floor. She heard television sets and the bass of a stereo as she ascended the stairs. She made the landing and knocked on the door marked 3B. She put her cell phone in her front pocket and kept her badge case and file in her hands. There were footsteps behind the door, and then the door opened.

A young man who was not Melvin Lee stood in the frame. He was tall and thin and had a long lupine face. His eyes were nothing eyes and told her only that he was high. She had seen this look, absent of all humanity, on some of the young offenders in her case files. She had seen it more frequently in the last couple of years.

"Melvin Lee," said Rachel, badging the young man.

"I ain't Melvin."

"I'm *looking* for Melvin," she said, keeping her eyes on his and her tone firm. "I'm Miss Lopez. Melvin's probation officer."

"Yeah, okay."

"Is Melvin around?"

"He out. He gonna be back soon."

Rachel smelled marijuana from inside the apartment. She slipped the badge case into the rear pocket of her jeans.

"I'll come back," said Rachel. "Tell him I was here."

Rachel turned to go.

"Hold up," said the young man, and Rachel stopped.

"Yes?"

"I'm sayin', he only gonna be out for, like, ten minutes, somethin' like that. He only buyin' a pack of smokes."

"Who are you?"

"Rico."

"My question is, what is your relation to Mr. Lee?"

"Melvin my father," said Rico. "Come on in and wait, you want to. He ain't gonna be but a bit."

Rachel hesitated. She tried to remember if Lee had a son. She didn't think it was in his file. He had omitted it, maybe, on the form. Not unusual, but still a lie. A violation, along with the weed, if there was any left. If the boy hadn't flushed it down the toilet already.

She needed to note these things for the record. It wasn't enjoyable, but it was her job. She stepped inside the apartment. The boy named Rico closed the door behind her.

They stood, awkwardly, in the living room. Rico did not ask her to have a seat or offer her something to drink.

Rachel looked at her watch. "I'll wait five minutes. Then I have to go."

The boy shrugged.

"I was supposed to see Melvin at his place of employment yesterday," said Rachel. "But I misplaced the location. He works at that car wash, right?"

The boy nodded.

"Where is that again?"

"You don't think I know?"

"I'm asking. Like I say, I had it written down somewhere —"

"But you mis-*placed* it." Rico smiled. There were gaps between his rotten teeth. "It's that one up there on Georgia."

"Right," said Rachel.

"Now you remember, huh." Rico looked her over. The smile was frozen on his face.

It was hot in the apartment. The window unit is running, thought Rachel, and still it's hot.

Rachel glanced past Rico to the table in front of the couch. Nothing there but a couple of video game controllers and an empty orange soda bottle.

"Lookin' for something?" said Rico.

Rachel said nothing. Rico chuckled.

"How old are you?" said Rachel, feeling a flush of anger.

"Seventeen."

"And your father is, what, thirty?"

"'Bout that, I guess."

"So you were born when he was thirteen. That means you were conceived when Melvin was twelve?"

"Huh?"

"You father was twelve when he got your mother pregnant. Is that what you're telling me?"

"I ain't never done the math, lady."

"It's Miss Lopez."

The boy stepped forward and stood close to Rachel. She could smell his foul breath.

Rachel did not step back. "What are you doing?"

"Gettin' a closer look at you. You mind?"

Rachel stared into his eyes. If she looked away or backed up, she would lose.

"You old," said Rico. "But that don't make no difference to me. I'll fuck you in every hole you got."

"You're about to get yourself *and* Mr. Lee in a whole world of trouble," said Rachel. She felt a nerve twitch at the corner of her mouth as she spoke.

"Who gonna cause that trouble?" said Rico. "You? Or maybe you think your police friend gonna come in here now and *cause some trouble*. Thing is, he gone, *Miss Lopez*. Way the smoke came off his tires on Sherman, looked to me like he had to take a call."

"I'm out of here," said Rachel, and she turned to go.

She heard Rico laughing behind her.

"Come on, Miss Lopez," he said. "I'm just playin' with you."

Rachel patted the front pocket of her jeans and felt her cell. She began to walk and heard his footsteps behind her.

"Hey," said Rico, "you forgot your badge."

She turned toward him, and as she turned she reached around to her back pocket and touched the rectangular outline of her badge case. She felt her stomach drop and the color drain from her face.

Rico held a serrated knife in his upraised hand. He brought it down violently and plunged the blade into her breast. She gasped at the pain as he withdrew it.

"*Popi*," said Rachel. Her eyes crossed and she screamed, "God!"

The knife swept down again. Rico's face was a grimace of effort and ambition, and the steel pierced her flesh and bone.

Rachel's howl filled the room.

TWENTY-ONE

HAD THIS FREAK come over to my crib last night," said the man who called himself King. "Big freak. Had some big legs and a *big*-ass ass on her too."

"She look like an animal?" said Momo, King's friend.

"Nah, man, she ain't look like that."

"'Cause that last female you had looked like an animal."

"Bull*shit*."

"Yes, she did."

"The woman I had last night looked good."

"But on the heavy side, huh?"

"A little."

"Like a big old beast."

"Your mother look like a beast."

"Your sister does."

"Your father."

"Go ahead, King." Momo turned to Melvin Lee. "Melvin, tell me King's last girlfriend didn't look like a horse and shit."

"I ain't getting into this," said Lee. "Not today."

Lee, King, and Momo were on dry detail at the car wash. King and Momo had both done time. They talked about women, and sometimes the Redskins, all day long. Normally, Lee joined them. But he wasn't in the mood.

Some days he didn't mind these two, but others, he wished he was working in the back with the one older dude and the two Spanish, the ones who prepped the cars before they rolled 'em inside. Out here in the front, where the cars came out clean and dripping, alls they had him doing was holding a rag, getting the excess wet off the vehicle, wiping down the interior, and all that. Like he wasn't even smart enough to point a hose at the wheels. Reminded him of those classes they used to stick him in before he dropped out of school, with all the kids couldn't read or add two and two, like he was one step off of retard himself.

Nearby, an older man stood beside his 7-Series and watched them dry it off.

"Get the hood," said the man, pointing to it. "Last time I brought my BMW in here you left drops on it. I can't be driving around in a water-stained vehicle."

"Get it, Momo," said King. "You heard the man."

Momo leaned over the hood and wiped it down. Good thing he did, 'cause Lee wasn't about to. Old man thinking he was something, had to tell them it was a BMW, like they were blind. An old BMW at that, an '89, two body styles back. Leather interior all cracked and shit, looked like the old man's skin. One of those bourgeois brothers, moved west of Rock Creek and forgot who he was.

Least they talked free around his kind. With the Caucasian customers, you said nothing, even when they were talking directly to you, out of pride. With the females, you kept your mouth shut too, unless they were feisty with you first. And then you didn't know how far to go. Some of these females, they'd complain to management if you took that man-woman thing past its limit, no matter who started it off.

The old man walked over to the tip box, which wasn't no more than a metal toolbox, padlocked shut, with a slit cut out the top. King had wrote this sign over it, said, "Tips please, this is how we feed our families," though King had fathered five kids and had never given one of them a thin dime. The old man pulled a dollar bill out of his wallet, doing it slow so they could see him, like he was giving them a thousand dollars instead of one, and shoved it down the slit.

"Dry the wheels too," said the car's owner.

"My man gonna get it," said Momo, meaning King.

King looked at Momo out the corner of his eye and crouched down to dry off the first of the wheels.

"So?" said Momo, standing over him as he did the task.

"What?" said King without looking up.

"You ain't finish the story. Did you do the freak or not?"

"What you think?"

"*How*'d you do her?"

"Woman that size, you got to ride her."

"Did you?"

"Like Seabiscuit."

"Bet she looked like that motherfucker too."

Lee finished wiping the black buckets and pulled himself out of the car. "You two can finish up. I'm gonna grab a cigarette."

"You ain't been on shift all that long," said Momo.

"Fuck y'all," said Lee. "I'm gonna have one anyway."

He dropped his rag and went into the pay area, which was separated from the wash bay by a long glass wall. Customers stood there and watched their cars roll down the line like there was something interesting about it, or like they were trying to catch a mistake. In the pay area a Korean woman, the wife of the owner, stood behind the register. In front of the counter was a display rack of little tree deodorizers, crown deodorizers for the African customers, maps, fluorescent key rings, El Salvador and Guatemala decal flags for the Spanish, and sunglasses that had been in style in 1985.

Wasn't no surprise that Koreans owned this joint. You threw a rock at any small business in the city, thought Lee, good chance you'd hit a slope's head. This woman here smiled and said the same thing, "Thank you so much," to all the customers as she took their money, and scowled at the employees when she saw them without a rag in their hands and said, "Where you go now?"

Melvin Lee passed her on the way to the bathroom.

"Where you go now?" she said.

"To pull on my rod," said Lee with a friendly smile. She understood the smile but not the words.

"Hurry up," she said.

Lee went into the bathroom, took a pee, then went out the back door and bummed a menthol from the old man who worked the pressurized hose. He lit the smoke and went around the side of the business, where a few cars were idling in line, and he dragged on the cigarette and let the cool of a Salem hit his lungs.

I get off paper, thought Lee, and I won't have to put up with none of this bullshit anymore.

Rico's silver BMW pulled into the driveway entrance.

Miller stopped alongside the brick wall of the building, where he could not be seen by the drying crew, and landed on his horn.

"Stupid-ass kid," said Lee, crushing the cigarette under his boot.

Lee walked to the BMW and stood by its driver's-side window. Miller's white T-shirt was streaked and splattered with blood. His eyes were electric and alive.

"What happened?" said Lee, a sense of dread hitting him like a slap in the face. "Thought I told you to stay put."

"Law came for you, Melvin," said Miller. "I took care of it, man. For *you*."

"Aw, *shit*, Rico."

"Melvin, you gotta get in the car. They gonna be comin' for you now, for real."

"Rico . . ."

"Get in."

Lee walked slowly around the car. He dropped into the shotgun bucket and looked over at Miller.

"Where we goin'?"

"My place," said Miller. "You gonna see where I stay at now."

• • •

DEACON TAYLOR LIVED IN one of the new condos around U Street, within walking distance of the Lincoln Theater, Ben's, and many nightclubs and bars. His place was nicely furnished, with a granite-counter kitchen and a bathroom with limestone walls and a huge jetted tub built to hold three. He was only blocks from where he did his dirt, but in terms of the lifestyle, he was far away.

Deacon was listening to some Ronald Isley when the

buzzer sounded at the front door. He checked his security camera and saw that it was police, the same Homicide team he'd spoke to earlier, come to see him for the second time that day. Deacon kept nothing in the apartment, no excessive amounts of cash and no guns or drugs, not even weed, so he was not worried. But he was curious to know why the MPD was back so soon. The men on the other side of the door identified themselves, and Deacon worked several locks to let them in.

"Yeah," said Deacon.

"It's us again," said Detective Steve Bournias, a stocky white man with a thin mustache.

"I can see that."

"Sorry to bother you," said Detective Reginald Ballard.

"We've got a problem, though," said Bournias. "Wonder if we can't get a little bit more of your time."

"This about those murders over on Crittenden? I already told you, I don't know nothin' about it."

"This isn't about those murders."

"Well, what *is* it about? I'm busy —"

"Fellow by the name of Melvin Lee, used to work for you. Probably still does, but that's neither here nor there."

"Now wait a minute —"

"Melvin Lee," said Ballard. "Lives on Sherman Avenue?"

"What about him?"

"We're looking for him. Our people checked on his place of employment, a car wash up on Georgia. Seems he showed up for his shift and then just kinda disappeared."

"So?" said Deacon. "What'd he do wrong, light up in a no-smoking zone, sumshit like that?"

"A little bit more serious than that," said Bournias. "Mr. Lee's probation officer was stabbed in his apartment this afternoon. Stabbed repeatedly, Mr. Taylor."

"You don't look so good," said Ballard. "You wanna sit down?"

"I don't know nothin'," said Deacon, the words automatic.

"This isn't the usual cost-of-doing-business bullshit," said Ballard. "To use a knife is personal to begin with. To use it with that kind of anger is something else again. Makes us think that maybe your boy has issues with women."

"I don't know nothin'," said Deacon.

"Get your shit," said Bournias. "We're gonna do this in the box."

"Lawyer," said Deacon.

"Yeah," said Reggie Ballard tiredly. "Okay."

• • •

LORENZO BROWN WAS TURNING up Sherman, coming off his chaining call, when he saw the ambulance and police cars blocking the street. Neighborhood residents were out, looking at one row house in the middle of the block like they were waiting on something to happen there or someone to be brought out. And then he saw Miss Lopez's Honda parked along the curb. He had sat in it enough times to know it was hers. She had those green little tree deodorizers hanging from her rearview to take away the smell of her cigarettes.

Lorenzo found a place to park the truck. He went into the crowd. Kids rode their bikes around the residents and police like buzzards waiting on the kill. Lorenzo found two youngish women who looked like they belonged on the street.

"'Scuse me," said Lorenzo to one of the women. "You know what's going on?"

"Woman got herself shot or somethin'," said the woman.

"I heard she got stabbed," said her friend.

"In that house?" said Lorenzo.

"In that house right there," said the first woman.

"White woman, what I hear," said the friend. "She musta had business here or somethin'."

Lorenzo's blood jumped. He felt a little dizzy in the heat.

"Is she dead?" said Lorenzo, dreading the answer.

"I don't know," said the friend.

"She another statistic now," said the woman.

One of the kids riding bikes made a pistol out of his fingers and pointed it at the back of one of the police.

Lorenzo walked toward the house. He approached the police line where they had stationed uniformed officers and where the yellow tape hung. He went right to a white policeman and stood beside him.

"Excuse me, officer," said Lorenzo.

The police looked him over, studied his uniform, read the rectangular nameplate on his chest.

"Yeah?"

"Is the victim a white woman?"

"*What?*"

"I might know the victim. If her name is Rachel Lopez, I know her."

"Who are you?"

"I'm one of her offenders."

"Hold up a second," said the police, grabbing hold of Lorenzo's biceps. Lorenzo did not try to pull his arm free. The police shouted into a crowd of police knotted by the row house door. "Hey, Sarge, come here!"

A black policeman with stripes on his sleeves came to the white police who was holding Lorenzo. The black policeman was well built and had grief and fire in his eyes.

"What?" said the Sergeant. "Donald Peterson" was etched on his nameplate.

"This gentleman says he knows the victim. Says he's one of her offenders."

"Is she alive?" said Lorenzo.

Sergeant Peterson took Lorenzo by the same arm and led him back toward the street. He held him tightly. There was anger in the way his fingers dug into Lorenzo's skin.

"Tell me she's alive," said Lorenzo.

"Shut your mouth," said Peterson. "'Less I tell you to talk, you keep your mouth shut."

Peterson roughed him putting him into the car.

•   •   •

THE HARDEST PART was seeing her under that sheet, the blood staining it in big sloppy circles that seemed to grow as they carried the stretcher down the steps. Her colorless face was nearly covered with a breathing mask. The rescue squad men and women worked on her as they made their way to the ambulance, but they might as well have been working on one of those dummies you'd see in a store window, way she looked.

The other hard part was trying to keep the recognition and surprise off his face when the sergeant asked him if he knew of a guy named Melvin Lee. Rachel Lopez, Peterson said, had been stabbed in Lee's apartment. A neighbor on the third floor had heard her screams.

"But the neighbor didn't call the police," said Peterson. "Rachel did. She had a cell on her. I guess she regained consciousness, at some point, long enough to do that." Peterson stared through the glass like he was watching her struggling to hold the cell in her trembling hand, struggling to make the call. "I saw her arrive here myself nearly two hours ago. She lost a lot of blood."

Lorenzo had already told Sergeant Peterson, in thumbnail, about his past and his relationship to Rachel Lopez. Peterson had asked him if he was aware that Lee worked for Deacon Taylor, the counterpart to Nigel Johnson in the Park View game. Lorenzo explained that he had been in prison for a while and no longer kept track of the local players or cared to know their names.

The interview questions softened, as did the eyes of Sergeant Peterson, as it became clear that Lorenzo had nothing to do with the attack and, in fact, considered Rachel Lopez to be a friend. Lorenzo had the feeling that Sergeant Peterson was a friend to her too.

Peterson said that Rachel's file, found in the apartment, contained Lee's employment information. An MPD unit had already gone to the car wash where Lee worked, but Lee had disappeared. His car, an old Camry, was still on the premises.

He wouldn't be in that car, thought Lorenzo.

"What you need to tell me now," said Peterson, "is that you don't know anything about this."

"Nothing," said Lorenzo.

"And you've had no dealings with Melvin Lee. You don't know where we could find him."

"I don't know anything," said Lorenzo, telling the lie as naturally as he took breath. "I don't know Lee and I don't know where to find him."

And if I knew, I wouldn't tell you.

Through the windshield of the patrol car, they both watched the ambulance pull away.

"You can go," said Peterson.

"Is she gonna make it?"

"I don't know," said Peterson. "You want to help her, say a prayer."

"I will," said Lorenzo.

And someone, thought Lorenzo, needs to pray for me too. While they're at it, pray for the motherfucker who did this to my friend.

TWENTY-TWO

LORENZO BROWN DROVE NORTH. He parked the Tahoe
in the court behind the Humane Society alley and
went through the screened back door, past the cat kennel,
and through the lobby without speaking to Cindy or anyone else. He took the stairs up to the second floor, keeping his footsteps as quiet as possible so as not to alert Irena
Tovar to his presence. Her door, as always, was open. He
did not look in that direction and went directly to his own
office at the opposite end of the hall. Jerry, out on calls
most likely, was not at his desk. Neither was Mark Christianson.

Lorenzo phoned Nigel Johnson, got his message box,
and left his direct number at the office. He then found his
report file from the previous day and the notepad on which
he had written down the license plate numbers of the cars

parked on the edge of Fort Dupont. The phone on Lorenzo's desk rang, and he lifted the receiver.

"Officer Brown."

"Officer Brown. I like that."

"Nigel. Need your help on something."

"Go ahead, boy."

"Black Holmes still in the cut, right?"

"Long as he breathin'."

"And his mother works for Motor Vehicles, doesn't she?"

"Uh-huh."

"You been good to Black?"

"You *know* I have. His mother gets an envelope every month."

"I need her to run a plate for me."

"Look, you're damn near police yourself. Don't you have a way you can get that done?"

"Not this time."

"Okay. What do you need?"

"I got the car and the license plate. I need the address of the owner."

"What car?" said Nigel, as if he already knew the answer and did not like it.

Lorenzo gave Nigel the plate number of the silver BMW and listened to silence on the other end of the line.

"You there?"

"Why?" said Nigel.

"I'm lookin' to find Lee and Miller."

"So am I. Matter of fact, Deacon and me gonna meet at dark, and we gonna discuss it. But I told you to stay out of this. I'm gonna handle it my own self."

"That ain't gonna work for me, Nigel."

Lorenzo told Nigel of the assault on Rachel Lopez. He

told him about Lee's Camry being left at the car wash, and how he felt certain that Rico Miller had done the crime.

"Last thing Melvin lookin' to do is go back to prison," said Lorenzo. "He had no reason to go at Miss Lopez like that."

"And you think Miller had a reason."

"That boy don't need a reason. In his fucked-up mind, maybe he thought he was helping Melvin. I had money to bet, I'd say Miller did Green and Butler too."

"That woman gonna make it?"

"I don't know. She got cut up bad. She's over at Washington Hospital Center now."

"You gonna be there at the office?"

"Yeah."

"I better call Black's mother before she leaves out the building. It's near quitting time for her."

"I'll wait to hear from you."

Lorenzo went down to the basement to check on the dog he'd brought in from Congress Heights. Mark Christianson was in the kennel, staring down into the open cage where Lincoln, the aggressive pit, had been. Some of the other dogs were making noise, looking for attention. Their barks and yelps echoed in the cool cinder-blocked room.

"Irena put Lincoln down?" said Lorenzo.

"She had it done while I was out on calls." Mark looked at his bandaged hand, as if the bite was the reason the dog had been destroyed.

"It ain't on you," said Lorenzo.

"I know it."

"You believe in God, right?"

"I believe there's someone higher than us."

"But do you believe that he's up there moving us around like chess pieces or somethin'?"

"Of course not."

"Neither do I. Things happened to that dog on this cruel earth to make it the way it was. Wasn't its fault, but still. It's not like God is gonna step in now, point his finger down from heaven, and touch that animal, make it so it can live around people and other animals the right way."

"What's your point?"

"Irena did her job. 'Cause that dog was too far gone to change its ways. He had to be put down. You see that, don't you?"

"Yes."

Lorenzo went to the cage where the cream pit bull lay. She had been treated by a vet with dressings and bandages, and was awake on her belly, her snout resting between her paws.

Lorenzo crouched down, whistled softly, and put his knuckles up against the cage. "How you doin', girl?"

The dog whined happily and tried to crawl forward, but thought better of it and stayed put.

"That your hold?" said Mark.

"I got her earlier today. Impounded her from an apartment down in Southeast."

"Have any trouble getting her out?"

"No," said Lorenzo.

Cindy called out to Lorenzo from the top of the stairs. Someone was on the line for him and did not want to leave a message.

Lorenzo stood and tried to walk past Mark. Mark put his hand around Lorenzo's biceps.

"You all right?" said Mark.

"Why?"

"You look different."

I look the way I used to, thought Lorenzo. You never knew me when I had this kind of hard on my face.

"I'm fine."

"You feel like having a beer tonight or something?"

"I got plans tonight," said Lorenzo.

"I know what happened down there in Congress Heights. I came down to back you up after Cindy radioed in the call, but you had already left. Someone on the scene told me what went down."

"Uh-huh."

"I thought you said there wasn't any trouble."

"There wasn't."

"You're good at this," said Mark. "I don't want to see you blow it."

"Thanks for gettin' my back," said Lorenzo, gently pulling his arm free.

"You need to talk or somethin', you phone me. Anytime."

"I got to get this call."

Lorenzo went up the stairs. Cindy told him that she was not his personal secretary, and he passed her without comment or breaking stride. Up in his office, he picked up the phone and took it off hold.

"Nigel?"

"I got it."

"A home address?"

"Car's not registered to Lee or Miller. Man by the name of Calvin Duke owns it. He stays down around Thirty-fifth, in Northeast. Black's mother say he owns a whole rack of vehicles, according to the computer."

"What, he got a used-car lot, somethin' like that?"

"Or he rentin' cars out," said Nigel.

"How you know that?"

"Lawrence Graham keeps his ear to the street on that kind of thing. Says Duke's got a rcp in Northeast. Maybe we ought to talk to him. If that BMW is a hack, Duke's got to know the place where he can collect the rent."

"Right."

"I'd like to find out where those two are at before I parley with Deacon."

"Pick me up at my place," said Lorenzo.

"Now?"

"I need time to change into some street clothes."

"I'll see you in fifteen minutes."

"Gimme an hour," said Lorenzo. "I gotta walk my dog."

Lorenzo left without speaking to Irena Tovar. Typically, at the end of his shift, he'd go to her office, sit before her desk, and discuss his cases and how he was coming along on the job. He knew he would not be able to look her in the eye today.

Lorenzo went to his Ventura, parked on Floral Place. He cooked the ignition and headed for Park View.

* * *

NIGEL JOHNSON PICKED UP the count from Ricky Young on Morton Street. This was normally DeEric Green's duty, and Nigel had not done it himself for some time. He was mindful of any 4D cruisers or unmarkeds as he drove down the street, past his people and Deacon's, who were standing on hot corners, dealing with the drive-through customers and the walk-up fiends trying to buy on the short. He received the cash from Young in a shoe box through the window of his Lexus. Then he navigated the circle back by the apartments, returned to Georgia, hung a right and another right on Newton, and took it to 6th, where his mother stayed. He was certain he had not been followed.

He took the shoe box, and some Breyers mint chocolate chip he had picked up on his way downtown, and went inside the house.

It smelled like her cooking. This was what he waited for, something he could never get from the phone calls he made to her three, four times a day. That smell. That and her music, which was playing now on the stereo he'd bought for her. It was the *Claudine* sound track, Gladys interpreting Curtis, singing about "the makings of you." The stereo was part of the elaborate entertainment center in the living room, which also included a plasma television set and a DVD player she could never seem to operate, also high-end.

Deborah Johnson came from the kitchen, walking down the high-shag carpet to take him in her arms. She smelled like perfume, the sweet kind she favored.

"Hello, son."

"Mama."

Deborah was a big woman, five-foot-ten and up around 260 pounds. She was pretty, with nice skin, looked like deeply burnished wood, and neatly styled hair. She always wore makeup, red lipstick and blue eye shadow, despite the fact that, except for Sundays when she went to church, she rarely left the house. She was fifty-four years old.

"Here you go," said Nigel. He handed her the shoe box first, then the ice cream.

"Thank you, baby. You got my flavor."

Nigel nodded. He worried about her heart, but he wasn't going to deny her the treats she loved.

"Let me put this stuff away," said Deborah.

"All right."

"You gonna have a plate of somethin'? I've got a nice ham and sweet potatoes to go with it."

"Little bit, Mama."

"Ham's cold."

"How it should be in the summertime."

"I'll be right back."

Nigel watched her go, pushing her weight forward, using the side-to-side movement of the heavy. While she was preparing his food in the kitchen, she'd run the cash through the electronic counting machine she kept back there in one of the cabinets. She liked to do that soon as he made the delivery.

"Sit yourself down," she said over her shoulder.

He had a seat in the living room. The couch and chairs had plastic slipcovers on them even though Deborah could afford to let the furniture wear down natural and change it out any time she wanted to. He couldn't convince her, entirely, that she didn't have to worry about pennies anymore. Once poor, always poor, that's what folks said.

He bought her jewelry and picked out her dresses from the oversize department at places like Nordstrom and Lord and Taylor. She never asked for these things but was thankful for them and wore them proudly. She bragged to her friends at church about her son the businessman, "my entrepreneur," who had the NJ Enterprises shop up on Georgia, and they went along with the charade, which she knew to be a ruse herself. She rarely spoke of it with Nigel and never with anyone else.

He had set up several accounts at different banks around town, the deposits never exceeding ten thousand dollars. The bulk of the remaining cash was kept here in her house. He wanted to make sure that she was taken care of in the event of his death or incarceration.

There was no one else in his life. He had fathered a couple of children when he was young but had paid the mothers off in lump sums and did not have much contact with them. He had one older brother, a successful Realtor in Raleigh, North Carolina, who had clean-breaked from the family long ago and had not seen D.C. since he'd left town. Nigel had never known his father. He'd gone looking for him, based on some cryptic information his mother had given him on a rare night when she'd had a second glass of wine, and discovered that the man had been dead for twenty years. It was said by the man's son, a crackhead who technically was Nigel's half brother, that the father was buried in a pauper's grave. Nigel had felt nothing upon hearing the news.

Nigel lived in a modest apartment near his storefront, up in Manor Park. After the expense of his rent, his mother's mortgage, her clothing and jewelry, his clothing and jewelry, his vehicles, the vehicles he bought for his men, his payroll, the rent on his storefront, and all the extras a man in his position had to have, there was little cash left. This was the secret that many drug dealers on Nigel's level kept. They could not save and were not rich.

It wasn't money that kept Nigel in the game. It was the power, of course, and the fear that he would lose what he had and, once out, be qualified to do nothing else. But it was also the responsibility he felt he had for those under him. From the beginning, he had told himself that he was providing opportunity and a sense of family for those who otherwise had no chance of attaining either. He knew now, and had known for some time, that this was bullshit drug

dealers repeated to themselves and one another to ratio-
nalize their lifestyles. More than just bullshit — it was a
dirty lie.

He had told this lie to his best friend. He had told it
to many other young men. The last young man he'd told it
to had been Michael Butler. Michael Butler, who at seventeen years of age would soon be in the ground, covered in
maggots. Nigel had spoken to him early on about the
opportunity that was waiting for him up the road. Instead, Nigel had shown him a horrifying death and an early
grave.

"You wrong," said Nigel under his breath.

His mother touched his shoulder. He had not heard
her reenter the room.

"What's that, baby?"

"Talkin' to myself, is all. Must be getting old."

"I'm heating the potatoes up. Won't be but another
minute."

"Okay."

Deborah Johnson came around the sofa and had a seat
beside her son. The Gladys Knight CD played beautifully
in the room. Gladys singing joyously about "a happy
home." Nigel remembered his mother wearing the grooves
out on her vinyl copy, back in time.

"Lorenzo called me today," said Deborah.

"He told me he spoke to you."

"You two gonna hook up?"

"Yes."

"Lorenzo's good," said Deborah, touching her son's
hand. "You watch out for him, hear?"

"I will," said Nigel.

"You ought to call him, tell him to come over, have
some of this ham."

"He busy right now."

"What's he doing?"

"He's out there on Otis, I expect." Nigel smiled a little, looking toward the living-room window that fronted the street. "Walkin' his dog."

· · ·

SHADOWS HAD LENGTHENED on the playground. Lorenzo watched the children doing what children did on summer evenings, getting in the last of their games before supper got called or darkness fell. He remembered being out here with Nigel when he'd first moved over from Congress Heights to stay with his grandmother, Nigel his first Park View friend. Nigel dreaming on a pair of Superstar three-stripes he'd seen in a store window, focusing on what he wanted, what he was gonna get, even then. Asking Lorenzo if there was anything he wanted, 'cause when he, Nigel, got his hands on some money, he was gonna buy his boy something too.

Lorenzo stood in the tall grass by the dusty baseball diamond, holding his dog by the leash, his other hand holding a plastic bag fashioned as a glove. I have come a long way, he thought, with a shit bag in my hand.

Jasmine did her business, and Lorenzo cleaned it from the grass. He tied off one end of the bag, walked through the alley that ran behind Otis and Princeton, and put it in someone's trash can back there. He cut out of the alley's T, went along Georgia, and turned the corner where the old neighborhood market, owned and operated by a Jew named Meyer, had been. Meyer, it was said, used to extend credit to the neighborhood's residents, but his business was gone, and he was long dead. Lorenzo headed up Princeton Place.

He had taken this route out of habit and now, nearing Rayne's house and his grandmother's house beside it, he was sorry that he did. Rayne was out on her porch, and little Lakeisha was up there too. At least Lorenzo was on the other side of the street.

"That Jazz Man, Mama?" he heard Lakeisha say.

Lorenzo tugged on the leash as Jasmine's head turned toward the little girl. He glanced at the house and saw Rayne standing by the railing, looking at him with bewilderment as he kept going without a word. He waved weakly but did not make eye contact with Rayne. Lakeisha called out to him and his dog, and he walked on, wincing at the sound of disappointment in her innocent voice.

Don't do that, little princess. Don't call me over. You and your mother don't need me in your life.

He didn't look at his grandmother's house at all. He just went on his way.

Back in his apartment, Lorenzo changed into loose-fitting jeans, a sleeveless T, and a short-sleeved button-down shirt. He tied a pair of Nike 20s tight on his feet. In the living room, he moved the hope chest and inspected the contents of the area beneath the cutout he had made in the floor.

Nigel called from one of his cells. He was out in the car, on Otis, waiting. Jasmine whimpered and came to Lorenzo as he hung up the phone.

"I'm comin' back," said Lorenzo. "You just go and lie down in your bed."

The dog walked into the bedroom. Lorenzo went to meet Nigel.

TWENTY-THREE

CALVIN DUKE LIVED ON 35th Street, off Ames, between
Minnesota Avenue and the Anacostia Freeway, in
his grandmother's house in Northeast. His backyard, like
most of the yards on the one hundred block of 35th Street,
was deep and wide, and ended at an alley. Past the alley
were the railroad tracks, and past the railroad tracks were
the Anacostia Freeway, the green of Anacostia Park, and
the brackish water of the Anacostia River. It felt like country here. Many of the residents on 35th maintained boun-
tiful gardens of vegetables and flowers in their backyards.
In Calvin Duke's were several cars.

Nigel Johnson and Lorenzo Brown cruised down 35th
in Nigel's Lexus, going along slowly so as not to miss
Duke's residence. Lorenzo spotted the house, and Nigel

swung his sedan into a space along the curb. They walked together to the front door.

An old woman answered their knock. Her skeletal frame was no more than a hanger for her housedress. Sparse white hair topped a scalp dotted with raised moles. Her eyes were sunken in their sockets. She had removed her teeth. To Lorenzo, she had the look of one of those shrunken heads he'd hung on his doorknob when he was a kid.

"Yes?" she said.

"Is Calvin in?" said Nigel.

"You some kind of police?"

"No, ma'am. We're lookin' to talk to him about a car."

"My grandson's out back, burnin' a steak."

"We'll just go around there, then, that's okay with you."

The old woman shrugged. "Mind that dog."

They walked down to Ames and then cut into the alley. Crepe myrtle and hibiscus were in bloom and plentiful among the vegetable gardens in the backyards. The smell of their blossoms hung sweet and heavy in the humid early-evening air.

Approaching the back of the old woman's residence, they saw the large figure of a man standing over a brick-walled barbecue pit built up on a concrete slab. He held a green bottle in one meaty hand and a grilling fork in the other. Smoke came up off the grill. A black rottweiler stood by the man's side, looking up at its master, then at the grill, and again at its master.

A large portion of the fenced yard was paved, and on the pavement sat three cars: a late-model Mercedes coupe, a new Cadillac XLR convertible, and a two-tone '63 Impala tricked with mags, new pipes, and air shocks. What wasn't paved was untended and dotted with excrement.

Nigel and Lorenzo stood at the fence. The rot barked lazily but did not leave its master's side.

"I help you two with somethin'?" said the man, raising his deep voice.

"You can if you're Calvin Duke," said Nigel. "We wanna talk about a rental."

"Who sent y'all?"

"Fella I spoke to down at the supper club," said Nigel. "Said you were the man."

"I guess you in the right place, then." Duke, around forty, big and round, light of skin, and moley like his grandmother, smiled. "You done found the Dukey Stick."

"Mind if we come in?"

"Come through the gate."

"What about that animal?" said Nigel to Lorenzo.

"That dog ain't gonna hurt no one."

They went through the gated portion of the fence, passing a freestanding garage that had been converted into some sort of office for the fat man. They walked by the cars, waxed and detailed, and stepped up onto the concrete slab. A T-bone steak sizzled on the grill over glowing coals. The bricks at the top of the pit were not mortared to those below them and sat crookedly. A couple of empty Heineken bottles were set atop the bricks.

Lorenzo whistled softly. The rot came to him at once, and Lorenzo rubbed its scalp. The dog's ears were scarred and carried open pink sores. Its eyelids curled inward.

"Champ supposed to be a watchdog," said Duke good-naturedly. "But he don't watch nothin' but what's on this grill."

"You got a fly problem with this dog's ears," said Lorenzo.

"That so."

"You clean up the feces in the yard, that'll discourage some of it. But you got to treat this animal's ears now. It needs treatment for its eye condition too."

"Oh, so now I'm gonna clean up the *feces* in my own yard." Duke looked Lorenzo over with amusement. "You wanna clean shit, you clean the shit out your own yard, hoss. 'Stead of comin' into my yard and telling *me* to clean mines."

"Dog needs treatment," said Lorenzo.

"What're you, some kind of dog police, sumshit like that?" Duke laughed expansively to let them know they were all friends.

Lorenzo stared at Duke.

Duke looked away and drank off some of his Heineken. He put the fork down on the grill and patted his fat thigh. "C'mere, boy."

The rot moved back toward his master but did not get too close. Duke reached down to pet him, and the dog backed up a step, then bent his head down timidly and allowed Duke's touch.

"Anyway," said Duke. "What can I do for you boys?"

"We're interested in one of your cars," said Nigel. "Silver BMW, the Three-thirty model."

"It's out."

"I can see that."

"How about that pretty Impala over there? Imagine drivin' that pretty-ass motherfucker down the street. Females be gettin' wet behind it."

"We lookin' to talk to whoever rentin' the BMW."

"Why?"

"That ain't your concern."

"It is if it's about my car. And don't try to act like you police."

"Be better for you if we were," said Nigel.

"Now you gonna tweak on me, big man?"

"I haven't yet."

"Comin' in here, *on my property*, makin' demands."

"I'm gonna ask you nice, but only one more time. We gonna need the name and address of the man who's rentin' the Three-thirty. You give us that, we gonna be on our way."

"I can't help you," said Duke, the boldness withering in his voice.

"The BMW," said Nigel.

"Look, I got rules. I might be part of this underground economy out here, but still, I got the same rules any other business got. I can't be givin' up the confidentiality of my clients."

"Fuck all this," said Lorenzo. He reached over and picked the fork up off the grill by its wooden handle.

"Hey," said Duke.

Lorenzo walked around Duke and backed him up so that his wide bottom hit the barbecue pit. Some bricks came loose off the top. Both bottles fell to the concrete and one of them shattered. Lorenzo pushed the fork toward Duke's face, and Duke closed his eyes and turned his head. Lorenzo touched the tines of the fork to Duke's neck, denting it, and Duke screamed. His voice was no longer rich and deep. Lorenzo stepped back. Smoke came off Duke's neck.

"You burned me," said Duke, as if Lorenzo had only hurt his feelings. He rubbed at the marks, like those of a snakebite, that were already showing there. Champ stood where he was and watched.

"The name and address," said Nigel.

"I got to get it from out my office," said Duke, just above a mumble.

"Don't come out the office with nothin' but that information," said Nigel. "Hear?"

Duke nodded without looking at either of them. He walked to the garage, used a key to open it, and went inside.

Lorenzo stabbed the fork into the T-bone on the grill, lifted it, shook it loose, and let it fall to the ground in front of the rot. The dog's nub of tail wiggled furiously as he took the steak in his teeth and trotted off to a corner of the yard.

Nigel chuckled. "You ain't lost nothin'."

"Some shit just *stay* natural," said Lorenzo.

"Thought you was gonna break a beer bottle off. Or maybe take one of those loose bricks and throw it through the window of that Impala."

"I thought of that. Car that nice, I just couldn't fuck with it."

"You made do with that fork, though."

Duke came out of the garage and handed Nigel a piece of paper. Nigel looked at it, folded it, and put it in his pocket.

"Nah," said Duke. "Nah, uh-uh." He had noticed Champ getting down on the T-bone. "Why'd you have to go and do that to a man too?"

"He deserves a steak, way you mistreat him," said Lorenzo. "And don't even think of beating that animal, 'cause I can see by the way he cringes that you do."

"Who the fuck *are* y'all?" said Duke.

"We ain't nobody you ever seen or met," said Nigel. "You understand?"

"Yeah, I know."

Lorenzo pointed a finger at Duke. "I'm gonna be back to check on that dog."

Nigel and Lorenzo went down the alley as dusk settled on the streets. Lorenzo felt good and he felt strong.
He was energized by the violence and comfortable walking beside his friend.

"Rico Miller rented the car," said Nigel. "He stayin'
here in Northeast."

"Lee gonna be with him too."

"I gotta get up with Deacon before we do anything."

"You can drop me by the hospital, pick me up when
you're done."

"Right." Nigel side-glanced Lorenzo. "Givin' that
man's T-bone up to his own dog, that was a nice touch right
there."

"Man wants you to take him serious, you'd think he
might pick a better name than Dukey Stick."

"It's a George Duke song."

"Who?"

"My mother had the LP," said Nigel. "That's how I
know."

* * *

THE WASHINGTON HOSPITAL CENTER, on Irving Street, was
walking distance from where Lorenzo and Nigel had
grown up. In their youth, both of them ate in the canteen
when one or the other had extra coin, and both of them
stole candy bars from the gift shop because they could.
Lorenzo knew that the WHC specialized in heart bypass
surgery as well as the usual emergency treatments, including shock trauma cases and victims of violent crime, so it
wasn't a surprise to see people who came from money min-
gling with middle-class and poor in the ER waiting room.
For a little while, all were equal in here.

The hospital kept a separate space, away from the reception area and general waiting room, for those receiving counsel, those grievers who were temporarily unstable, those receiving bad news, and those under watch by police. Lorenzo sat in the general area and kept an eye on that room. He had seen a police officer enter and then Sergeant Peterson, the police who had roughed him earlier in the day, go in after him. Also, it looked like a reporter or something standing outside the door. Had to be, because the man had a notepad and pen in his hands. A couple of women carrying paper coffee cups went in behind them. One of them was big, wore a bright pantsuit and plenty of makeup, and had a revolver holstered on her hip. Plainclothes police, Lorenzo reckoned. The other was a young white girl, college age or a little beyond. Both women looked as if they had been crying.

Lorenzo sat there for an hour or so. He watched the doctors coming from surgery, entering quickly in their scrubs, talking to families in groups of twos and threes, and leaving just as quickly. He watched the sergeant come out of the special room, go to the water cooler for a drink, and recognize Lorenzo, sitting there in his street clothes, as he passed. The sergeant did not stop to speak to him and walked back into the room. Lorenzo thumbed through a car magazine without recalling a word he read. Then he saw a surgeon go into the room where all of Rachel's people were. And right after that, he heard a woman scream. He felt certain that it was a scream of grief. It was the same kind of emotional release he'd heard come from mothers and girlfriends at funeral homes and cemeteries when he'd been deep in the game. Hearing it, and the sobs that came after, he felt some life leave him.

Lorenzo got up out of his chair and walked to the

nearest restroom. He washed his face with cold water. Then he left the hospital and went to the drop-off spot by the front doors, where he had said he'd be, to wait for Nigel.

. . .

SERGEANT PETERSON, unable to be still, had left the room for just a moment to get a drink of water, when he saw Rachel's offender, the drug dealer turned dog catcher, sitting out there in the general lobby. He didn't stop to talk to him. He assumed the man was there to wait on news about Rachel. This man had seemed all right, given who he was, but Peterson had more important things to do than hold some con's hand.

Rachel's surgeon came into the room a short time later, over to where Peterson and two of Rachel's coworkers, a probation officer named Moniqua and a young assistant, sat. They all got up out of their chairs as the doctor entered.

The doctor explained the nature and location of the wounds, and the massive loss of blood. Rachel had been stabbed in the chest and through the hand, and sliced across the face. There was the possibility of neurological damage. She was "lucky," said the doctor, that the blade had not entered her heart or lungs.

"The next twenty-four hours are crucial."

"She gonna live?" said Donald Peterson.

"I'm optimistic," said the doctor. "Yes."

Moniqua let out a scream that sounded like death itself. It was her way of letting go of all the pressure she'd been feeling at her friend's ordeal. In Peterson's experience, people dealt with this kind of thing their own way.

Moniqua and the assistant hugged and cried. For his part, Peterson rapped his fist on the table and said a silent prayer of thanks.

Later, when he'd got himself together, he remembered the offender out in the main waiting area.

Peterson decided to go out there and tell the man that his probation officer was going to make it. But when he went to where the offender had been sitting, the dog catcher, or whatever he was, was gone.

TWENTY-FOUR

EACON TAYLOR SAT under the wheel of his E-Class, parked on Iowa Avenue, with Marcus Griffin beside him. Griff's midnight blue Infiniti was parked on the street as well. In view was Roosevelt High. Across from the school, a group of young men sat on the porch of a row house, smoking marijuana and drinking from bottles in paper bags.

"Here go his Lex," said Deacon, watching as Nigel Johnson's import rolled slowly down the street.

"Looks like he got Graham with him," said Griff.

"That ain't no surprise."

"What you want me to do?"

"Watch my car, is all. Me and Nigel gonna go down to the track, walk around it some."

"And do what?"

"I'm gonna listen, mostly," said Deacon. "When I come back, I'll tell you what I learned."

Nigel parked on Iowa. He got out of the Lexus with two cigars in hand and walked across the street. Deacon met him in the middle of the street, and the two of them shook hands. Nigel offered Deacon a cigar and Deacon accepted. Nigel lit Deacon's cigar, then put fire to his own. They agreed to go down to the sky blue running track that encircled the football field in Roosevelt's bowl.

Griff leaned his back against the Mercedes and folded his arms. Graham affected the same pose against the Lexus. They stood on opposite sides of the street and stared at each other without animosity. They were playing their roles. As they stared, their bosses went along a high fence, entered the school grounds through an open gate, and descended the stadium stairs.

Down in the bowl, on the lighted track, Deacon Taylor and Nigel Johnson walked side by side, occasionally dragging on their Cubans. Nigel wore pressed jeans and a short-sleeved silk designer shirt. Deacon was dressed in a similarly casual, expensive way.

"You look good, big man," said Deacon.

"You too," said Nigel. "Prosperous."

"I'm tryin'. Game ain't gettin' any easier."

"Tell it," said Nigel. "All this death too."

"My sympathy for your losses," said Deacon. "Want to put that out front straight away."

"I appreciate that," said Nigel. "Losin' DeEric was one thing. But to lose Michael Butler over something that foolish —"

"I know," said Deacon. "I know."

"That boy was good."

"What I heard."

" 'Course, this whole thing got to rollin' off a misunderstanding started by my own. I admit that. I wanted to get up with you and make it right, but this thing happened before I could."

"I told my people to talk to Green. Make it known, in no uncertain terms, that he made a serious mistake. But understand, I didn't order no hit."

"I never thought you did."

"Rico Miller took it upon his self."

"What I figured."

"Now I got this other thing to deal with, the thing with the probation officer."

"You know about that?"

"I didn't know shit about it till Homicide come knockin' on my door."

"Bad business for all of us, Deacon. We can't be havin' our people involved in this kinda dirt. You fuck with police, even probation police, whole force gonna come down on you hard. I know Miller's your boy, but . . . question is, how we gonna handle this?"

"I'm not gonna handle it," said Deacon. "You are."

"You givin' me permission to do what I need to?"

Deacon nodded.

"Why?"

"Straight business, like you say. I can't control Rico no more."

"What about Lee?" said Nigel.

"Melvin with Rico, far as I'm concerned."

"He been with you a while."

"Police put him in the box, he gonna flip. Melvin can't jail again. He knows this."

"And when this thing gets done, how you gonna play it?"

"Gonna have to make a show of it. Throw the funeral, buy the T-shirts, the flowers. Say the strong words that need to be said. But that's where it's gonna end."

"What about your people?"

"Long as it's you behind it, they gonna be straight. You send some underlings to do this thing, it might make mine feel like they got the right to be heroic and shit. But ain't nobody gonna come at Nigel Johnson." Deacon looked Nigel in the eye. "You got my word."

They rounded the curve of the track.

"Where the police at on this?" said Nigel.

"They workin' the murders from last night. They got nothin' so far. Far as the probation lady goes, I don't know. They got to be lookin' hard for Melvin. But Rico must have left his prints all over that apartment. They put those prints into the system, they gonna identify him through his priors. Won't be long before they after Rico too."

"Means I don't have much time."

"You know where Rico at, right?" said Deacon.

"Northeast," said Nigel.

Deacon's eyes moved to Nigel. "He at that same place . . ."

"Forty-sixth and Hayes," said Nigel.

"Right."

They walked farther. Nigel thought of Lorenzo, back in high school, running this track at night in his jeans and basketball sneaks. Nigel watching him, cutting on his technique. Lorenzo bragging about how he'd smoke anyone in the forty, they had the mind to try him. Talking about running for the school, wearing the colors of the

Rough Riders. Nigel telling him that he had no business in school, that school was for faggots and suckers. That if he stuck with Nigel, the two of them were going to have it all.

"Shit," said Nigel softly.

"What?" said Deacon.

"Nothin'. I'm tired, is all. You ever feel that way?"

"Yeah," said Deacon, narrowing his eyes. "Sometimes I do get tired. Just like you."

• • •

NIGEL GOT BEHIND the wheel of the Lexus. Lawrence Graham slipped into the bucket beside him.

"I'm on," said Nigel.

"What about me?" said Graham.

"I'm gonna need you for somethin' else."

Nigel turned the key and put the car in drive.

"Where we goin'?" said Graham.

"Pick up Lorenzo at the hospital. Listen to me careful, 'cause we ain't got all that far to go."

Nigel drove up Iowa, passing the Mercedes on the other side of the street.

Deacon Taylor and Marcus Griffin, sitting in Deacon's car, watched Nigel pass.

"You two square it up?"

"Yeah," said Deacon. "We good."

"What's the plan?"

"Told you, I don't plan," said Deacon. "I look for opportunities."

• • •

NIGEL PICKED UP Lorenzo outside the hospital, where they dropped off the people going in for surgery and picked up those who were recovering. Lorenzo, slump shouldered, standing by an old head smoking a cigarette, looked like he'd been under the knife himself.

Graham got out, allowing Lorenzo to take the passenger bucket, and slid into the backseat.

"How she doin'?" said Nigel.

"She's dead."

Nigel drove back into the old neighborhood. No one spoke or reached for the radio. Nigel pulled into a spot on Warder Street, by Park View Elementary, and cut the engine.

"Why we stoppin' here?" said Lorenzo.

"Thought we'd walk some," said Nigel. "Talk."

"I'm done talkin'. I'm ready to go. You said you were lookin' for some clean hardware. I got everything back at my apartment that we gonna need."

Nigel looked past the headrest to the backseat. He tossed his keys over his shoulder into Graham's cupped hands. "Stay here, Lawrence."

Nigel got out of the car. Lorenzo hesitated for a moment, then got out too.

They walked onto the elementary school grounds, lighted in some spots and in others under a blanket of full dark. The silhouetted figures of two boys, no older than eleven or twelve, moved through the night. Marijuana smoke roiled faintly in the air.

Nigel had a seat on a wooden bench by the swings. Lorenzo sat beside him.

"You see them kids?" said Nigel.

"Yeah."

"'Bout the same age we were when we started out."

"They look to be."

"Smells like they're sampling the product. The way you used to do."

"I did love it," said Lorenzo.

"And I was all about business. Even before I started grindin', when I had my paper route and I'd bring you out with me before sunup."

"You were focused on getting the newspaper on the doorstep just right. So you could get those Christmas tips."

"And all you wanted to do was bust out streetlights."

"I had the arm to do it too," said Lorenzo. "I could wing some rocks. Someone should have put me up on the mound."

"That's what you *should*'ve been doin' with your youth. Pitchin' for some baseball team. Running track like you wanted to. 'Stead of gettin' high and following me."

"Past is past," said Lorenzo, echoing what he'd heard so many times at the meetings.

"Look, Lorenzo —"

"Don't apologize, Nigel. I made my choices."

"Right. At least you doin' good now."

"I get headaches."

"Damn near everyone go to work each day gets headaches. I'm sayin', I see you in that uniform, doin' something good out here, it makes me feel proud of you, man. Makes me think maybe I *didn't* fuck you over all the way."

"That uniform don't change who I am."

"Who you are is who you are today. Not what you were before you did your bid."

"Bullshit. You come on back to my apartment, you gonna see how much I changed."

"One thing ain't changed," said Nigel with a sad chuckle. "You still thickheaded."

A young woman pushing a baby carriage turned the corner off Warder, walked down Otis, and passed under a street lamp. Lorenzo and Nigel studied her with interest.

"What you think her thing is?" said Lorenzo.

"I don't know. Fine at fifteen, a mother at sixteen. Fucked and forgotten by some boy she ain't never gonna hear from again. She done made her own mother a grandmother at thirty-two. Now she livin' at home, a high school dropout with no skills, wonderin' what she gonna do with her life. Sitting on the couch, watchin' Judge Brown and the soaps, eatin' sweets and smokin' cigarettes. Fifteen years from now? She gonna be a grandmother herself, and that fine young girl gonna look like every other dusty-ass woman you see on the bus."

"You ain't been on a Metrobus for twenty years."

"You know what I mean."

"How about this?" said Lorenzo. "She made a mistake and she knows it. The boy who got her that way is working hard to rent an apartment so they can live together as a family. Her mother watches the baby during the day so the girl can stay in school, get her degree. And maybe her mother will raise the baby for a few years while the girl goes on to college. And that kid gonna watch an educated mother and a hardworking father, and by example, all those good things gonna rub off."

"Another way of looking at it, I guess."

"You ought to *see* all the people I meet on my job every day, Nigel. All the stories I hear."

"I can imagine," said Nigel. "The game, it's just a tiny part of what's goin' on out here. Remember back when they was callin' this town Dodge City?"

"That was reporters and shit, made that name up. The ones who were too scared to come into the neighborhoods they were writin' about."

"The everyday people who lived in this city *hated* that name."

"As they should have," said Lorenzo. "Drama City be more like it."

"Like them two faces they got hangin' over the stage in those theaters. The smiling face and the sad."

"City got more than two sides."

"Whatever it got," said Nigel, "you on the right side now. The side where people get up and go to work. Wash their cars out in the street, tend to their gardens. Watch their kids grow."

"Maybe. But I'm still gonna avenge my friend. Rico Miller? Shit, motherfuckers like him, they're in their element behind those walls. I ain't gonna *let* him have that gift. Boy needs to be put down like an animal."

"I'm not sayin' he doesn't deserve to die. I'm telling you you can't be a part of it."

"You don't need to worry, Nigel. I'm not goin' back over to where I been. I'm gonna be at work tomorrow and the day after that. But I'm still gonna do this thing tonight."

"It don't work that way."

"We'll see."

"You been out of it so long, you forgot how it goes. You go in, you got to go in fierce. Forget they're human. Forget that you're human too."

"I know it. Remember, I've done this before."

"But you cleaned your slate. Now, what, you gonna go and throw away your soul again?"

"What about yours?"

"Mine's been lost forever." Nigel looked away. "I'm sayin', this ain't you anymore."

"I'm on this."

"I don't want you with me, Lorenzo."

"I don't give a fuck if you do or if you don't," said Lorenzo, turning to stare directly into his friend's eyes.

"You that set on it?"

"I am."

"Thickheaded," said Nigel.

"C'mon." Lorenzo stood. "Let's get on over to my crib. Wanna show you what I got."

They walked down Otis toward Lorenzo's apartment. Lawrence Graham followed in the Lex.

TWENTY-FIVE

LORENZO BROWN ENTERED his apartment. Nigel Johnson and Lawrence Graham followed. Jasmine, as always, was waiting just inside the door. She backed up and growled at the sight of Nigel.

Lorenzo crouched, patted her belly, and rubbed behind her ears. His touch calmed her down.

"Dogs don't like me," said Nigel, taking a seat on the hope chest behind the living-room sofa. Graham stood with his back against the wall.

"That's 'cause they know you're scared of 'em," said Lorenzo.

"I can't forget that shepherd in the alley behind Princeton, took a piece out my hand."

"That was twenty years ago."

"I just told you I can't forget it." Nigel pointed to the

hallway. "Do me a favor and put that animal back in your bedroom."

"Yeah, okay. C'mon, girl."

Lorenzo went down the hall, Jasmine behind him. Nigel and Graham exchanged a glance. They heard the sound of Lorenzo's bedroom door closing and the footsteps of Lorenzo coming back down the hall.

"Where your hardware at?" said Nigel.

"You're sittin' on it."

Nigel got off the hope chest. Lorenzo moved it aside and pulled up the throw rug that lay beneath it. Under the rug was a rectangular cutout that was fitted in the hardwood floor. Where two sides of the rectangle had been grooved out, Lorenzo grasped the cutout and lifted it from its place. He leaned it against the chest.

In the space beneath the floor were two large metal toolboxes. Lorenzo lifted them out one by one. The muscles of his forearms rippled against the weight.

Lorenzo opened one of the toolboxes. Its inner tray had been removed to accommodate three handguns wrapped in oiled shop rags. Lorenzo unwrapped one of the guns, a Glock 17, and showed it to Nigel.

"It's live," said Lorenzo.

"What about the others?"

"They're carrying full loads too."

"Where you get these?"

"Remember Hoppy, stayed over there on Lamont?"

"Thought he was out of it."

"He back in."

"They clean?"

"Straw buys out of Virginia. Never been fired. Serial numbers still on 'em."

"Why?"

"Why I have 'em?"

"Yeah."

"For the reason I been sleepin' on the same side of the bed my whole life. It feels right."

"What else you got?" said Nigel.

"Forty-five Colt and a thirty-eight Special."

"And in the other box?"

"Extra magazines and bricks. Couple clean rags. A box of latex gloves."

"Lemme see the thirty-eight."

Lorenzo replaced the Glock in the toolbox and withdrew another gun. He unwrapped a Taurus seven-shot revolver with rubber grips and handed it to Nigel.

Nigel hefted the Taurus and turned it in the light. He released the cylinder, spun it, checked the load, and snapped the cylinder shut. He holstered the Taurus in his waistband.

"This is me right here."

"Let's do it, then," said Lorenzo.

"I need some water before we go."

"What, you want me to serve it to you? Water in the kitchen, same place it is in every house you ever been in."

Nigel went back to the Pullman kitchen. They listened to him bang a glass against another and heard the faucet run and the cry of the old pipes as the water ran through. It seemed as if Nigel was running the water for a long time. Lorenzo looked at Graham, and Graham shrugged.

Nigel returned, gun in hand.

"Let's go," said Lorenzo.

Nigel pointed the gun at Lorenzo's chest. "You ain't goin' nowhere, son."

Lorenzo stood motionless. Back in the closed bedroom, Jasmine began to bark.

"Dog knows," said Graham. "Funny how that is."

"Dogs don't like me nohow," said Nigel.

"Don't play," said Lorenzo.

"I'm not," said Nigel. "I'd rather see you dead than see you go back to where you were."

"That's a lie. You couldn't use that on me if you wanted to, Nigel."

"No," said Nigel, making a head motion to Lawrence Graham. "But he could."

Graham pushed away from the wall, stepped across the room, and took the gun from Nigel's hand.

"He tries to follow me," said Nigel to Graham, "you pull that trigger, hear?"

Graham nodded.

"Pull it seven times, you got to."

Graham nodded again. His eyes smiled.

Nigel closed both toolboxes and made certain they were secure. He picked them up and headed for the door. Graham, holding the gun on Lorenzo and not taking his eyes from him, backed up and opened the door for Nigel.

"Ni*gel*," said Lorenzo.

Nigel stopped walking but did not turn his head. "What?"

"You can't, not without me. You my boy."

"I never was," said Nigel. "But I'm gonna do you right this one time."

He walked out of the apartment. Graham closed the door with his foot and pointed his chin at the sofa.

"Have a seat," said Graham.

Lorenzo sat down on the sofa as Graham settled into the worn armchair beside it. He held the gun loosely, its barrel pointed at the hardwood floor.

"And don't try and act like you gonna rush me, either," said Graham.

They stared at each other and spoke no further. They listened to Jasmine barking in the other room.

• • •

RICO MILLER HAD downloaded an electronic version of "In da Club" to his cell phone, so that the song played when someone called. Someone was calling him now. He picked the phone up off the folding table in the living-room area of his bungalow and answered. It was Deacon Taylor.

Miller listened to Deacon as he watched Melvin Lee. Lee, slouched on a sofa Miller had spotted by a Dumpster one day, held a live cigarette between his fingers. The ash was long and about to drop. Smoke hung heavy in the air, turning slowly under the light of a naked bulb.

Lee's eyes, bugged in their sockets, had no life. His arms were thin and knotty, coming out of his shirt like twigs. Miller did not remember Melvin being so small.

Deacon talked on, smooth and precise. Miller's eyes narrowed as he listened to his voice. When Deacon was done, Miller said, "Yeah, all right," and hit "End" on his phone. He closed the phone's lid and placed it back on the table.

"Deacon," said Miller.

Lee stared straight ahead.

"He said he couldn't get you on your cell . . ."

"I been had it off."

". . . so he tried mines."

"He angry, right?"

"No. He's actin' real nice. Said he knew about the parole lady. I told him I had to, 'cause she was fixin' to violate you. He said that shit was unfortunate, but it had to be done. Said he understood."

"What else?"

"Told us to stay right here till he figures out how to put us somewhere safe." Miller licked his lips. "'You sit tight right where you at,' he said, like he knew where we was."

"What're you sayin', Rico?"

"Deacon be talkin' out the side of his mouth, Melvin. He done with us. Maybe he know where we at or maybe he tryin' to find out. Either way, he gonna send someone over here eventually. And when that someone come, he ain't comin' as a friend."

Lee put his cigarette to his lips and dragged on it hard. A rope of ash dropped to his lap. He made no move to brush it away.

"We need to move," said Miller. "Gotta lay up somewhere else."

Lee exhaled smoke. His cigarette hand shook as he moved it down to rest on his thigh.

"You stay here and keep an eye on the front," said Miller.

Miller walked back into the bedroom. Lee stared at the plaster wall before him, chipped and water stained, and the bedsheets covering the windows.

There ain't no place to run to, thought Melvin Lee. Lee felt the heat of his cigarette as it burned down toward his fingers, but he made no move to put it out.

Entering his bedroom, Miller kicked aside a PS2 controller and some magazines. He stepped on a game case and crushed it, not caring, has he crossed the room. None of his possessions had ever made him happy. They had no value now.

Miller went to the closet and parted the shirts and

jackets that hung on its rod. He freed the false wall, a sheet of particleboard fitted behind the clothing, and dropped it behind him. He removed his cut-down Winchester pump-action shotgun from the rack. He retrieved his Glock, his S&W .38, several bricks of bullets, a box of low-recoil shotgun load, and his harness and holsters. He placed everything on his bed.

Miller went to a dresser he'd bought for twenty dollars at the Salvation Army store. On top of the dresser sat the shoe box containing the count taken from DeEric Green's Escalade. Beside the shoe box was Miller's knife. He'd cleaned it and secured it in its sheath. He looked at his nickname, burned from top to bottom into the leather.

Creep.

His mother was the first one to call him that. That was, when she wasn't calling him a punk or worse. Berating him, slapping him in public at every drugstore or grocery they went to when he'd ask for an action figure or just a pack of gum. When he cried, she only slapped him harder.

"Gonna teach you not to cry," she said. "I ain't raisin' no sissies."

There was one time at this department store, around Christmas, when Rico was six or seven. He saw these ornaments, silver balls with people's names painted on them, hung on this big old tree they had set up in the middle of the store. He was standing beside the tree, trying to find his name on one of the balls, when he saw one had Ricky on it, right in front of him. He knew it wasn't his name exactly, but if he could take the ball with him, he believed his mother could paint over the *k* and the *y*, make them into an *o* somehow. Make it so it said Rico.

"There go my name, Mama," he said, pointing happily at the tree.

"That ain't your name."

"Can I have it? We can make it my name when we get home."

"Your name Creep," she said, yanking on his hand. "And I ain't got the time to be paintin' over shit. You don't need that thing no way."

He reached for it and pulled it from the tree. The ball fell and shattered on the floor.

"Now you gonna get somethin'," she said, slapping him so hard the store and all the Christmas lights in it began to spin. "You fuck up every goddamn thing you touch."

He cried, and hated himself for crying, as she dragged him through the store. He couldn't even look at his weak self in the mirror for the next few days.

That was out in public. In private, in their apartment in a rodent-infested, drug-plagued government housing project that someone had the nerve to call the Gardens, down near the Navy Yard in Southeast, his mother was worse. When she was drinking or sucking on that glass pipe, she beat him with her fists. Sometimes she whipped him with a belt. She never did beat on his little sister. Miller couldn't step to his mother, but he found a way to wipe that grin off his sister's face.

"My sister don't scream when you fuck her," he'd said to Melvin the day before this one, and Melvin had laughed.

Yes she do, thought Miller. She scream and sob, both at the same time.

He was on the street by the time he was twelve. Staying with a bunch of older boys in Southeast, working the corners, learning the game. In and out of schools, courtrooms, and juvenile facilities. The last was Oak Hill, out there in Laurel. Couple of tough ones had tried to step to him there, and he showed them who he was. He walked out of that motherfucker one day, just climbed the fence and went over it where some other kids had cut the razor wire down. Far as he knew, no one was looking for him. Since he'd left the Hill, he'd been in the wind.

Staring at his name burned into the sheath, he thought of his mother, and then that parole woman. How good it felt when he'd cut her across the face, plunged the blade into her chest, and stuck it through her hand when she'd raised it to protect herself. Thinking on it, his dick grew hard.

Miller slipped the knife into the shoe box alongside the money. He went to the bed and loaded the guns. As he worked, he ground his teeth. The sound was like a whisper in the room.

TWENTY-SIX

NIGEL JOHNSON LIFTED the trunk of his Lexus. A light inside the lid illuminated the two toolboxes he had placed there. He looked around the street, as he had done when he parked his car on Hunt Place, just off 46th, a short walk down to Hayes. He seemed to be alone.

Nigel opened both toolboxes. From one he extracted a pair of latex gloves and fitted them on his hands. From the other he removed the two automatics and peeled away the oiled rags that protected them. He wiped down the guns with one of the rags. He checked the Glock's load and holstered the .9 under his shirt, behind the waistband of his jeans, at the small of his back. He then inspected the Colt. It was a Commander, the government model .45 with checkered grips. He was more familiar with this gun than he was with the Glock; he would lead with the Colt. He did not take the extra magazines. There were eight rounds in the Colt and ten in the Glock. Eighteen rounds to kill two men. It had to be enough.

He holstered the Colt under his shirt, barrel down, the grip resting against his hard belly. He wiped the toolboxes with a clean rag and closed the lid of the trunk.

Nigel went along Hunt and turned right on Hayes, studying the alley layout behind them. He headed toward the corner at 46th. Many of the street lamps were in disrepair. The neighborhood was quiet and very dark. He neared Miller's house, dimly lit behind bedsheets that hung in every window.

Nigel walked quietly, moving around the side of the house. The backyard was mostly dirt and weeds. A rotted wooden porch with ripped screens was situated at the rear of the house. Beside the porch sat a small set of steps leading to a landing and a back door. A sheet hung in the door's glass. Near the door was a small window, the size situated above a kitchen sink. It was covered by a sheet as well.

Nigel looked at the door. He could kick it in and go in hard or stand out here in the yard and wait. His palms were damp, and he wiped them dry on his jeans.

Some light bled out to the yard from behind the sheets. Nigel stepped back into the shadows, drew the Colt from his belt line, and held it by his side.

. . .

"IT'S HOT," said Melvin Lee.

"Ain't hot to me," said Rico Miller.

"Hotter than a motherfucker in this piece," said Lee. "Don't you ever open no windows?"

"No. And we ain't gonna start now."

"Thought we was leavin'."

271

"Gonna wait till after midnight. Ain't no one on the road then. We can drive all night."

"Where?"

"Don't worry about where. Just sit there and hold that gun. Anyone comes callin', we gonna be ready."

The room stank of weed, perspiration, and cigarettes. A naked 150-watt bulb blew white light down into the space. Lee sat on the old couch near the folding table and chairs. He held Miller's .38 loosely between his legs. Lee didn't want the gun, but Miller had put it directly in his hand. Lee looked like a bug against the cream-colored couch. Sweat beaded on his forehead.

Beyond the folding table stood Rico Miller, his back against the wall. Miller held the cut-down shotgun barrel up, his fingers fitted in the pistol grip, the stock resting on his thigh. His eyes were pink from the hydro he'd smoked. His face held no emotion.

"I'm goin' out to have a smoke," said Lee.

"Have it here."

"Can't breathe in here. I'm going out."

"Go out the back, then, you have to," said Miller. "Don't be long."

Lee got up off the couch and stuck the revolver in his waistband. He did not look at Miller as he walked from the room.

Lee went down a hall and passed through the kitchen. At the rear of the kitchen he unchained the slide bolt from the door. He turned the dead bolt as well. He walked out onto the landing, pulling the door behind him but leaving it ajar. He went down the steps and stood in the residual light leaking from the kitchen. Listening to the crickets, looking out at the black of the yard, he reached into his back pocket for his cigarettes.

He shook a smoke out of the deck. He lit a match and bent his head down to touch tobacco to flame. Something leaped out of the darkness.

Nigel Johnson swung the Colt's barrel violently across Lee's face. Lee's nose shifted to one side; blood jumped up in the weak yellow light. He lost his legs and began to fall. Nigel clipped Lee's temple with the barrel as he went down. Lee fell to his back and lay still.

Nigel racked the Colt's slide and pulled back on its hammer. He stood over Lee, bent forward, and put the barrel of the gun to Lee's mouth. He raised his palm to shield the blowback. He thought better of it and stood straight.

Nigel walked up the steps to the back door of the house. He let his heart slow some, then pushed on the door and stepped inside.

· · ·

LORENZO BROWN STARED AT Lawrence Graham, gauging the distance between them. Graham still held the gun with its barrel pointed at the floor.

"Don't think on it," said Graham, reading Lorenzo's eyes. "They say you were fast when you were young, but you ain't young no more. And you never were that fast."

"You bein' kinda casual with that Taurus," said Lorenzo. "You givin' me ideas."

"Try me, you got a mind to."

Jasmine whined from back in the bedroom.

"I can't just sit here," said Lorenzo.

"Do what you got to."

"I'm gettin' up."

"That's on you," said Graham.

Slowly, Lorenzo pushed himself up and stood away

from the couch. He started to walk around it and head for the hall. Graham raised the revolver and pointed it at Lorenzo. Lorenzo studied the gun's cylinder and knew, and as it came to Lorenzo, Graham squeezed the trigger. The hammer fell on an empty chamber.

Graham squeezed the trigger six more times, as he had been told to do. Each snap of the hammer hitting nothing was like the strike of a nail in Lorenzo's heart.

"He said to squeeze it seven times," said Graham.

"Motherfucker," said Lorenzo.

"Bullets back in the kitchen, I expect. With that glass of water he got."

Lorenzo went down the hall and let Jasmine out of the bedroom. He returned with his car keys in hand.

"You comin' with me?" he said to Graham.

"Where?"

"To help Nigel."

"Too late for that." Graham looked at his watch, then back at Lorenzo. "Nigel in the belly of that motherfucker now."

* * *

NIGEL WENT THROUGH the kitchen, his back sliding against the counter, out of sight of the hall. Behind him, roaches crawled across the linoleum countertop.

"Melvin," said a voice from the living room. "Melvin!"

Nigel turned the handle of the cold spigot and opened it all the way. Water drummed against the porcelain bowl of the sink.

Nigel rechecked the safety on the Colt; the gun was live. He moved from the kitchen to the hall, holding his weapon out in front of him. He could see a portion of the living room ahead, and it was bright.

Show yourself, thought Nigel. I am gonna murder the fuck out of you tonight. He blinked sweat from his eyes.

He came into the living room. Rico Miller stood in the right corner of the room, his back against the wall. He held a cut-down shotgun, and it was pointed at Nigel. For a moment, neither of them moved.

"I knew you wasn't Melvin," said Miller. "Melvin got his own smell."

Nigel scanned the room: sofa, table, chairs.

"You kill him?" said Miller.

Nigel dove as the shotgun roared. The load blew off a portion of the sofa back, sending upholstery up into the air. Nigel landed behind the folding table, grabbed it, and stood with it in his hand. He heard the rack of the pump. The second shot hit the table square, like the slap of God. Its impact threw Nigel back to the floor.

Nigel crabbed backward furiously, the Colt still in his hand. He pointed the gun and squeezed its trigger. Smoke came off Miller's shoulder as he walked toward Nigel with the cut-down aimed low. The room flashed; hardwood erupted at Nigel's feet. Miller reracked the shotgun and fired as Nigel shot blindly into a shower of plaster and dust. Miller staggered through pink mist. The shotgun spun from his hands, and he dropped like meat to the floor.

A ringing sounded in Nigel's ears. There was a ripping pain where the shot had peppered his upper chest. His silk shirt was slick and darkened with blood. He tore the shirt open and examined his wounds. He stood, fought nausea, and kept his legs.

Nigel went to Miller's corpse. He fired a round into its head. He spit on Miller and walked from the room.

He moved back through the hall, straight through the kitchen, and out the back door. He walked down to the steps to where Melvin Lee lay unconscious in the grass. He shot Lee twice in the chest, holstered the Colt, and walked on.

A dog began to bark. A light came on in a nearby house.

Nigel went to the alley and followed it to Hunt. He saw a midnight blue Infiniti parked near his Lexus. He recognized it but did not stop. He needed treatment and he needed to get off the street. He went to his trunk and opened it. He heard a car door open and footsteps on pavement. He put the Glock into the toolbox but drew the Colt and kept it in hand. Its receiver had not slid open; he still had at least one round.

Nigel looked around the lid of the trunk. He saw Deacon's second, the one who called himself Griff, walking toward him. The hump under his shirt told Nigel that the young man was wearing a gun.

Nigel, his hands deep in the trunk, put his thumb to the long hammer of the Colt and locked it back. He rested a finger inside the trigger guard of the gun.

"Easy," said Griff, a friendly smile on his face, his hands raised as he approached Nigel.

Nigel could see that this boy was not much older than Michael Butler. Or Rico Miller, the boy he'd just killed.

"Don't come no closer," said Nigel. "I can see you're strapped."

"I ain't hidin' it," said Griff.

"Say why you're here. Speak plain."

"Deacon sent me. He figured you could use some backup."

"It's done," said Nigel.

Many dogs were barking now. Nigel was dizzy, and

there was a deep ache in his chest. He winced against the pain.

"You need help?" said Griff.

"We both gonna need to get gone now."

Griff looked him over. "Wish I coulda been there with you, big man."

Nigel closed his eyes. "You talkin' about your own boys. Don't that mean nothin' to you?"

Griff shrugged. "Deacon say kill 'em, that's what I'm gonna do."

Griff's answer chilled Nigel. Sickened, he removed his finger from inside the Colt's trigger guard. He pulled back on the hammer to release it, then eased it down.

"You all right?" said Griff.

"I'm tired," said Nigel.

Griff drew his gun and shot Nigel in the temple. The bullet's exit blew blood, bone chips, and brain matter into the trunk of the car. Nigel slumped forward, his body convulsing violently. Griff shot him in the back of the head.

Griff refitted his gun behind the belt line of his jeans. The gun was a Desert Eagle nine-shot .357 Magnum with a bright nickel finish. He had paid one thousand dollars for it from a straw-buy man in Columbia Heights, and it was his pride.

Gun works good, thought Marcus Griffin. He had wanted to try it for some time.

TWENTY-SEVEN

LORENZO BROWN OPENED his eyes. He stared at the cracked plaster ceiling and cleared his head.

Jasmine rose from her square of remnant carpeting and stretched. Her nails clicked on the hardwood floor as she came to Lorenzo and licked his fingers. He rubbed her neck and behind her ears.

I am in my apartment with my dog. This is mine.

Lorenzo sat up on the bed. From the clock radio came the smooth sound of Donnie Simpson bantering with Huggy Low Down on PGC. Huggy was doing his December roundup, talking about his nominees for Bama of the Year. Their familiar voices made Lorenzo smile.

In the bathroom, Lorenzo swallowed a couple of ibuprofens, a multivitamin, and a C. He exercised, ate a bowl of Cheerios, then showered and changed into his uniform and a winter coat. Going through the living room, he passed his grandmother's hope chest, now covering a permanently sealed cutout in the floor, and several packages, including a bottle of perfume, an Easy Bake oven he'd bought for his daughter, and a Cinderella Dream Trunk, all waiting to be wrapped. He took a chain leash with a looped leather strap off a nail he had driven into the wall. Jasmine emerged from the bedroom and joined him at the door.

Lorenzo's landlord had left the plastic *Post* bag under a brick on the front porch. Lorenzo took it and walked up Otis with Jasmine, passing row houses and government oaks. He came to the corner at 6th Street, the cut-through to Newton. There were no cars grouped down there where Nigel's mother stayed, and the curtains in her windows were drawn shut. Lorenzo would have to get over there for dinner sometime soon, bring her some of that ice cream she liked. She seemed to enjoy his visits.

Farther east, Lorenzo went by the row house of Joe Carver's aunt. Joe's F-150 was not parked on the street. The job on North Capitol had been completed, and Joe had moved on to a new construction site in Northern Virginia. These days he was always out of the house before dawn.

Lorenzo passed Park View Elementary, where mothers were dropping off their children for the last classes before the holiday break. He cut north on Warder, turned on Princeton Place, and walked down its hill. There he saw Lakeisha, wearing a lavender coat with fake fur around its collar and a clear plastic book bag on her back, coming up the street. Her mother was several steps behind her. Lorenzo planned his walks so that he would see Rayne and her daughter here the same time each day.

Jasmine whined, her tail wagging mightily as she

strained against the leash. Lakeisha met them and crouched down to pet the dog and let Jasmine lick her fingers. Rayne, looking good with the latest haircut, came to them and touched Lorenzo's hand.

"Hey," said Rayne.

"Morning," said Lorenzo, telling her what she wanted to know with his eyes.

"Jazz Man love me?" said Lakeisha, looking up at Lorenzo, smiling, showing him her teeth, which had finally come in full.

"In her heart," said Lorenzo.

"I want a puppy for Christmas, Mama," said Lakeisha.

"That's not gonna happen," said Rayne.

"You can share Jasmine with me," said Lorenzo.

"*And* I want a Cinderella Dream Trunk," said Lakeisha.

"You never know," said Lorenzo. "You be a good girl, you might get it."

"But you're *not* getting a puppy," said Rayne.

"Don't y'all wanna know what I want?" said Lorenzo.

"I already know," said Rayne.

"You and my grandmother been conspirin', huh?"

"She's just being neighborly," said Rayne.

"Hmm."

"I better get her to school," said Rayne. "We on this weekend?"

"I'm plannin' on it," said Lorenzo, looking down at Lakeisha. "You have a good one, little princess."

"Okay, Mr. Lorenzo. Bye, Jazz Man."

He watched them walk up the street. When he saw them reach the school grounds, he moved on.

At the park, near the baseball diamond, Lorenzo stamped his feet against the cold while Jasmine defecated in the grass. He slipped his hand inside the plastic bag, made a glove of it, and picked up her steaming feces. He turned the bag inside out and tied it off. A couple of teenage boys, school age but not in school, walked across the field and chuckled at him, standing there wearing a uniform and holding a bag of shit, as they passed.

Go ahead and laugh, thought Lorenzo. I don't care.

• • •

LORENZO DROVE SLOWLY down Morton Place. He was going to pick up a cat on a spay call at the Park Morton apartments before heading up to the office. Gray snow, the remnants of the previous week's storm, was patched along the curbs. Touts and runners, boys in their midteens, stood on corners, doing their dirt. They wore long white T-shirts under their parkas and down coats. Some had bandannas tied around their necks or legs. All worked for Deacon Taylor.

Within days of Nigel Johnson's murder, the majority of the drug business in the southern portion of Park View had gone over to Deacon Taylor. It was said that this had been his ambition all along. In the transfer of power, Deacon had absorbed most of Nigel's people. Among them was Lawrence Graham.

The police had quickly triangulated the murders of DeEric Green and Michael Butler, the murders at 46th and Hayes, and the assault on Rachel Lopez. Rico Miller's prints, left at Melvin Lee's apartment, were matched to the prints on the shoe box full of money found in his house. The shoe box carried the prints of Green and Butler as well. Also, police had the murder guns and the knife used in the assault. What police did not have was a lead in the killing of Nigel Johnson. They had forensic evidence but no witnesses or anyone who would talk.

The breakthrough came, as they usually did, through information triggered by an arrest in an unrelated crime. A Columbia Heights resident, Jason Willis, was picked up for heroin distribution and, as was procedure, asked if he knew of any recent murders in the area that he would be willing to "clean up" for police in exchange for a consideration come sentencing time. Williams, facing his third felony conviction, claimed that he had personal knowledge of a murder committed in August by a young man named Marcus Griffin, an enforcer for Deacon Taylor. Griffin had bragged on the murder to Williams one night when they were sharing some weed. Griffin was promptly arrested and charged. In his apartment, police found the murder weapon, a Desert Eagle .357 Magnum with a bright nickel finish. In the box, Griffin confessed to the killing of Nigel Johnson. The markings on the slug removed from Johnson were deemed to match the .357. When asked why he had not disposed of the weapon earlier, Griffin explained that he could not bear to part with such a "pretty gun."

In exchange for detailed testimony against Deacon Taylor, who Griffin said had ordered the hit, Griffin would get a ride in the Witness Security program. Griffin was currently in custody in a low-numbered cell in the Correctional Treatment Facility, a privately run unit near the D.C. Jail. The CTF, otherwise known as the Snitch Hive, housed government witnesses and informants. Griff would be looking over his shoulder for the rest of his life. As for police and prosecutors, they would finally get their shot at Deacon Taylor, whom they had been after for some time.

So Deacon, it seemed, might soon be done. But as Lorenzo drove down Morton, it looked as if nothing had changed. Deacon's troops were still out there, working his corners. And if they were to go away, there would always be other young men to replace the Marcus Griffins, Lawrence Grahams, Nigel Johnsons, and Deacon Taylors. Lorenzo understood why boys went down to the corners; he had been one of them, and he knew. Still, the knowledge didn't lessen the bitterness he felt.

Lorenzo picked up the cat, a Persian, from a woman in Park Morton and drove north. Going up Georgia Avenue, he saw single mothers moving their children along the sidewalks, young girls showing off their bodies, church women, men who went to work each day, men who did nothing at all, studious kids who were going to make it, stoop kids on the edge, kids already in the life, a man smoking a cigarette in the doorway of his barbershop, and the private detective with the big shoulders talking to a white dude on the sidewalk in front of his place, had the sign with the magnifying glass out front. It was a city of masks, the kind Nigel had said hung in theaters. Smiling faces and sad, and all kinds of faces in between.

* * *

"THAT'S IT," said Lorenzo Brown. He reached out and turned down the volume of the CD player in the dash. "Can't take it anymore."

"I was listening to that," said Mark Christianson, behind the wheel of the Tahoe.

"Said I can't take it."

"That's the New York Dolls."

"I don't care if it's the Yankees *and* the Knicks, I do not want to hear it. Man's got a personality crisis, he needs to keep it to his self."

They drove slowly down the alley behind 35th Street in Northeast. They passed houses with deep backyards, once lush with vegetable and flower gardens, now only showing the muted shades of winter.

"Where is it?" said Mark.

"Where those cars are at, up ahead."

They came upon the house they were looking for. A restored Impala, a Mercedes coupe, a silver 3-Series BMW, and mounds of excrement, both dried and fresh, sat in its yard. Farther back, a black rottweiler stood on a concrete deck beside a pit-style grill constructed of brick. The male rot came forward, passing a freestanding garage, and stood at the fence. He looked at the truck and its occupants, and barked one time. Lorenzo rolled down his window and whistled softly.

"You all right, Champ," said Lorenzo, and the dog wiggled his rump.

"Looks like he's got entropia."

"And those scars on his ears are from flies. The owner never does clean the feces out his yard."

"You got a name?"

"Calvin Duke. I spoke to him already. He still ain't learned."

Mark took a couple of photographs, then backed out of the alley and drove around to the front of the house. He idled the Chevy on 35th Street as he wrote out the Official Notification form.

"Irena says you haven't been in to sit with her for a while," said Mark, not looking at Lorenzo as he made notations on the warning.

"She worried about me?"

"She likes you, Lorenzo."

"I like her too. But I don't feel the need to visit with her every day like I used to. I figure this work thing is gonna go on for a long time. I can't be lookin' for her to hold my hand forever."

"All I'm sayin' is, you ever need to talk to us —"

"Y'all are there," said Lorenzo. "I know."

Mark put a long strand of black hair behind his ear and touched the handle of the door. "You coming along?"

"I think I'll hang out here. Last time we spoke, me and Duke didn't see eye to eye."

Ten minutes later, Mark returned, tossing his clipboard into the backseat. "I'm ready for lunch."

"You go on," said Lorenzo. "I got something else I need to do."

• • •

"I AIN'T NEVER gonna be cured of this sickness I got," said a light-skinned man with big freckles dotting his nose. "But I feel better today than I did yesterday. And yesterday? I felt better than I did the day before. So thank you for letting me share."

"Thank you for sharing," said the group.

"Anyone else?" said the guest host, an addict who had lost it all and recovered three separate times.

"My name is Shirley . . ." said the short young woman with the deep chocolate skin and almond eyes.

"*Hey, Shirley.*"

". . . and I'm a substance abuser."

The meeting room, in the basement of the church on East Capitol, was full to capacity. The holidays were especially tough on addicts and alcoholics, not only because it was the season of temptation, but because of the painful memories of families betrayed and lost. The chairs of all four rows semicircling the scarred lectern where the host stood were occupied today.

Rachel Lopez smiled hearing Shirley's voice. In the same row, down toward the left side, sat Lorenzo Brown.

"I saw my little girl today," said Shirley. "She was going into her school, over there at Nalle Elementary. My grandmother was walking her in. My baby was wearing this pink quilted coat I bought for her and a matching backpack for her books and stuff. I had it all on layaway. I'd been payin' on it for a while, and I got it out before Thanksgiving. She looked real pretty in that coat today.

"I was standing behind this tree, the same tree I stand behind most mornings when I watch her go in. And she saw me there. Either she saw me or sensed me, I don't know how. She stopped and said something to my grandmother, and my grandmother let go of her hand. My baby walked right over to where I was standin'. I'm not gonna lie, I was shaking. I didn't know what to say. But she helped me out and said somethin' first: 'Thank you for my coat, Mama.' I said, 'You're welcome, sweetheart,' and she leaned forward then. I bent down, and she kissed me on my cheek, and I brought her in for a hug and smelled her hair. She smelled the way I remembered her. I was . . ."

Shirley's voice cracked. She lowered her head.

"My little girl goes to Nalle," said a woman in the last row, breaking the silence that had fallen in the room.

Shirley wiped tears off her face. "This here is gonna be the best Christmas I had in a long time. I got a job over at that big dollar store over on H Street. It's seasonal employment, and I ain't doin' nothin' but cleanin' the bathrooms they got, but still. God bless all of you. And thank you for letting me share."

"Thank you for sharing."

"My name is Sarge . . ." said the grizzled man with the dirty Redskins cap, seated near Shirley.

"Hey, Sarge."

". . . and I'm a straight-up addict. I had a funny thing happen to me the other night, thought y'all might appreciate. I got this efficiency down by the Shrimp Boat, has this little common patio on the back. I was out there, cooking a rib-eye steak on that hibachi I got."

"In the cold?" said a man.

"You know that don't stop me. I even had my music set up, this box I got plays cassettes *and* CDs. I was listening to this old song I like, by this boy out of Philly, singin' on how he about to bust a nut 'cause he wants to get with this girl real bad, and he don't have the control to put it off. 'Love Won't Let Me Wait,' that's the name of that song."

"Norman Conners," said the same man.

It's Major Harris, thought Lorenzo. Nigel's mother had the record.

"It's Major Harris," said Sarge. "Not that it matters, but I'm tryin' to paint the whole picture for you, and the details are important. Now, normally when I'm cookin' out and listenin' to a little music, I get the urge, you all know this. And I ain't talkin' about the urge for sexual companionship, case you think I am. I don't try to get with females too much anymore. I just do 'em wrong anyway."

"Hmph," said a man.

"I ain't sayin' I don't *like* females," said Sarge.

"You gonna tell your story?" said Shirley.

"I already did," said Sarge, "in my roundabout way. I'm sayin', I didn't get the urge to get high that night, the way I usually do when I cook on the grill. And I guess what I'm really tryin' to say is, well, you know I been critical sometimes, bringin' negativity up in these meetings. But this shit here . . . this works. Anyway, it's workin' some for me."

"'Bout time," said a man, followed by some easy laughter from the group. Even Sarge cracked a smile.

"I ain't done." Sarge cleared his throat. "There's been this one friend I made here, in particular, who helped me out. . . ." Sarge's eyes cut toward Shirley for a brief moment. He tightened his cap on his graying head. "I just want to thank that special friend. And all a y'all, matter of fact. Thank you for letting me share."

"Thank you for sharing."

"Would anyone else like to say something?" said the host.

"My name is Rachel Lopez . . ."

"Hey, Rachel."

". . . and I'm an alcoholic. I've been sober for three months and nineteen days."

The group applauded. Lorenzo closed his eyes. He prayed for his daughter, and for Rayne and little Lakeisha, whom he had grown to love like his own.

". . . I thought my drinking gave me power. I thought that in bars, at night, I could do what I hadn't been able to do with my parents or my offenders. That I could exercise some kind of control. I had to hit bottom to see that I was all wrong. I had no power. I was just a drunk, and I was alone."

Lorenzo said a prayer for all the people who had looked after him and were looking after him still: Mark Christianson and Irena Tovar, his grandmother, and Miss Lopez.

". . . I'm dating a man, a police officer. I don't know

where it's going, but it's good today. And that's what I'm focusing on now: today."

Lorenzo said a special prayer for the soul of Nigel. When he was done, he opened his eyes.

". . . so thank you for letting me share," said Rachel Lopez.

"Thank you for sharing."

The basket was passed around the room, and then the group gathered in a large circle. Lorenzo stood beside Rachel, her hand on his shoulder, his on hers. The group recited the Serenity Prayer, and then the Lord's Prayer, and said "Amen."

"Narcotics Anonymous," said the guest host.

"It works if you work it."

• • •

OUTSIDE THE CHURCH, the group dispersed quickly, as the weather did not encourage loitering or idle conversation. Some got into cars with their friends and sponsors or walked toward their residences or places of employment. Others gathered in the Plexiglas bus shelter on East Capitol, out of the wind.

Rachel and Lorenzo stood on the edge of the parking lot as Rachel found a cigarette, lit a match, and cupped her hands around the flame. Mark Christianson had pulled the Tahoe into the lot and was waiting. They could hear muffled barking sounds coming from inside the truck. It sounded like more than one dog.

"That you?" said Rachel.

"Yeah. My partner was supposed to go to lunch. He must have made an unscheduled stop instead."

From the driver's-side window, Mark smiled at

Lorenzo, then made woof actions with his mouth and wiggled his eyebrows.

"He looks nice," said Rachel.

"He's odd," said Lorenzo. "But I guess he's all right."

Lorenzo looked her over as she smoked. A shock of gray had come into her hair, a thick streak against the black. It had appeared soon after the assault. There was a horizontal scar, a thin razor line on one of her cheeks, and a large circular scar, like a heat scorch, in the palm of one hand. That hand had yet to recover its full dexterity. The largest scars were on her chest. The stitch marks were prominent and would be there for the rest of her life. He could see part of them now, pink and raised, coming from the V-neck of her sweater beneath her open coat. She looked small. She looked like she had aged ten years.

"You ought to quit them cigarettes," said Lorenzo.

"Hard to quit everything at once," said Rachel.

Shirley and Sarge, walking together, emerged from the church and came toward them. Sarge kept on without a greeting. Shirley stopped to say hello.

"Can I get a Marlboro, Rachel?" said Shirley.

Rachel shook one from the deck. Shirley put it behind her ear and accepted Rachel's matchbook, gotten at a convenience store, as well.

"You comin'?" said Sarge, calling to Shirley from the sidewalk.

Shirley smiled at Rachel and Lorenzo. "Y'all have a blessed day."

"You also," said Rachel.

Shirley joined Sarge. The two of them walked down the street.

"I got calls to make," said Lorenzo.

"So do I," said Rachel. "You been to the clinic lately?"

"I been meanin' to."

"You need to get over there and drop a urine."

"You know I'll be droppin' negative too."

"No doubt."

She looked into his eyes. Both of them smiled.

"All right, then, Miss Lopez," said Lorenzo, touching the sleeve of her coat. "Let me get on out of here and see what my partner's got in that truck."

"Stay on it, Lorenzo."

"I plan to."

Lorenzo went to his vehicle; Rachel went to hers. There was light left in the day, and work to do.

ACKNOWLEDGMENTS

Thanks to Adam Parascandola, Mitch Battle, and Rosemary Vozobule of the Washington Humane Society for their valuable assistance, and for all their good work. Likewise, my thanks go out to the police, probation officers, ex-offenders, and members of Narcotics Anonymous in Baltimore and Washington, D.C., who allowed me to look into the world that would shape the foundation of *Drama City*. Shout-outs to Reagan Arthur, Sloan Harris, Alicia Gordon, Michael Pietsch, Heather Rizzo, Tracy Williams, and Betsy Uhrig, who were among the many people who helped make this happen. And: Emily, Nick, Pete, and Rosa. Remember: "D.C. Don't Stand for Dodge City."

All Orion/Phoenix titles are available at your local bookshop or from the following address:

Mail Order Department
Littlehampton Book Services
FREEPOST BR535
Worthing, West Sussex, BN13 3BR
telephone 01903 828503, *facsimile* 01903 828802
e-mail MailOrders@lbsltd.co.uk
(Please ensure that you include full postal address details)

Payment can be made either by credit/debit card (Visa, Mastercard, Access and Switch accepted) or by sending a £ Sterling cheque or postal order made payable to *Littlehampton Book Services*.
DO NOT SEND CASH OR CURRENCY

Please add the following to cover postage and packing

UK and BFPO:
£1.50 for the first book, and 50p for each additional book to a maximum of £3.50

Overseas and Eire:
£2.50 for the first book plus £1.00 for the second book and 50p for each additional book ordered

---

BLOCK CAPITALS PLEASE

name of cardholder ....

address of cardholder ....

delivery address
(if different from cardholder)

....

....

postcode ....

postcode ....

☐ I enclose my remittance for £.................................

☐ please debit my Mastercard/Visa/Access/Switch (delete as appropriate)

card number ☐☐☐☐☐☐☐☐☐☐☐☐☐☐☐☐

expiry date ☐☐☐☐   Switch issue no. ☐☐

signature ....

prices and availability are subject to change without notice